THE
MOM PROM
MURDER

THE
MOM PROM
MURDER

TRISH EVANS

StoneArch Bridge Books

Westlake Village, California

The Mom Prom Murder: A Novel

Published by
StoneArch Bridge Books

Library of Congress Catalog Number: 2020910364
ISBN 978-1-7332349-6-2 (paperback)
ISBN 978-1-7332349-7-9 (Epub) / 978-1-7332349-8-6 (Mobi)

For more information visit
trishevansbooks.com

For Michael

CHAPTER 1

ANYONE LIVING WITHIN the boundaries of the little township of Calivista Heights, California, had more than likely encountered Vickie Mack at one time or another. And it is most certain that anyone who had encountered Vickie Mack had also harbored serious thoughts aimed at her demise. So, while there was an element of shock the night of the Calivista Heights Elementary School auction when Vickie Mack's body was found stuffed inside the trunk of Auction Item Number Four, no one was truly surprised or even upset, not for very long anyway. No, the only shock related to Vickie Mack's murder—in fact the only thing that kept her memory alive for many weeks to come—was the more-than-convincing circumstantial evidence surrounding two very unlikely prime suspects: Rachel Berger, a loving wife and mother of one; and Emily Fryze, mother of two and recently separated from her husband of nine years.

No sudden earthquake could have thrown as strong a jolt into Calivista Heights as the shocking rumors and titillating hearsay surrounding Rachel and Emily. As gossip vibrated along grocery store aisles, at local gas pumps, even between bathroom stalls at the Calivista Heights Public Library, one thing was certain: no one young or old, rich or poor, friend or foe, doubted that Rachel Berger and Emily Fryze were absolutely guilty of the murder of Vickie Mack. However, not surprisingly and without exception, the very same residents—the unofficial jurors of Calivista Heights who judged the two housewives guilty of premeditated murder—also unanimously determined the *bumping-off* of Vickie Mack to be justified, completely and utterly warranted and wholly defensible. Not a single citizen challenged this biased public opinion when discussing the murder. Consequently, just one day after Vickie's untimely demise, a movement was formed by one of the town wags and, even though Rachel and Emily had been released without bail and had been living in their own homes since the morning after the murder, middle-aged women took turns standing on the four corners of Vista La Mar and Cliff Side Drive waving homemade signs with the words "Free Berger and Fryze." Countless passersby were greatly disappointed to learn that free hamburgers and French fries were not being offered. Needless to say, Rachel Berger and Emily Fryze had unwittingly become the town's first and, to anyone's knowledge, *only* cult heroes.

Calivista Heights was not the typical Southern California suburb with overly populated neighborhoods, overly populated schools and overly populated jails. The only overly populated thing about Calivista Heights was the number of overly wealthy, overly educated, overly coiffed housewives who employed full-time nannies to help raise their overly indulged children. In fact, Calivista Heights residents prided themselves more on the well documented statistical research revealing the average household's annual income to be floating somewhere in the $350,000 range than on the township's noble heritage. Founded in the late 1800s by earnest evangelical Lutherans, Calivista Heights became an enclave of like-minded refugees from severe Midwestern winters who built functional cottages lacking any ostentatiousness. Few of Calivista's current residents cared to know how or when the original Lutheran descendants had assimilated into today's eclectic collection of Presbyterians, Methodists, Mormons, Episcopalians, Catholics and a growing number of *non-affiliateds*. For the most part, Calivista Heights had remained unnoticed and insignificant until the 1980s when younger, silver-spooned couples raised their noses at the red-tile roofed, mass-produced, cookie-cutter "developments" sprouting indistinguishably from Santa Barbara to San Diego. Instead, those who could afford it swarmed into Calivista Heights, and by the year 2000, a collection of grand and pretentious Palm Beach-inspired mansions had replaced most of the original one-story beach cottages. And with its early recovery from the 2008 economic meltdown, Calivista Heights residents, the rich and not-*as*-rich, now openly patted each other's backs whenever the local paper proudly reported that the average price of a single family VCH—Very Calivista Heights—home fluctuated between $1,700,000 and $3,000,000 depending on whether a bear or a bull was flexing on Wall Street.

The Calivista Heights community openly oozed an arrogant sense of superiority, not only due to its lack of available, affordable homes, but also because Calivista Heights could boast "no Targets, Costcos or Home Depots." National chains need not apply. No fast food restaurants. No major or minor shopping malls. No movie theaters. Even neon signs atop stores were forbidden, according to long-standing Calivista Heights city codes, a remnant of those good old austere Lutherans. Two gas stations, two grocery stores (one for the moderately wealthy, one for the more pampered shopper), a hardware store-pharmacy combo, a bookstore, three family owned restaurants and three banks were about all the Calivista Heights Chamber of Commerce listed on its roster. Truth be told, unless one lived or worked in Calivista Heights, there was no good reason to drive through its narrow, destination-less streets.

Vista La Mar was the only road allowing access into and out of town. The road began where a canyon intersected with famed Pacific Coast Highway and took its name from a once spectacular ocean view (now blocked by a massive Luxury Condominium structure). Winding its way upwards past the high school, through the secluded town and then looping and twisting its way back to Pacific Coast Highway, Vista La Mar followed the contour of an ancient canyon—truly a road less traveled—and was not considered to be a shortcut to anywhere.

To most residents, the only drawback to their town being small and somewhat isolated was that Calivista Heights wasn't big enough or bad enough to warrant a police station of its own. It had never had one. Because of this and due to its relative remoteness, Calivista Heights had always fallen under the jurisdiction of the West Los Angeles Police Precinct. Existing without its own police station increasingly had become a source of concern for Calivista Heights residents, and this concern, or rather this *deficiency*, began to feel like a thorn in its side but not as painful as the thorn that pricked the sides of every West Los Angeles police officer stationed at

Precinct #25. Everyone from rookies straight up the ladder to the division chief knew that a call from the Calivista Heights area code would not constitute enough of an emergency to pull patrol cars away from the rougher parts of town where murders, robberies, car thefts, drug busts and other inner-city criminal activities were the norm. Every WLAPD #25 officer also knew that a CVH call would inevitably involve more time, paperwork and political savvy than any other call to the station. It was extraordinarily rare, but occasionally a house robbery required a patrol officer to venture into Calivista Heights to make an official report. This would happen only after one of the town's private security patrols confirmed, just short of swearing on his mother's grave, that the LAPD would not be dealing with another complaint regarding local juvenile delinquents who partied too loudly while driving their Porsches or Audis through Calivista Heights Park, leaving wheelie tire tracks on the park's well-manicured grass.

Once a week the *Calivista Post*, a "must read" for all Calivista Heights residents, printed editorials and numerous Letters to the Editor foaming with consternation over the town's lack of police security. But the viewpoints and opinions in the Editorial Section seemed almost mild-mannered, even docile, compared to the distressed observations and energetic complaints printed in the ever popular "A Penny for Your Thoughts" section of *The Post*. Week after week, pleas and demands were made for a full-time police car to roam the "increasingly dangerous" streets of Calivista Heights. In reality, it was not because of the limited influence of the "Penny for Your Thoughts" entries but was instead due to the powerful sway of a handful of Calivista Heights citizens who happened to be high-ranking judges or county supervisors or other influential leaders throughout Los Angeles that the Chief of Police, Kenneth Beady, felt he had been ramrodded into giving Calivista Heights what it wanted.

Just five weeks before the Vickie Mack murder, the headline of the *Calivista Post* proudly hailed, "Full-Time Police Patrol at Last!" *The Post* triumphantly proclaimed a "long fought victory" in securing the services of Officer Douglas Mew, twenty-five years of age and a recent graduate of the Police Academy. However, the taste of victory and the jubilant, warm welcoming of Officer Mew by the citizens of Calivista were short lived, for it very quickly became apparent that Officer Mew had not been stationed in Calivista Heights to serve and protect but rather to serve and collect . . . as the town's full-time parking enforcement officer.

The essence and meaning of this move by Chief Beady was definitely not lost on the Calivista Heights citizens. Seven days and two hundred and sixty-three parking citations since Officer Mew's arrival, the *Calivista Post* spewed out letter upon letter, editorial upon editorial, written by angry citizens proclaiming, "Police Chief Beady will end up being the last one to laugh." Week after week, the "Penny for Your Thoughts" section was infiltrated with venomous complaints aimed at the officious Douglas Mew who had a miraculous gift for knowing when a parking meter's green light was seconds from turning red. To add more salt to the wound, the intrepid Officer Mew obviously enjoyed his newly acquired power and fame and showed no mercy for anyone while writing a parking ticket—which is why it could have been said that next to Vickie Mack, Officer Mew was the most talked about and most hated person in Calivista Heights.

Critics of Officer Mew continued to dominate the "Penny for Your Thoughts" section of the town newspaper until the week following Vickie Mack's murder. Suddenly, the *Calivista Post* had a new focus for its front-page headlines and its legions of "Penny for Your Thoughts" readers: "Emily and Rachel: VICK-tims or Mack-Murderers?"

CHAPTER 2

DETECTIVE MICK SELBY was on duty Friday night, April 19th, the evening of the Calivista Heights School Auction. Phones had been ringing at Precinct #25, but not with the same urgency of most Friday evenings.

"Selby! Calivista Heights. Line three!" the desk clerk called out.

"No way! Where's Mew?" Selby barked to the desk clerk. What he meant and what was clearly understood by the desk clerk was *No way was he, Detective Mick Selby, going to get stuck with a Friday night call from Calivista Heights!*

"He's the Heights' meter maid! Besides, he's off tonight," the desk clerk shouted back at Selby. The clerk truly loved when Calivista Heights calls came in and every detective within earshot abruptly headed for the bathroom or a hallway or any corner that would keep them from being pulled into a Calivista Heights call.

"Uh-uh! Get someone else to take the call," Selby argued.

"You're next on the docket. Besides, the lady on the line says it's a 911."

"Geez!" Selby looked around for his partner. Not there. He looked at his watch, noted that it was 11:18 p.m., and then groaned with displeasure as he picked up the phone and pressed the blinking light. "Detective Selby," he announced and then paused, listening to the caller.

"Okay. Okay, calm down," Selby loudly insisted. "When?" Selby reached for a pen to jot down the bits of information he could decipher. "Lady . . . travel trunk . . . tangled mess." He paused, listening but not fully comprehending what he was hearing. "What the—? Can you repeat that?" Selby said with controlled annoyance.

Off to one side, the bathroom door opened just enough to allow two sets of eyes to peer around the opening.

"Did you say a woman's clothes are tangled in a trunk?" Mick Selby pushed his chair away from his desk, shaking his head in disbelief. Stifled laughter leached from the walls of the men's bathroom and the next-door copy room. The bathroom door closed with a loud *thud* just as Mick turned his head, shooting stink-eyes toward the bathroom door. No one was brave enough to receive Mick's glare.

"Okay," he said into the telephone. "Not tangled? A woman? Right? With a tiara? Right?" Mick hit his forehead with the palm of his left hand. The desk clerk's arms and head collapsed onto the reception desk, his body convulsing with laughter.

Mick lifted the phone away from his ear and stared daggers at three officers who had dared to slip back into the room and were now standing close enough to hear Mick's conversation without appearing to be eavesdropping. One of the officers casually picked up a file, flipped through its contents and then pointed to a specific page, pretending to show it to the officer next to him. Both officers nodded their heads and furrowed their brows to appear engrossed in the file's contents while the third officer leaned his bobbing chin between the shoulders of the other two and silently did all he could to stifle his laughter.

"I'm sorry, ma'am. Tell me one more time. Slowly." Mick Selby listened as he looked up at the ceiling and filled his cheeks with air. "Okay, then, *sir*. I'm sorry for the mistake," Selby apologized. "Yes, yes. You are absolutely right. Nerves can make a voice sound higher pitched."

More laughter spilled from the bathroom and from the cluster of officers loitering around the water cooler.

"I'm sending officers out right now," said Selby. A long pause ensued as Mick listened. Then, "No!" he yelled with authoritative force, his face turning dark as he shouted into the phone. "Don't let anyone take anything from the trunk!" Another pause. "No! Do *not* take the body from the trunk!"

There was a long pause as Selby listened to the caller, then responded, "I don't care if they . . . Geeze! Just get everyone away from the trunk, okay? Okay. And keep them away. Thank you, ma'am . . . I mean sir! We're on our way." With that, Detective Mick Selby slammed the phone into the cradle.

Guffaws belted from every corner of Precinct #25 where a dozen uniformed, grown men and women were now painfully bent over in gut-splitting laughter. Selby angrily pointed at the desk clerk and everyone else in the office. "That's enough, you clowns!" he barked. The room became silent as Selby grabbed his jacket, adjusted his utility belt and glared at the group of officers. "Where's Roma?"

"Ohhhh, a-*ROAMMMMM*-ma," sang a chorus of officers.

The door to the men's bathroom opened and a tall, dark-haired Hispanic man stepped through the doorway, holding a paper towel and pretending to dry his hands.

"What's up?" Detective Aaron Anthony Roma asked innocently, as if oblivious to all that had just transpired.

"We're going to Calivista Heights," Selby announced.

"What? Is there a Poodle on the loose tonight?" Roma smirked as he looked at the room full of peers, all of whom were laughing, even as Selby glared at the officers. Roma was enjoying the moment way too much as far as Selby was concerned.

"What's da matter wid ya, Roma? Ain't no poodle this time. It's a freak'n poodle skirt that's loose at the Beaumont Beach Club," mocked one officer.

"Very funny," Selby scoffed angrily as he shoved the front door open and left the building. Roma followed him out the door, pretending to fluff a poodle skirt around his waist.

"Be brave, detectives," called out another officer loud enough for Selby to hear as he and Roma walked through the parking lot to their unmarked car. Roma looked across the roof of the car and noticed Selby glaring at him.

"What?" Roma asked, feigning innocence.

"We might be dealing with a murder, you nincompoop!" Selby yelled, opening his door and slipping into the driver's seat.

Roma paused to let that sink in for a second before sliding into his seat. "A poodle murder?" As usual, Roma didn't know when to stop. "Maybe a pink, poodle-skirt murder?" He snickered to himself, then looked at Selby.

Selby stared at his partner with enraged, stone-cold seriousness, which caused Roma to instantly sober up. He turned on the lights and siren of their unmarked car.

*

Detective Selby swerved their squad car into westbound city traffic, skillfully maneuvering between cars and pedestrians. He was grateful this call had come late at night since traffic was light, making it easy to quickly merge onto the westbound Interstate 10.

Detective Roma glanced quickly at Selby, whose silence and prolonged anger made Roma uncomfortable. "Okay. I get it. This is a real live Calivista catastrophe," Roma said trying to break the ice.

"There's a dead body, Roma!" Selby barked at his partner.

More silence.

"Or so the caller said," Selby scoffed, hinting that he knew this could very well be another knuckle-headed faux emergency from the affluent part of town.

"So, just where is the body?" Roma asked.

"In a trunk at one of the private beach clubs," Selby answered.

"Which one?" There were three private beach clubs located equal distance from each other along Pacific Coast Highway.

"The Beaumont."

Their car quickly approached the westbound side of the McClure Tunnel where Interstate 10 instantly transformed into Pacific Coast Highway. Whether traveling east or west through this short passageway, it never ceased to amaze Mick how one was instantly transported to an alternate universe. The landscape of the gritty, southwest side of Interstate 10, where run-down, graffiti-stamped apartments were jammed beside brightly lit gas stations and sketchy Seven Elevens, morphed the moment the car exited the tunnel heading west. No cut-rate gas stations this side of the McClure Tunnel; no dodgy liquor stores; and no titanic-sized billboards suggestively offering a better sex life if one drove the newest pickup truck. The west side of the tunnel instantly revealed soaring scenic cliffs—the palisades—always a threat to come tumbling down in the next California earthquake. Just across the highway was the expansive Pacific Ocean, free for rich and poor alike to enjoy, right? *Wrong*. Roma and everyone in Precinct #25 knew not to get Detective Selby started on this, his favorite pet peeve. Why was it okay for an endless row of bloated beach mansions, crammed side-by-side along the highway, to completely block one of the most beautiful views in the world? Sure, one could argue that the ocean view wasn't completely blocked, because the same multi-million-dollar beach houses did allow views of the Pacific Ocean between their closely built properties—very fleeting views. Despite Selby's sense of injustice that this side of the universe belonged only to the very rich (the Tunnel being the unofficial but definitive line of demarcation between the haves and the have nots, between the lucky and the unlucky), emerging on the ocean side of the tunnel never failed to give him a rush, an instant feeling of hope and goodwill, and a glorious breath of salty, beach air.

The fog from the marine layer was unusually thick for a late spring night, preventing the detectives from seeing any more than two or three car lengths ahead. Blinding streaks of red and blue light boomeranged back and forth between the wall of fog and their windshield, making it difficult to drive with any real speed. Selby could barely tell that he'd passed the mile-long stretch of mansions and was approaching the Beaumont Beach Club until Detective Roma pointed ahead to the club's entrance.

Selby swerved their car sharply left and then down a swooping drive-way. As if from a disco ball, muted flecks of white light swirled around a stately marquee announcing the Beaumont Beach Club. The unmarked police car pulled to a stop, its red and blue lights disrupting the festive tranquility that had been created by strands of miniature white lights wrapped around a row of palm trees. A large group of tuxedoed, middle-aged men, all visibly upset and agitated, stood in front of the club's gigantic wooden front doors, shielding their eyes from the unmarked car's bright lights, while frantically motioning the officers to hurry toward the valet hut.

"They look like a bunch of freak'n penguins waving their fins at us," Roma scoffed. "No valet?"

Selby jammed the car into park, looked at the mob of men by the door, then turned to Roma. "Our welcoming committee."

CHAPTER 3

"HOLY CRAP! WHAT took you so long to get here?" squeaked the king penguin as he waddled up to confront Selby.

Yep, he's the "ma'am" on the phone, Selby thought to himself as the assemblage of tuxedoes gathered around the two detectives. The squeaky speaker was in his mid-fifties, well fed by all appearances, with a fat face and fleshy neck that made him look much older. *A cardiac arrest victim waiting to happen.*

"Good evening, *sir*, do you have something to show us?" asked Selby with authoritative calm.

Selby and Roma were immediately escorted into a large, dimly lit foyer with walls covered in gold, velvety wallpaper. Small groups of sobbing women huddled along the walls while husbands and boyfriends hovered over them making futile attempts at consoling the distraught women.

A lone security guard stood at the opening to a cavernous ballroom. One of the two massive ornately carved wooden doors to the ballroom was closed, the other was wide open with the guard acting as a sentry, blocking the entrance. He was a short man with squinty brown eyes and jowls that hung like a hound dog's ears, pointing to a rotund belly semi-hidden by a sloppy, ill-fitting security uniform. Pinned to his chest was a gold-plated I.D. that read: D. Burns. Burns held his walkie-talkie up to his ear as the two detectives approached. He then snapped to attention, clicking off his walkie-talkie, giving Detectives Selby and Roma a commanding nod of his bulky head, a gesture that caused his chin to sink into his goiter-like neck. When the two detectives acknowledged him with stoic stares, Burns tried to square his shoulders, an unsuccessful attempt to show he had everything under control.

"The body is secure in the trunk, and I made everyone leave the room, if you see what I mean," said Burns tilting his large head toward the lobby and then toward the ballroom.

"Okay," said Selby.

He and Roma waited for the rotund guard to step aside to let them through the door but Burns stood his ground. "Ah, except for her, if you see what I mean," he apologized, nodding his head once again toward the ballroom.

A deep-throated, primeval wail resounded from inside the ballroom, causing Roma to wince. His first thought was that it sounded like an animal in distress.

"That's the dead lady's mother," said the guard, cocking his head toward the stage. "I tried to get her away from the corpse, but she went berserk, so I let her stay there until you guys arrived, if you see what I mean."

"Anyone else in there?" Roma asked.

"No, just her. I told her husband I'd let him stay with her, but he said he needed a drink. He was already pretty soused, if you see what I mean," the guard added.

"No, I don't see what you mean. Where's the husband now?" Selby asked.

"Over there by the bar. He's the one arguing with the other guy 'cause they won't open up the bar for him." The guard pointed behind the two detectives, then added, "You see what I mean?"

Roma and Selby looked across the lobby at two men leaning against a marble bar, both wearing shiny patent leather dress shoes, expensive tuxedoes, fat, black bow ties, crisp, heavily starched white shirts, and colorful cummerbunds wrapped around two substantial, not-very-well-hidden potbellies.

Yep, thought Detective Selby, *these are the kind of men who own their own tuxedoes, and probably more than one. No rentals here.*

"See what you can find out over there," said Selby to Roma. "And call in some back-up. I'll be in here."

Roma pulled out his cell phone as he walked across the lobby, calling dispatch and simultaneously listening to the argument in the bar.

"My gaw-forshaken schtep . . . schtep . . . schtepdaughter is a corpsh up for sale at dish gaw-forshaken aucshhhon and ya-wone lemme have a drink?" slurred the shorter of the two men. The crown of his head sprouted the archetypal old man's ring of baldness, framed by thinning hair dyed sunset-yellow that swooshed around and below the shiny chrome-top. Roma immediately thought of a grass hula skirt on a heavy Hawaiian male dancer.

Selby stood in front of Burns, who was still blocking the door to the ballroom.

"I've had my hands full, if you see what I mean," the guard jerked his head, first in the direction of the drunks at the bar, then back toward the ballroom, where the wailing continued.

"I see what you mean," Selby said. "Detective Roma is calling in more support. Now, if you don't mind," Selby said as he gestured for Burns to move aside. "I'd like to take a look at the body."

"Yes, sir." The guard stood at attention, almost saluted and then pivoted to let Selby walk into the ballroom. Taking short, skippy-steps, the guard followed on Selby's heels, eager to be included on the law enforcement team.

Selby turned around and held his hand up for Burns to stop walking. "Hold on," Selby commanded, peering at the guard's badge. "Burns, is it?"

"Yes, sir."

"Okay, Burns, I need you to go back out there and make sure everyone in the building stays put until we can speak with each person." Selby couldn't help himself from adding, "If you see what I mean."

"Yes, I do sir," Burns responded with a brotherhood nod, as if he and Selby were now *simpatico compadres*. Then he turned and shuffled toward the lobby, saluting Detective Roma who had now entered the ballroom to rejoin Selby.

Selby and Roma walked into the large ballroom and began weaving across the emerald green carpet toward the stage, sidestepping around the dinner tables, noting crumpled napkins on empty seats, dessert plates with half-eaten chocolate brownies (now soaked and mushy with melted whipped cream) and discarded auction plaques with large black numbers printed on both sides. Roma spotted three or four tables where the oversized floral centerpieces seen on all the other tables were missing.

Like a whale slowly rising to the surface of the ocean, the woman on stage lifted her broad shoulders and hunched-back, then tilted her neck and head backwards while releasing the most disturbing sound either officer had ever heard. *Worse than a cow in labor,* thought Selby.

The woman was wearing a long black dress adorned with thousands of twinkling fake diamonds. Her shoulders were capped at the top by short, black, sparkly strings like a 1920's flapper that made a tap-tap-tapping noise as they swayed up and down to the motion of each of her heaves.

Selby carefully walked up the five steps to the stage and quietly stood in front of the wailing woman. He quickly took note of a large, old-fashioned canvas-and-leather traveling trunk, the kind that went down with the Titanic. The lid of the trunk was closed, secured shut by two thick, black canvas straps that wrapped around the trunk's diameter, their ends coming together with copper hook-and-eye buckles. The antique padlock, screwed to the front and center of the trunk, worried Selby but he refrained from saying what he was thinking: *Please tell me someone didn't go and lock that thing up and take the key with them.*

Selby carefully looked around the area of the trunk while Roma gingerly approached the large, sobbing woman in the sparkling evening gown. He kneeled down on one knee and leaned into the woman's face. "Ma'am, I'm Detective Roma, and I'm here to try and find out what's happened. I understand that—"

"My beautiful daaaaughter has been murdered and is in that, that *thing!*" screamed the woman into Roma's face. "Those *two women* had it in for my sweet Vickie! They're the ones who did this to, to, my daaaaughterrrrr." The animal moaning resumed with a vengeance and the woman began hitting her breasts with clenched fists.

Roma thought it odd that with all the moaning and groaning and wailing, not one tear or tear streak showed on her cheeks or around her eyes. Her heavy mascara and thick, powdery makeup were perfectly pancaked in place. No nose drool. No red eyes.

"I understand you are terribly upset, but I need to help you off this stage and away from this crime scene so that my partner and I can gather the evidence," said Roma.

"You don't need *ev-i-dence!* Talk to Rachel Berger and Emily Fryze! They did it!" she wailed, thrusting her arm in the direction of the lobby.

Roma looked up at Selby and was grateful to hear several approaching police sirens accompanied by more wails from this slouching and rising whale of a woman.

Within moments, three police officers entered the ballroom and hurried to the stage. One immediately relieved Roma of caretaking the distraught mother. Two other detectives entered the room with cameras, white latex gloves, yellow crime scene tape and the other paraphernalia needed to secure the area and begin the forensic investigation.

"We don't even know for sure if the victim is in there," griped Selby as he pulled on the tight latex gloves.

"Might still be a pink poodle, huh?" Roma quipped, hoping for a little chuckle from his partner. Selby glared at the closed trunk, then at Roma.

"Not say'n, just say'n," Roma barely whispered.

After photographs were taken of every angle of the closed trunk and investigators had dusted everywhere for fingerprints, Selby and Roma each unbuckled one of the canvas straps. Selby carefully jiggled the padlock, relieved to find it was not locked.

Roma watched Selby examine the rim of the trunk's lid. The two men made eye contact with each other, then very slowly, at a snail's pace, Roma raised the top of the trunk. He had a fleeting thought—this was like an episode of "Let's Make a Deal" where he, Roma, was the anxious contestant waiting to see if he'd won something grand or ended up hearing the show's canned "whaaa-whaaa" for losers. Roma was about to make a game show pronouncement when the top of the trunk opened just enough to reveal the contents inside.

"Whoa!" Roma whistled loudly. "That ain't no poodle, is it?"

Selby slowly shook his head as the two men stared at the flaming red hair, glassy-dead eyes and thick pancake makeup on the lifeless face of Vickie Mack.

CHAPTER 4

"MRS. BERGER?" ASKED Detective Mick Selby as he opened the door of the interrogation room at the West Los Angeles precinct headquarters.

"Yes!" Rachel answered way too abruptly. Her dark brown eyebrows jolted to the tip of her widow's peak giving her a comical look of panic.

"Ahhh," Selby faltered for a moment. He bit his upper lip between his teeth and looked down onto the notepad in his right hand. "Before we get started . . . ah, I would remind you again, you have the right to remain silent. What you say can and will be used against you. Do you understand?"

"Yes," replied Rachel. She had seen this a million times on television.

"Good. Would you like some coffee?"

"No." Rachel had wanted to tell him that she hated coffee but thought better of it.

"Water?" Detective Selby pressed even though it was plain to see that offering a beverage was not helping this very tense, very attractive forty-something woman to relax.

"No!" She quickly shook her head with her eyes closed. The pounding of a migraine throbbed in her left eye, and Rachel desperately wanted to ask for a Diet Coke but thought better of that, too.

"Anything?"

"No thank you," she said, softening her tone.

Selby tried one last time. "This could take a while."

A while? The unrelenting migraine pressed harder against her eye. Rachel knew very well that without her Imitrex medication, the migraine would push its way into her temple and then travel, slowly and excruciatingly, to the trunk of her neck where it would torture her for hours, maybe even days. Without her medicine, Rachel knew her only hope for some kind of relief was to shoot some caffeine into her system.

"Actually, I could kill for a Diet Coke," she blurted out. *Oh, my God! What did I just say?* Rachel screamed inside her throbbing head. "No, no," Rachel quickly corrected herself, raising her hands as if gesturing, *don't shoot, I surrender.* Then slowly, carefully, she added, "I would love . . . love . . . a Diet Coke."

"Okay, I believe you," Mick responded, mimicking Rachel's *don't shoot* position.

Rachel dropped her hands to her lap. "I would never do that!"

Detective Selby cocked his head. "Do what?"

"I would never kill for a Diet Coke!" Rachel's left hand flew to her mouth as she wondered what was making her say these things.

"Well," said Selby hesitantly, "there you have it." Selby knew that if this woman was involved with the murder, getting a confession out of her would be effortless.

"It's just a saying I use a lot . . . *I could kill for a Diet Coke* . . . I don't mean it literally," Rachel stammered. "Really," she almost whispered.

Selby squinted his eyes, looking at Mrs. Berger. She reminded him more of his wife than of the typical Calivista women. He noticed she was wearing a simple, sleeveless black gown that showed only a hint of cleavage and a necklace with a plain gold chain and a small white pearl. Everything about Mrs. Berger seemed understated compared to the other women he'd questioned earlier that night at the Beaumont Beach Club. Unlike the other women, Mrs. Berger's shoulder length dark hair was not teased or perfectly coiffed with large amounts of hairspray. Her natural, unassuming beauty, *sans* false eyelashes and caked makeup, was in stark contrast to the other female partygoers.

"I've been addicted since college," Rachel confessed.

Mick waited, knowing there had to be more.

"To . . . to coke."

Mick waited again.

"Not coke-coke! *Diet* Coke," said Rachel, hurrying her explanation.

"Huh," Mick nodded, but he wasn't sure what to make of it.

"I've never even had that other kind . . . of coke," said Rachel. "Just Diet Coke."

Selby squinted his eyes again and slightly cocked his head which immediately made Rachel think he didn't believe a word she was saying.

"I, I, I'd never kill someone for a Diet Coke. Never!" Rachel instantly played back in her mind what she had just said. "Look, I didn't kill Vickie for a Diet Coke!"

Detective Selby's face was the perfect deadpan.

"That would be ridiculous!" she continued, realizing she had put herself on the defensive.

"It would, wouldn't it," agreed the detective with a straight face.

"Or for any other reason," Rachel quickly interjected.

The detective scrunched his face, as if he'd just suffered a brain freeze. Rachel exhaled a long gust of air. "TMI," she sighed.

"Excuse me?" said Selby.

"Too much information." Rachel shook her head.

Selby felt the upward twists at the corners of his mouth. "No, no. Not too much . . . ahh . . . not TMI. Not TMI at all." He reached for the door behind him. "Let me get you that Coke," he said, then paused, looked back at Rachel and pointed his left index finger at her. "*Diet* Coke, that is . . . then we can talk."

Rachel gave a prompt nod of her head before he disappeared. Looking down at her lap she saw that her hands were clenched so tightly that her knuckles were whiter than white . . . as if she were praying. That wasn't a bad idea, she thought. "Oh, God, what is happening? I sound like I'm guilty of murder! Please, please help me here!" Rachel gripped her hands even tighter until they hurt. "Oh! It's too hard to pray at a time like this," she said aloud to herself, then continued. "But if ever there were a time for you to intervene, it would be now, God."

Rachel loosened her hands and noticed that her wedding rings were absent from her left ring finger. *Not again!* It was such a bad habit. Because her hands tended to become dry in winter and spring, she was always taking off her rings to rub hand cream into her dry skin. She usually remembered to put the rings on again, but not always. *Shoot! They're probably at school, in the girl's bathroom, on the sink,* she thought. She remembered making a last stop at the school office to pick up extra copies of the auction program. She'd been so busy loading her car with everything she needed that night for the auction she didn't think to use the bathroom at home before she left. By the time she'd reached the school to retrieve the programs, she desperately needed a bathroom. Rachel remembered washing her hands in the girls' bathroom then carefully placing her rings on the rim of the porcelain sink so she could rub a drop of hand lotion between her cracked fingers without clouding the diamond.

Once before, she'd left her rings in the school's bathroom and guess who'd found them? Vickie Mack. And so, of course, out of the kindness of her dear, sweet, pinched-up heart, Vickie had driven to Rachel's house just to return them. Rachel recalled Vickie saying, "They're such sweet rings. Such a *tiny diamond.* I knew they were yours immediately. Honestly, Rachel, I thought I'd be doing you a favor by letting them remain lost so you could get Conrad to replace them with something more . . . *substantial . . . more impressive.* But then, there's the sentiment, isn't there?"

Rachel knew all too well how much Vickie Mack relished those moments when she could demean and degrade someone else under the pretense of doing a kind and noble act. But Rachel also realized that somehow, over time, she'd allowed Vickie's little remarks to cause her to surreptitiously, almost covetously, take note of the million-dollar diamonds so many Calivista women flaunted on their left hands. They were all so Very Calivista Heights, *sooooo VCH,* as she and Emily had nicknamed anyone who literally or figuratively wore the pretentious, self-important airs so typical of Calivista's upper echelon.

Rachel had never before placed any importance on acquiring or wearing expensive jewelry and when she and Conrad moved to Calivista Heights, she mockingly observed how daily accessorizing was an Olympic sport for the average Calivista Heights wife. Rachel and Emily often likened VCH women to the gaudiest of Christmas trees, the fake ones with limbs flocked pink and purple and drooping with heavy designer ornaments and too much silver and gold tinsel.

So, wondered Rachel, when did it happen? *When did I become suscepti-ble to the insidious lure of the very same jewelry-goddesses I once made fun of?* It might have been just before their fifteenth wedding anniversary when she asked Conrad if she could add two deep blue sapphires to bookend the beautiful and lovely-but-small diamond he'd given her on their engage-ment? *And how was I able to convince myself that I had not become what I had so ridiculed about other VCH women? How could I be so disingenuous?*

Waiting for a Diet Coke at 2:15 in the morning in a sterile interroga-tion room inside the West Los Angeles Police Station, battling a raging migraine, Rachel realized with shock and shame that she had, indeed, become the worst kind of VCH woman. *Oh! That Vickie Mack! Why did I care what she or anyone else thought? So what if Vickie or anyone else thought my wedding rings looked like they came from a bubble gum machine?*

"Stupid, stupid, stupid!" Rachel groaned out loud pounding her fist on the metal table and, at the same time, wondering what a jail cell might look like from the inside.

CHAPTER 5

"STUPID?"

Rachel turned and saw Detective Selby standing in the doorway holding an unopened can of generic diet soda in his right hand and a white, Styrofoam cup in his left.

"This is all we have. It's not cold and it's not Coke, but it *is* diet," said Selby placing the can and cup on the table.

Rachel hated generic sodas and worse than anything, she hated *warm sodas of any kind. Was this a sign from the heavens of some divine displeasure with her? How many times had she promised God, not to mention Conrad, that she would quit Diet Coke?*

"So, tell me what's so stupid," said the detective.

"Oh, nothing, really. I just noticed my wedding rings are missing. Again. It's not a big deal. I leave them everywhere. I probably left them at home or in the lady's room at the club . . . or maybe in the girls' bathroom at our school. I do that a lot."

"Huh," said Selby, taking his place across the table from her.

"Thank you," said Rachel, hoping there would be ice in the cup. She looked inside. No ice.

"You know something?" said Selby. "If my wife were missing her wedding rings, she'd be pretty freaked out."

Rachel was mortified, realizing she'd sounded so VCH to the detective. *I'm sure he thinks I'm just another rich housewife who can afford to replace her wedding rings any day of the week.*

"But Detective, I do freak out when I lose my rings," said Rachel, fumbling to find the right words. "I, um . . . I just seem to not notice them missing until it's too late to remember where I last took them off."

"I understand," Selby said.

Rachel detected a degree of sympathy in the detective's voice, which gave her a smidgen of hope *that maybe she wouldn't be spending the night in jail.* She looked at the fairly attractive, middle-aged detective with salt and pepper hair that was cut a little too short. He looked to be in good shape and unlike most TV detectives, Detective Selby lacked the ubiquitous paunch, balding head and bad attitude. In fact, he seemed like a nice, normal, levelheaded man, and his wife was probably a nice, normal, levelheaded woman . . . who would never take off her wedding rings.

Rachel looked down at the soda can, then popped off the tab. A weak, cheerless fizz sound trickled through the opening. *This will never stop my migraine,* Rachel thought, even as the migraine worked its way down her neck.

"Okay then," Selby huffed as if worn out by the trip to the soda machine. Rachel waited for Selby to say more. He didn't, so she glanced down at the soda and reluctantly took a sip. The detective remained silent.

Just ask me some questions, Rachel begged silently. She took another sip of the warm soda. *Disgusting!*

Though anxious to begin the interrogation, Selby hesitated, trying to decide if he should first tell Mrs. Berger that a major soda fizz mustache had lingered across her upper lip. It was not an easy thing, questioning an attractive woman with a fizzy moustache.

"Ah," Selby faltered as he reached over to a filing cabinet behind him and grabbed a tissue box. "You might, ah, want to just . . . here." He pulled a tissue from the box and mimed wiping his upper lip.

"Oh," said Rachel as she reached for the tissue and self-consciously wiped her lip. "Thank you," she whispered.

"I'm just a little curious, Mrs. Berger, how you and Mrs. Fryze got mixed up with such a loony bunch of people."

Rachel was stunned to see the detective smiling at her. She tried to return the smile, but instead gave a heavy sigh of confused gratitude.

"I don't really know," she said, slowly shaking her head.

Selby smiled and shook his head too. Rachel felt the tension in her back ease up a tiny bit, and she returned Selby's smile. She and Emily had asked themselves the very same question the moment they agreed to be co-chairs of the Calivista Heights Elementary School Auction. She still had no answer.

"The beginning is always a good place to start," Selby nudged, still smiling.

"The beginning?" asked Rachel. She inhaled slowly and deeply while feeling the throb of her migraine pounding at her temples. "I don't exactly know when the beginning began," Rachel spoke softly.

But she really did know when the beginning began. It began with Vickie Mack! It began three years ago, the day Rachel and Emily first met Vickie. Instantly, Rachel's mind was flooded with the memory of their first encounter with that despicable, loathsome, awful, terrible, appalling woman. But Rachel was certain this was not the beginning the detective wanted to hear about, so she remained silent.

"Okay then," said Detective Selby, realizing his first question was too open-ended. He decided on a different approach. "Tell me about this auction of yours. It looked like a pretty posh event. Lots of expensively dressed people, real expensive cars in the parking lot, expensive booze and some pretty expensive things being sold at the auction tables. I noticed one item was a twelve-night stay at a castle in Austria. That's pretty amazing. If there hadn't been a dead woman in a trunk up on the stage, I might have stayed for dinner and dessert."

"Well, you *do* know, it is Calivista Heights," said Rachel, wondering why the detective was being so casual. *Is he trying to make me relax so I'll slip up and absentmindedly tell him I murdered Vickie?*

Detective Selby noticed a subtle grimace wash across Rachel's face. "I'm sorry, Mrs. Berger. I guess you and, ah—" Selby stopped, then looked down at his notes. "You and Mrs. Mack were close friends. Her death must be very upsetting."

"I am upset, but to be perfectly honest, Vickie and I were not close friends, not at all. I might as well tell you that I hate her . . . or hated her, but I never wanted her to actually die. Well, except maybe in that momentary way one thinks after being battered over and over again by someone, but that's only because Vickie Mack was the meanest, awfulest, most conniving, most despicable person I've ever known."

"Whew. Don't hold back, Mrs. Berger." The detective smiled again, then continued. "Are you the only one who thought Mrs. Mack was mean and conniving?"

"No," Rachel replied. "She hurt a lot of people besides me."

"Huh," said Selby thoughtfully.

"I didn't like her, but I didn't kill her."

"Can you think of any particular reason why someone *would* want to kill her and then throw her into a trunk as *the grand finale* of the auction?" Detective Selby knew he was making light of a tragedy, but he couldn't help himself.

Rachel flinched. "No," she said with a not-so-convincing tone in her voice.

The door behind Detective Selby opened, and Detective Roma stepped halfway inside the doorway. He nodded at Selby. "Need to see you for a sec."

Selby nodded at his partner, then reached for a yellow pad of paper at the end of the metal table and slid it over to Rachel.

"I won't be gone long, but in the meantime, please write down the day's timeline, you know, everything you did this morning all the way to when you found Vickie Mack's body. We'll call that the beginning. Okay?"

Rachel stared at the yellow-lined tablet then looked up at the two detectives.

"Okay, but I need a pen or something," she said to Selby. *Give me some crayons and I'll draw some pictures,* she said silently to herself. Her migraine was making her defiant.

"Uhhh . . . sure." Selby looked around the room for a pen, but finding none, he pulled a pen from Roma's breast pocket and handed it to Rachel.

"Here. Detective Roma has a whole lot more of these," said Selby as he and Detective Roma left the room and closed the door.

Rachel's head vibrated with pain.

*

Fifteen minutes later, Detective Selby walked through the door and returned to the seat across from Rachel. He was holding a square Polaroid photo.

"Ah, Mrs. Berger, I forget, what did you say your wedding rings look like?" Selby tilted his head, as if trying to recall something.

"Umm," Rachel was confused. She didn't think she'd described them to the detective. "My engagement ring is yellow-gold with a round diamond and one blue sapphire stone on each side. And the wedding ring is a yellow-gold band."

"Now, that's interesting," Selby said as he slowly pushed the Polaroid picture across the table for Rachel to see.

Rachel stared in utter shock. One mangled, obviously broken hand filled the entire photo. Two rings, identical to the ones Rachel had just described, encircled the pinky finger of the terribly swollen left hand. Rachel let out a sudden and involuntary gasp. Her left hand jolted from her lap and her eyes fixed themselves to her own ring finger . . . *sans* rings.

"Is that Vickie's hand?" Rachel gasped.

"That would be correct," said Selby.

Rachel looked directly into Selby's eyes with dismay. "Are those mine?" she squealed.

"You tell me," replied Selby, pokerfaced.

"They look like my rings, but . . . but . . . how?" Rachel frantically sifted through her brain to find an explanation for why her wedding rings were on the very dead and bloated, left pinky finger of her nemesis, Vickie Mack. *Ohhhhh! That Vickie! She must have found them that afternoon in the school bathroom.*

CHAPTER 6

EMILY FRYZE'S ENTIRE body shook with fear as her mind zigzagged with images of Vickie Mack's body slumped like a ragdoll and stuffed inside the 1930s steamer trunk. The most expensive auction item in the school's history was supposed to be inside the trunk, not a dead body. How had she, Emily Fryze, a native of Calivista Heights and a graduate of Calivista Heights Elementary School, no less, ended up in a windowless interrogation room waiting to be questioned about—and maybe booked for—the murder of Vickie Mack? And, how *did* Vickie Mack end up dead inside a trunk? That definitely was not part of the plan she and Rachel had conjured up as co-chairs of the auction. Instead of Vickie Mack's body, there was *supposed* to have been a large blue and silver envelope with eight luxury cruise ship tickets that Emily was *supposed* to lift from the bowels of the trunk and parade across the stage in hopes of eliciting higher and higher bids for Auction Item Number Four. Their plan was for Rachel, in her stunning, black Donna Karan cocktail dress, to pull two additional items from the trunk—a sparkling princess tiara and a red velvet bowtie—and for Rachel to place the tiara on her head and fasten the bowtie just above her modestly plunging neckline, additional hints that tickets to the renowned New Year's Eve Gala at Vienna's Hofburg Palace were included.

"Oh, my God! The bowtie!" Emily moaned as she experienced a sudden flashback—seeing the voyager trunk yawn open and the red bowtie lying like a grotesque mustache across Vickie Mack's upper lip."

"Bow tie?" someone asked from across the room.

Emily's trance ended as she took in a tall, attractive, thirty-something Hispanic man leaning against the doorframe, holding a cup of coffee in his right hand. She had been driven to the West LA precinct by two women police officers, and she expected one of them to interrogate her, not this handsome man who, Emily judged, was about her age. Detective Aaron Roma's slightly unruly hair was brushed all the way back to the collar of his dark blue sport coat. It was way past midnight, and Emily was tired and more than a little stressed, but that didn't stop her heart from involuntarily skipping a beat as the detective walked toward the table where she sat and carefully placed the coffee cup in front of her. Emily started to reach for the cup, but her hands shook so hard she quickly dropped them to her lap.

"The bow tie?" Detective Roma asked again, hesitating.

Emily half-nodded with a *yes*, or was it a *no*? The detective couldn't tell, and he couldn't focus, either. This beautiful, thirty-something woman had captured his interest in a way that had nothing to do with the Calivista Heights murder case.

Detective Roma feigned tying a bow tie at the front of his neck. "We don't usually wear bow ties when questioning people about murders, not on Friday nights anyway." Impressed with his own quick sense of humor, Roma smiled until he realized his little joke caused Emily to burst into tears.

Ahh, Jeeeze, Detective Roma thought to himself. *I was just trying to help the lady relax. Why do women always have to cry? What good does that ever do?*

"Here," said Roma, pushing the coffee closer to Emily. Her tears and sobs were suddenly accompanied by a succession of violent, unladylike hiccups. Roma looked around the room, desperate for a box of tissues. Instead, he saw Detective Selby peering into the room through the door's rectangular window. Roma stared back at Selby and mouthed, "What?"

Selby pretended to hold a cup in his hand and then mouthed the word, "Water."

Emily burst forth with another thunderous, almost violent hiccup causing her blond, shoulder length hair to fly upwards. Roma instantly thought of the Flying Nun. He'd had a crush on Sally Field ever since he was a kid.

"Ah, I'll be right back." Roma patted the table twice and retreated to the hallway.

Ignoring Selby, Roma strode past him to the water cooler. He yanked at the limp paper cup hanging from the dispenser and proceeded to fill it to the brim with ice-cold water.

Emily's syncopated hiccups and sobs from the interrogation room mingled with the sound of burbling water bubbles floating to the top of the cooler. Carefully carrying the cup of water, Roma took a deep breath and walked back toward the room, pausing just long enough to stare-down Detective Selby with a defiant look that said *I've got everything under control.*

Then, seemingly out of nowhere, a sharp and shrill hiccup, more like a scream, burst forth from the interrogation room, so loud and primal it made Roma jump, which in turn caused the cup of ice water to spill onto his crotch, where he experienced something akin to a brain freeze but not in his brain. Roma fixed his eyes straight ahead but still saw from his peripheral vision Selby holding his right hand across his face to stifle a guffaw.

Mustering all the mental strength he could pull together and pretending he felt not an ounce of pain or embarrassment, Roma entered the room with an air of practiced nonchalance, slid into his metal chair and offered Emily the now half-filled cup of water.

Emily sipped. Roma stared into her beautiful blue eyes.

A peaceful calm prevailed . . . until . . . Emily belted out yet another round of gulping hiccups. The detective waited in silence, wondering how such a beautiful woman with a knockout figure had managed to look so appealing despite the grotesque utterances coming from her mouth. Roma realized he would just have to wait for her unpredictable attacks to end.

Not quite five minutes passed before Roma attempted to break the ice. "By the way, I am Detective Roma."

Emily nodded and, with a wave of her hand in the direction of the nameplate on Roma's left breast pocket, acknowledged that she had figured this out all on her own.

"And you are Emily Fryze," he said, noting the absence of a wedding ring on her left hand.

"Nice to meet you Detective Aroma," said Emily, carefully pronouncing his last name as if describing a pleasant odor. She realized it was an odd thing to say, *nice to meet you*, but it was nice to meet him, except it would have been nicer, she thought, if it had been under different circumstances.

"Ah, actually, it's A. Roma," he corrected her and pointed at the capital 'A' that was *clearly* followed by a period, a space and then a capital 'R' for Roma.

Emily double sniffed and nodded her head indicating that she understood what the handsome detective was trying to say. "Yes. A-roma."

Aaron Roma hated the way his badge somehow caused everyone to blend the 'A' and the 'Roma' together, but never more than at that very moment when the beautiful Emily Fryze had mispronounced his name. He decided to let it go for now.

"You okay?" he asked kindly, hoping the hiccups would not return.

"I think so," Emily answered.

"I have to be honest with you, Mrs. Fryze."

Emily held up her hand to stop him. "I should probably tell you that I'm about to become . . . *ex*-Mrs. Fryze." Emily wasn't really sure why she had blurted out this personal information, especially since she and Pete were only *separated*, not yet *divorced*.

"Oh. Okay." Aaron Roma nodded his head. "I'll make a note of that." He looked at her a second longer than normal, experiencing an unexpected sense of exhilaration.

"I'm not really sure if it's pertinent, but—" Emily suddenly hiccupped again.

"No, no, everything is pertinent to an investigation," Roma said, "especially when something like this . . . this possible, um, homicide happens."

Emily gulped when she heard the word *homicide*, then nodded her head in agreement.

Something about the *soon-to-be-ex-Mrs. Fryze* had Detective Roma feeling off-balance, slightly unhinged. Roma rotated his neck then cocked his head toward the lobby of the police station where many of the auction guests were still waiting to be released. "You know, some people out there are pretty sure you and your friend, Mrs. Berger, had something to do with, umm, what happened to Mrs. Mack."

Emily stifled a shriek, then responded in disbelief. "What?" She inhaled a half-breath and the violent hiccups erupted all over again.

"Well, yes . . . but that doesn't mean they're right." In fact, Aaron Roma truly hoped the quick-to-judge auction attendees he'd interviewed earlier were wrong.

"There is just no way! Why we never—" She stopped mid-sentence, giving way to a loud half-belch, half-hiccup.

Roma realized that questioning Emily Fryze was not going to happen without her constant outbursts. He scooted his chair backwards to the metal filing cabinet in the corner of the room and reached for a tablet of lined paper.

"I'll tell you what," Roma said between two more of her hiccups. "You just write down everything you can remember about tonight."

"Everything?" Emily's head and shoulders jumped up from the force of another hiccup.

"Yup," said Roma. "Everything you can remember. Think you're okay to do that?" Roma realized that he sounded far more compassionate toward *this* murder suspect than he had to others.

Emily smiled in appreciation of Roma's warm tone of voice and nodded her head. She valiantly tried to suppress another explosive hiccup.

"I'll be back in about fifteen minutes," said the detective as he stood up and walked to the door. "Maybe by then—" He smiled and made a cute, endearing gesture that somehow suggested a hiccup.

Emily could not take her eyes off him as he left the room, even admiring the way he walked. *He has such a strong but kind way about him.* Then, tapping her head to snap herself out of her daze, she forced herself to stop thinking what she had been thinking and began reconstructing the day in writing as if composing an impromptu essay in a high school English class:

I woke up at about 6:30 this morning. After I showered and got dressed, I woke up my two children, got them dressed, and then made their breakfast. Around 7:45 Robbie Berger knocked on our door, that's Rachel Berger's son; it was my day to take him to school. I drove Robbie and my children, Max and Molly, to school; actually, Molly, my daughter doesn't go to school yet. She's only two years old. But after I drove Robbie and Max to school, I drove Molly to Miss Anna's who sometimes babysits for me. Then I drove back to my house and loaded some of the auction items that had been stored in my garage into the back of my car. Then I drove to the Beaumont Beach Club to help the decorations committee get everything set up for the night. I called Rachel, my co-chair, to remind her to pick up the rest of the Auction Programs at the school office. She said she had been delayed by Vickie Mack who happened to be in the girl's bathroom at the same time Rachel was in there. Rachel was a little upset with Vickie, because Vickie wouldn't stop badgering her about the secret auction item.

Rachel arrived at the club about an hour later, and we worked until an hour before the auction and then took turns going to our rented room at the club, where we changed into our dresses for the evening. I remember Mrs. Smart, Vickie Mack's mother, arriving early and asking if we'd seen Vickie. Neither Rachel nor I had seen her at the club all day and, to tell the truth, we were grateful we hadn't. Of course, we didn't say that to Mrs. Smart, who was anxious because she wanted to be the first to see Vickie in the 'designer gown' Vickie had ordered for the occasion. Around 5:30 p.m., people started to arrive, and things got busy and crowded and loud and really, really hectic. All through the silent auction, Vickie's mother and stepfather kept asking about Vickie's whereabouts and just when it was time to close all the silent bidding and herd our guests into the ballroom, Mr. and Mrs. Smart insisted that we extend the silent auction another 45 minutes. We knew Mrs. Smart wanted everyone to see her daughter stroll down the winding stairs in her "gorgeous, one-of-a-kind gown" and that Mr. Smart wanted to extend the silent auction so he could grab a few more drinks before the bar closed for the night. Lots of people complained, because they were hungry, but we were forced to extend the time because the Smarts are our school's biggest donors. When Vickie didn't show up an hour later, we had to finally close the silent bidding. The guests found their assigned dinner tables, and the meal was served.

Rachel and I were supposed to sit with our husbands (well with her husband, Conrad, and my soon-to-be ex-husband, Pete), at the same table with Vickie Mack, the Smarts and the Vandees, but Pete wasn't there because his plane from Atlanta was delayed. Rachel and I didn't get to sit down for dinner because we were tied up with lots of little emergencies backstage. (Do you want me to write about all the emergencies?) And then while the dinner plates were being cleared, Rachel and I went onstage to thank all the volunteers and to *introduce the auctioneer for the Live Auction event. The auctioneer was a little weird; actually, he was very weird, but he got people to bid large amounts of money for the items. And then when the auctioneer started to call out bidding for the last item, the secret mystery item hiding in the steamer trunk, Mr. Smart, Vickie Mack's stepfather, started bidding against himself. (By the way, he did the same thing at the last auction. His wife makes him do it.) He bid a ridiculous amount of money and made the auctioneer say 'going, going, gone' and everyone seemed to be having fun and laughing. But then when Mr. Smart opened the trunk Mrs. Smart started screaming. And there was Vickie Mack, Mrs. Smart's daughter, all twisted and dead with my daughter's plastic, princess tiara on her head and the red bowtie on her lip.*

Emily stopped herself from adding that Vickie Mack had *once again* managed to ruin a perfectly good time. The door to the interrogation room opened. Emily looked up and smiled at the handsome detective. "I've written down most of what I can remember, Detective Aroma," Emily said wearily.

"A. Roma," he corrected. "A, *period,* Roma," he said. Normally, Aaron wouldn't have bothered to point this out a second time, but Emily Fryze's smile and effortless beauty had made him ill at ease. Somehow, he cared that she got it right.

"Ahh, that's right," remembered Emily, wondering why he insisted she get his name right. *Maybe he's a little insecure . . . revealing the kind of vulnerability Pete lacked. There was something reassuring and honest about vulnerability in a man.*

The detective reached for the tablet and began slowly reading each of Emily's pages, frequently looking up and making eye contact with her, sometimes smiling, causing Emily to squirm uncomfortably in her chair.

"Well," said Detective Roma when he finished reading her missive. "You certainly have had an eventful day."

Emily opened her mouth to answer, but all that materialized was an outrageously loud hiccup, like a vocal exclamation mark.

Detective Roma was immediately lovestruck.

CHAPTER 7

IT HAD BEEN a very long night for Dr. Conrad Berger. To start with, his good friend and former neighbor Peter Fryze was supposed to have been in attendance at the Calivista School Auction. Without Pete's presence for some comic relief and comradery, the evening had become unbearable. The past eighteen months had put a strain on both men, but especially on Pete. Conrad knew from their after-tennis conversations over coffee that Pete still had hopes of repairing his wobbly marriage and eventually moving back home with Emily and their two kids. This was the only reason why Pete had promised Emily he would attend the auction—he was convinced it would earn him a few points and show Emily that he could be a supportive husband even if he wasn't living at home.

Conrad didn't believe a word of Pete's text, which had arrived just as the Auction was beginning, offering up a lame excuse about some sort of "delay due to unusual circumstances."

Conrad had responded in a text back to Pete: *B.S. You owe me, big time!* Fuming, Conrad wondered what had happened to the vow the two men had made eighteen months ago, *their pledge*, the unbreakable promise they'd made to help each other survive the dreaded Auction Night come hell or high water.

Even as Conrad strolled through the Silent Auction room sipping on a vodka tonic, looking at items he'd been hearing about for months, he tried to suppress any anger towards Pete. But he really was annoyed, which led him to dream up several diabolical plans to get even with his pal. One thing for sure, Conrad would show no mercy on Pete during their Saturday morning tennis game. *None.* Oh, and maybe, just maybe, he, *Doctor* Conrad Berger *'would be called to the hospital for an emergency surgery'* the very hour of Pete's daughter's princess birthday party—the party Conrad had promised to attend in support of Pete.

To add to Conrad's frustration, the Silent Auction portion of the evening, which took place during the *hors d'oeuvres* and cocktail hour, had been extended for an extra forty-five minutes solely because the very self-important Mrs. Valerie Smart, Head of the school's Board of Trustees *and* mother of Vickie Mack, had complained to Rachel and Emily that there had not been *nearly* enough time to view and bid on the endless auction items. Rachel had whispered into Conrad's ear that the delay was really because Valerie's daughter had not yet arrived, and Mrs. Smart did not want her dear Vickie to miss out on making a grand entrance down the long, winding staircase from the hotel lobby into the ballroom.

For the last two months, Rachel and Emily had received endless hints from Vickie regarding her *specially designed formal gown* created as "a tribute to our brave soldiers returning from Afghanistan." What this had to do with a school auction, Rachel and Emily had not a clue. But they already knew the colors and theme of her dress from the "little hints" Vickie had kept slipping into their conversations, knowing the two ladies were "desperate to hear the gown would be, *surprise,* red, white and blue."

Conrad had promised Rachel, no, *he had sworn on his last breath* that he would not be late to the auction, which meant he had worked through his lunch hour nibbling on one of Robbie's Lunchable packets, the kind with four measly slices of cheese, four round pieces of some kind of meat and four dry crackers, so he would arrive at the auction earlier and hungrier than any of the other guests. While dreading the event, he had been looking forward to a dinner of filet minion and baked potato, washed down with a nice Cabernet. But when the silent auction was extended by forty-five minutes Conrad knew dinner would either be cold, overcooked, or both, a situation he soothed by a second vodka tonic.

Dinner seating assignments for the auction had been another prolonged and exhausting task for the two chairwomen, with "up-front" tables being very much in demand. After all, the evening was known by everyone as The Mom Prom, an evening in which the young and beautiful mothers of Calivista Heights, in full movie star makeup and dressed in colossally expensive gowns, would parade into a beach club ballroom with the grandeur of a hundred Marie Antoinettes, stopping at each table to speak (with feigned interest) to the very same women they had regularly snubbed and gossiped about every day while on the playground watching their kids before school.

Conrad was supposed to have been seated between Rachel and Pete, a seating arrangement he and Rachel had agreed upon months before. But with Pete being MIA, Conrad had ended up sitting alone, watching the Mom Prom procession with no one seated on either side of him. No sooner had Rachel and Emily arrived than they had abandoned the dinner table to attend to undisclosed emergencies, *crises* he assumed were related to the live auction and most likely related to "the mystery item," which had been nothing but a nuisance ever since donations had started piling up in his garage six months ago. Now, with dinner finally being served, Conrad felt like a wallflower, unpopular and friendless with two empty chairs to his left and one empty chair to his right.

"Looks like you couldn't get a date for the prom."

Conrad turned to his right and saw Lionel Smart leaning over the vacant seat between them.

"I've been stood up," replied Conrad with a smile. "Twice."

"Ain't that a shame," said the old guy.

Conrad couldn't quite hear Lionel above the clanking of dishes and the cacophony of a few hundred voices all talking at once, so he leaned closer to Lionel and directly into a full gust of Scotch whiskey headwinds wafting from Lionel's breath.

"Beg your pardon?" said Conrad, ducking to avoid the next squall.

Lionel nodded his head, slurred a few unintelligible words, then squinted at Conrad as if seeing him for the first time.

"Mom Prom. That's what we of the opposchit schex call it." Lionel opened his left eyelid and winked as if letting Conrad in on a secret. "All this," Lionel waved his hand across the ballroom, "makes the ladies feel like they're back in high school." Lionel lifted his drink, took a swig of it, then added another wink just for Conrad. "Mom Prom. But don't tell *them* that." Lionel "hitch-hiked" his right thumb in the direction of his wife and the anorexic but expensively bejeweled Mrs. Vandee. The two women, seated next to each other, were in deep conversation and oblivious to Lionel's minor insult.

Conrad politely laughed, then Lionel guzzled the rest of his Scotch and abruptly turned his back on Conrad. Feeling snubbed and ill at ease, Conrad reached out to pull his steak closer but was dismayed to discover that an eager waiter had removed his plate during the few seconds in which he had leaned toward the whiskey headwinds.

"Conrad! Con! Connie!" called Lars Von Vander Somethingorother whose name no one on God's green earth could pronounce or spell or even remember. Lars and his wife Elsie, together known as The Vandees, or just The Vees, were on the School Board and big-time donors. "C'mere, Connie!" Lars was gesturing for Conrad to come over and sit next to him. Despite feeling that he might be forced to play *one-man-musical-chairs all night*, Conrad picked up his glass of vodka and moved over to the chair next to Lars.

"You're the husband of one of tonight's big honchos, aren't you?" It appeared that Lars was drinking only water that night.

"I guess you could say that," Conrad responded.

"So, I'm betting you know what that big mystery auction item is," boomed Lars.

It was like he was speaking to the entire room.

"Afraid not. It's a mystery to me, too," said Conrad in total honesty.

"Ah, come on, Con-man, you have to tell me if it's worth the money my wife is making me bid on it!" Lars laughed loudly at his pun, then coughed until his face turned beet-red.

"Honestly, Lars, I don't know what's in the trunk, but Rachel hinted that it's going to be worth all the suspense surrounding it."

"Surrrrrre you don't know." A killer cloud of garlic breath spewed from Lars's lips to Conrad's nostrils, causing Conrad to lean back as if hit in the chin by a phantom's right hook. He didn't know which was worse, a burst of garlic breath or a gust of sour Scotch whiskey.

"Think whatever you want, Lars, but Rachel didn't tell me a thing about the last auction item," said Conrad with a polite smile.

"Well, it better not be that damn puppy-dog your wife and her partner were going to give away or I'm going to be damn angry," Lars said to Conrad. "I've heard that dog's crazy!"

"I promise you it's not the *damn puppy dog*, Lars. He's at my house as we speak." Conrad shook his head. "And for all I know, he's turning our piano bench into kindling."

"Happy to hear that, Connie!" Lars V shouted then turned his back on Conrad.

This had actually been the longest conversation Conrad had ever had with Lars Vandee. Aside from greeting each other at various events, the two men had never had a noteworthy conversation with each other. Lars was predisposed to interact only with the largest of the school's donors. Even though Conrad and Rachel were not among them, Conrad felt that all of Rachel's volunteering duties at the school more than made up for their modest donations to the School's Annual Fund Drive. In fact, it would be impossible to put a price on the amount of time and talent Rachel had put forward over the last eighteen months, not to mention all the leftover pizza dinners (some moldy around the edges), the mounds of unfolded laundry, weekends without Rachel, weeknights without Rachel, the bed without Rachel, the endless Go Fish card games with Robbie *sans* Rachel, movie nights without Rachel, even family birthdays and some minor holidays without Rachel. In Conrad's mind, all of this amounted to far more than the largest School Fund donation, including the sum total of Lars V's contributions.

Suddenly, a high-pitched, screeching audio feedback caused everyone to look toward the stage. In her long black gown, her blonde hair pulled back into a French twist, Emily Fryze was staring at the microphone, looking utterly baffled as to how to stop the unpleasant feedback.

"Oooffta," she said holding the microphone away from her mouth. "I'm so sorry."

Her words caused a new ripple of audio feedback, amplified in waves, causing everyone in the room to reach for their ears. Emily winced at the sound, then looked behind her, desperately hoping someone with technical ability would come to her rescue.

Within seconds, Cupertino Flores, the school's custodian, scurried onto the stage and took the microphone from Emily. Cupertino held his shoulders high with his head sunk between them, displaying for everyone his painful discomfort at standing on a stage in front of a room full of important people. Cupertino fiddled with a button or two on the stem of the microphone, and the screeching stopped.

"Way to go, Coop!" shouted Lionel Smart. "Whoop-whoop for Coop!"

A few other semi-inebriated men joined the chorus, making Cupertino even more self-conscious. "Yea, Coop! You da man Coop! Coooooop!!"

Catcalls kept on coming during the thirty seconds it took Cupertino to show Emily how to use the microphone, and then, as if it would make him less visible to the people who had employed him for the past three years, Cupertino Flores tip-toed from the stage to hide behind the heavy gold curtains.

"We definitely owe Mr. Flores a big thank you," Emily said into the microphone. "Not just for helping with this microphone, but for all the things he does to keep our school in top shape. What would we do without our own Cupertino Flores?"

The crowd took Emily's cue and began clapping and then slowly, table by table the dinner guests collectively stood up to pay further homage to their multi-talented, underpaid, underappreciated, hardworking custodian.

After a few moments, it was apparent to Emily that Cupertino was not coming back on stage to acknowledge their appreciation, so she intervened. "I know Cupertino appreciates your appreciation. So, thank you one and all." Emily paused for a moment. "I want to let you know that the most important portion of the evening, the Live Auction, will be starting in ten minutes, so you have just enough time to review the pamphlet with details of the live auction items, except Auction Item Number Four. I promise there will be hints given along the way to help you figure it out. So, get ready to raise those bidding paddles!"

Emily carefully returned the microphone to its stand and left the stage as loud chatter from the guests began anew. Some people eagerly reviewed their auction pamphlet; others headed for the restrooms or began checking their cell phones for messages, probably wondering how much longer they would have to be there. It had already been a long evening.

Conrad stood up and scanned the room in hopes of seeing Rachel, but it was obvious she would not be coming out from behind the curtain to join him. Discouraged, Conrad turned to sit down but discovered Mrs. Vandee was sitting in his seat, all glittery and giddy and . . . looking for trouble.

CHAPTER 8

"HELLO, DOCTOR CONRAD Berger," sang the anorexic Mrs. Vandee in a low and sexy voice. "Mind if I sit with you for a while?"

"Not at all," Conrad lied. He suddenly felt hot, so he took off his jacket and placed it over the back of Rachel's vacant chair. The moment he sat down, Mrs. V pressed her mouth to his left ear.

"My husband has garlic breath, *againnnnn*," she whispered with utter annoyance. "It's impossible to sit near him."

"Oh, I hadn't noticed," Conrad lied again.

"And you lie like a rug," giggled Mrs. Vandee.

Conrad was at once ill at ease and tongue-tied.

"He eats anything and everything with garlic," she added, leaning her thin body close to Conrad's. "Not very promising for any bedroom festivities, if you catch my drift." She rolled her eyes at Conrad, who forced an awkward smile in return.

"Hmm," was all Conrad was able to muster. He was getting angrier by the minute at Pete Fryze for abandoning him tonight.

Conrad nervously glanced in the direction of the stage and felt a moment of relief at seeing Rachel standing at the podium. But this was short-lived because, Rachel was obviously huddled in a serious discussion with Emily and Cupertino, which most likely eliminated any remaining prospect of his wife joining him at the dinner table.

"I see you are getting a little low over there," Mrs. V said, pointing to Conrad's mostly empty cocktail glass.

"Looks like it, doesn't it," he said, looking at the ruby red, unnaturally long, perfectly manicured fingernail tapping at his cocktail glass. The half-melted ice and watered-down dregs of his vodka tonic were all that remained.

"Well, if you ask me," teased Mrs. V with a wink, "you need a refill."

"Too late. The bar's closed for the night," said Conrad.

Immediately, Conrad felt grateful Rachel and Emily had decided not to have an open bar for the Auction Night, unlike prior auctions where too many patrons had far too many free drinks at their disposal throughout the entire event. Everyone still talked about the previous auction where Vickie's stepfather, Lionel Smart, had stood atop a dinner table, hooting and waving his auction paddle in the air to prevent the auctioneer from closing the deal on a pair of size seventeen-and-a-half basketball shoes signed by Shaquille O'Neil.

To save herself and her mother, Valerie Smart, the embarrassment of a possible repeat performance by Lionel, Vickie Mack had demanded at an auction committee meeting months earlier, that there be no liquor of any kind, not even wine, during the entire evening.

In deference to her role on the committee, not to mention the memory of Lionel's show-stopper, Rachel and Emily had been inclined to consider Vickie's request, but they were promptly bombarded with alarm and vitriol from parents who vowed to not attend the fundraiser without the availability of the happy juice. So, Rachel and Emily compromised by permitting a "closed bar" that would be available *only* during the silent auction hour; in other words, no free alcohol, but guests could pay for their own drinks until the dinner hour. The bar would be closed for the night after that. As for dinner, Rachel and Emily had conceded to popular demand by providing one complimentary bottle of red wine and one complimentary bottle of white wine at each table during the dinner; all this much to Vickie's ire.

"Who needs a bar when you have . . . *thissss*," Mrs. Vandee crooned in an overly suggestive tone of voice. Conrad watched as Mrs. V retrieved a narrow, tubular object from inside her diamond-studded handbag. For a few seconds Conrad stared at it, then squinted both eyes so he could read the light blue lettering on the white paper sleeve of the tube Mrs. V held in her hand. The letters appeared to spell out "TAMPON," but Conrad was certain that could not be right. With a blank look on his face he glanced at Mrs. V, then back again at the object.

"Doctor Berger, surely you know what this is," she giggled like a schoolgirl with a silly secret.

"Ah, well, I'm not really sure." Conrad rotated his neck uncomfortably.

Mrs. V leaned forward, next to Conrad's left ear and whispered, "It's a fake tampon holder. Shhhhhhhh"

"Ah, well, there you are," Conrad said, mystified and befuddled.

"A fake tampon holder," Mrs. V repeated, snorting a giggle through her nose.

"Aha," Conrad responded. He looked around the table desperately hoping for someone, anyone, with whom to make eye contact, someone to pull into some other conversation, *any* conversation. Across the table, Mr. Vandee was huddled in deep political dialogue with Valerie and Lionel Smart. None of them were paying even the slightest attention to Conrad or the tampon-wielding Mrs. V.

"Can you guess what's inside my secret little tampon?"

"Well, I'm guessing it's a, ah, you know, a tampon?" Conrad rolled his neck around once again trying to work out the knot that had become lodged at its base. *All of this because Pete Fryze had missed his flight from Atlanta.*

"No, silly," Mrs. V twittered some more. "I said it's a *fake* tampon thingy."

"Well, then, you've got me there," said Conrad. Tampons, real or fake, were not topics he wished to discuss at a black-tie dinner with anyone, including his own wife. *Wasn't there some kind of statute, written or unwritten, that prevented women from discussing gender-specific issues like tampons to males, especially at formal events?*

"Look what I'mmm dooo-ing," sing-songed Mrs. V, even as she nuzzled closer to Conrad, who instinctively moved away from her.

Conrad watched Mrs. Vandee pull on the tampon sleeve to reveal a plastic tube filled with an orange-colored liquid. Then with the long, ruby-red nail of her thumb, she boldly flicked off its plastic cap and shamelessly raised the tube to her puckered lips. Conrad's chin dropped, and he could not help becoming bug-eyed.

"Mmmmm. Vintage Scotch—1967 Macallan! Want some?" She looked at Conrad with seductive eyes and lightly shimmied her shoulders. "Since those mean old auction ladies decided to close the bar so early, I decided to bring my own *reinforcements*." She giggled and shoved the tampon/booze holder into Conrad's hand. "There's a lot more where this one came from."

"Ohhh, no, no! No thanks," said Conrad, pushing the tampon back into Mrs. V's hands.

But Mrs. V would not be denied. She tilted the tampon *thing-a-ma-jig* over the rim of Conrad's cocktail glass and released a healthy stream of whiskey.

"My God, Elise, put that thingummy away!" bellowed Mr. V from across the table.

Guests from the surrounding tables craned their necks to see what "that thingummy" was. Mrs. V instantly dropped the fake tampon/whiskey container into Conrad's glass. "I'm just sharing a little something with my buddy Doctor Berger!" screeched Mrs. V back to her husband for all to hear.

Every muscle in Conrad's body stiffened as he knew there was no explaining what everyone was looking at. Afraid to make eye contact with anyone, Conrad just stared at the oversized, upside down tampon with rusty orange 1967 Macallan Scotch Whiskey swirling inside his glass, while everyone within eyesight gawked at him, wondering how a tampon ended up in his cocktail glass.

"What you got over there, Connie-my-man?" roared Lionel Smart.

"It's called preservation for the evening," trilled Elise V as she pulled a second female preservation unit from her glittering purse and waved it in Lionel's direction.

"What did you say you have in there?" Lionel teased.

"Lionel!" sneered Valerie Smart.

"Whaaat?" Lionel said with false innocence.

Valerie glared at her husband. "That is a woman's tampon," she said between her gritting teeth.

"Oh, Valerie, don't be so juvenile," reprimanded Mrs. V. "This little thing isn't what it looks like. It's just a fake hiding place for an itty-bitty touch of Scotch."

"Then at least be a little discreet and take it to the lady's bathroom, for god's sake," sneered Valerie Smart.

"Whoa, whoa, wait a minute," Lionel pleaded. "My dear Elise Vandee, please don't be stingy! Come over here and share some booze-in-the-tube with me." Lionel opened his arms wide, inviting Mrs. V to join him. "We can't let the Con-man have all the fun."

Mrs. V happily accepted Lionel's invitation and sashayed Marilyn Monroe-style around the table, finally plopping onto old Lionel's lap. A very jovial Lionel eagerly wrapped both his arms around Mrs. V's tiny waist. "Pour it down the hatch!" said Lionel, opening his mouth wide so Mrs. V could make a direct deposit of the entire contents of tampon-flask-number-two into the old guy's gullet.

As expected, Lionel Smart was living up to his raucous reputation by inciting numerous guests to pay closer attention to the boisterous goings-on at his table. Conrad glanced at the table next to his and was mortified to see that two women were staring at his cocktail glass with the upside-down, fake tampon. Blue neon letters loudly displayed the name of the feminine product.

"Sheesh!" hissed Conrad, knowing this was exactly the kind of madness everyone relished and gossiped about for days to come. With one swoop of his right hand, he reached for the female flask, rammed it into the breast pocket of his white shirt, and then, attempting to appear casually indifferent, he crossed his arms over his chest. Unfortunately, this caused an icy cold wetness to ooze through his shirt. He slowly looked down only to see that his soaking wet breast pocket looked like a mini billboard flashing the word TAMPON off and on.

Mercifully, a parade of waiters holding coffee and dessert trays, funneled into the ballroom and swarmed between tables, causing everyone around him to return their attention to their respective tables. Conrad waited a moment, looked around to be sure he was no longer being observed, then stealthily removed the tampon from his Scotch-stained shirt and stuffed it into the front pocket of his tuxedo jacket that was hanging on the back of Rachel's chair.

At that very moment, the house lights were raised to their full fluorescent glory.

"Hallelujah! It's finally showtime!" Lionel Smart jumped up from his seat ejecting Elise Vandee from the old man's lap and sending her flying face first onto the floor.

CHAPTER 9

WITH THE OVERHEAD lights beaming at full wattage from above, the grand ballroom had lost its warm, romantic mood and had taken on the glaring ambiance of a hospital operating room. Conrad recalled Rachel complaining a few weeks earlier that Vickie Mack had insisted there be bright, glaring lights during the live auction. "When bidders can clearly see what they are bidding on, they'll open their checkbooks even wider," was what Rachel had remembered Vickie saying.

Guests had adjusted to the glare and were sipping coffee and nibbling at their desserts while they reviewed the descriptions in their auction books and, perhaps, had begun thinking about their bids for the four Live Auction Items.

"Hey, Doctor Connie," yelled Lionel from across the table. "There's information on all the items but one. Mystery Item Number Four doesn't tell me a thing!" He was holding up the auction booklet for Conrad to see.

"I'm sure there will be hints about it before the bidding," said Conrad.

"I'm telling you, Mr. Husband-of-the-Co-Head-Honcherito, if they start hinting about that crazy dog, I won't offer one single dollar," said Lionel with contempt. "Got it?"

Emily and Rachel walked onto the stage arm-in-arm to loud clapping and cheers, rescuing Conrad from having to respond to Lionel's belligerence. Conrad was pretty sure the generous applause was not because both Emily and Rachel looked beautiful in their long black evening gowns, which they did, nor because everyone appreciated all the hard work and long hours it took for the two women to organize an evening like this. Conrad sensed the warm welcome was, in truth, an expression of relief that the last event of the evening was finally about to begin and soon, with some luck, everyone could go home.

"Thank you," said both Emily and Rachel into the microphone.

"Before we begin the Live Auction, we'd like to thank everyone for being here, and we'd like all the wonderful volunteers who helped to make this evening possible to please stand up," said Rachel with genuine gratitude in her voice.

While women throughout the room stood to receive recognition and applause, Conrad looked at his wife and her best friend and was flooded with memories of the last few days—how crazy it had been and how upset and agitated Rachel and Emily had both become. He'd never seen Rachel so nervous and tense. Conrad knew it was because of the dog—*the damn dog*—the dog that had been donated to the Auction Committee and had been touted by Vickie Mack as The Biggest Auction Item Ever. Rachel and Emily had never been convinced that a puppy would be the big auction night winner that Vickie Mack and the rest of the committee thought it would be.

Vickie Mack! That woman had made Rachel's and Emily's lives a living hell from the moment it was announced that *they, not Vickie Mack,* would be heading up the next year's auction. When she wasn't appointed to head the auction—but *was* appointed to the Auction Donation Committee— Vickie had decided in her own self-delusional way that Rachel and Emily had stolen her rightful leadership position from her! Just the thought of Vickie Mack angered Conrad, but now that he was thinking of her, *where was she?* She was supposed to be sitting at this table with her mother and stepfather.

"Valerie," said Conrad, leaning across the table towards Mrs. Smart. "I thought your daughter would be sitting with us tonight."

"Well," huffed Mrs. Smart to Conrad, as if blaming him for Vickie's absence. "Vickie was supposed to be *right here,* in this very seat!" Valerie Smart pointed to the seat next to her. "I can only imagine that she's backstage helping your wife and Emily Fryze. *Again!* Vickie is such a selfless person, always giving of her time. Lord knows your wife and Emily could never have pulled all this off . . . without her," said Valerie, ending her little tirade with a grand wave of both her arms.

"All I can say is, she better not be backstage helping out with that damn dog!" chided old Lionel, pointing his index finger directly at Conrad who wondered how and when the dog had become *his* fault.

"Lionel, you have my solemn promise there is no dog backstage," said Conrad sternly enough for Lionel Smart to know that that he, Conrad, was tired of hearing about the damn dog. "He's probably finished chewing on our piano bench and is now hanging from the dining room chandelier," Conrad added, hoping to lighten the mood at the table.

The applause throughout the ballroom had trickled down to nothing and all the women volunteers had now taken their seats.

"And so, without further ado," Rachel said from the stage, "we'd like to introduce you to our auctioneer for the evening. He is one of Calivista's very own, who most of you remember from the very funny and very popular TV show, *The Bizzaro Family!* Please welcome Ted Lloyd!" warbled Rachel.

Rachel had always sounded strong and confident when speaking in public, so Conrad wondered why her voice had faltered this time, as if she were nervous.

On cue, the dinner guests stood up from their seats, applauding and cheering as Ted Lloyd emerged from a table near the stage. He waved to the crowd, kissed his wife and then paused on each of the five steps leading to the stage to turn and wave at his adoring fans.

"Someone should tell Ted Lloyd this isn't the Oscars," said Lionel to no one in particular.

As Conrad remembered all too well, Ted Lloyd was not the auctioneer Rachel and Emily had wanted to hire for the evening. They had interviewed several professional auctioneers, two with scheduling conflicts, two others who had retired, and one *still available* who kept showing Rachel and Emily magic tricks and mentioning how he liked performing his tricks while conducting an auction. Rachel and Emily weren't yet worried, because they were scheduled to meet a highly recommended auctioneer who *was* available the night of the Calivista auction.

That's when Vickie Mack had entered the picture. Again. It was Vickie's brilliant idea that a trained, professional and licensed auctioneer would not be necessary. So enamored was Vickie with the school's "only famous TV star and parent" that on behalf of the entire school community she *personally* invited the faded TV personality to be the auctioneer for the night. Vickie had waited to announce her "Big Get" at the School Board meeting, where Rachel and Emily were scheduled to present an update on the Auction Committee's progress. In fact, Emily and Rachel had barely mentioned their progress regarding the professional auctioneers when Vickie Mack stood up.

"Please let me interrupt you two lovely and well-intentioned women for just a moment. I have the best news *ev-ver* that is going to save you from an *auctioneer disaster!*" Vickie stormed up to where Rachel and Emily had been standing and physically edged them away before proceeding to tell the Board her *best news ev-ver.*

Needless to say, Vickie had convinced the Board that having Ted Lloyd serve as the auctioneer was, in Vickie's words, "a brilliant idea and would be of great savings to the committee, especially since Ted Lloyd *would probably, well, most likely,* donate his time for free."

Well, as Rachel and Emily learned later, Mr. Fading TV star was *delighted* to be the school's auctioneer though *highly insulted* by the misguided assumption that he would "donate" his esteemed name and valuable time to the school *for free*. In fact, Ted Lloyd ended up charging far more for his services than any of the potential professional auctioneers, but that didn't matter to Vickie Mack, because *on her own* she had found "a famous personality" to host the Auction, guaranteeing to the Board the biggest success *ever.*

"Just think what a coup this is for our little school. I'm going to announce it in the *Calivista Post*. All the other schools will be so envious," Vickie told the School Board that night in her signature, sugary voice.

*

The crackling sound of a microphone under assault by Ted Lloyd was enough to jar Conrad out of those painful memories and back to the Auction.

"Well! Hellllloooo everyone at Calivista Elementary Schooooool!" shouted a loose and much-too-relaxed Ted Lloyd. Cheers and hooting erupted from the audience.

Well, thought Conrad, *maybe this balding old coot has the chops to pull off the role of auctioneer after all.* He craned his neck a bit so he could see Rachel's reaction as she and Emily stood to the side of the stage in front of the curtain.

"Let me just say right off that you all look more despicable and debased than any group of people with whom I've ever had the displeasure of consorting!" Ted boldly yelled to his audience.

Less vociferous cheering and far fewer hoots responded to this unusual, somewhat confusing greeting from one of their school's very own, once-famous TV star, Ted Lloyd. Conrad looked at Rachel, whose right hand now covered her mouth as if in horror.

"Ahhhh, come on," Ted reprimanded the audience. "You know what I mean. We're all in this together, aren't we?" Ted spread both arms wide to include the entire room full of people. A smattering of puzzled but still supportive cheers and applause answered Ted's bizarre call for unity, as if the audience were in a bunker together.

Conrad noticed several people clearing their throats and some whispering from behind raised auction pamphlets.

"Well, okay, you know what they say, if you can't take a joke . . . we'll just have to get this thievery, this highway robbery underway!" Ted Lloyd yelled at the top of his lungs. "Is everyone ready to *rummmbulllllle?*"

CHAPTER 10

A NERVOUS QUIET had filtered through the cavernous ballroom, broken only by a few whispers fanning from tables here and there. The handful of men who had shouted out their "whoo-hoos" in response to Ted Lloyd's opening monologue, had instantly received the ever-forceful stink-eye from their wives. Those husbands were now behaving and sitting quietly in their seats.

"Soooo, what do we have first on the *deal 'em and steal 'em* docket?" Ted Lloyd bellowed into the microphone.

Visibly alarmed, Emily Fryze stepped away from the curtain, walked to where Ted Lloyd stood and politely pointed to the cue cards that had been placed on the podium, the very same list of auction items with which he, the auctioneer, was supposed to have become familiar prior to the auction.

Emily and Rachel had begged the fading actor to review the auction items with them, but the self-aggrandizing Ted Lloyd used their only meeting with him to expound upon the advantages of his being "a star" with what he described as his "God-given gift to *ad lib* in surprising and entertaining ways." He had told the ladies that he had begun his career as a stand-up comedian "with tremendous extemporaneous talent," and saw no need for *any* preparation. In fact, just the opposite; he preferred to go in cold.

"Oooo-la-la!" Ted Lloyd said loudly in response to Emily standing beside him. "Mmmm, what shall the starting bid be for this lovely lady? What did you say your name was?"

Aghast, Emily turned several shades of red and pointed again at the cue cards, even as nervous giggles rippled through the audience.

"Well, you're no fun," Lloyd said as he leaned toward Emily, using the microphone stand to steady his balance. "Okay, I have here the first lively item to be liveried-off to all you salivating dupes out there! Open your checkbooks!"

From the stage, Emily watched in alarm as a friend of hers, a wealthy and generous donor, stood up from her table near the front and abruptly left the ballroom, followed by her dutiful husband.

"Oh, come on," Ted spitefully called out with both hands cupped around his lips. "Don't get your panties in a bunch. I'm just funning with you."

Horrified by what she had just heard, Emily quickly covered the microphone with one hand and whispered, "Mr. Lloyd, please. Please just start with this item."

"Of course, my lady," Ted responded with mock chivalry, then bowed with a sweep of his right arm.

Emily hated being patronized, and it took all of her inner fortitude to keep her emotions in check. She fixed her eyes angrily on Ted Lloyd's eyes. Ted met Emily's glare and decided to appease her.

"Well, I see we have here . . ." Ted paused. He looked at the cue card, then at Emily. "Where is it?"

Emily pointed to the clear plastic case sitting on a table, only two steps to Ted's right. A backlight illumined a basketball signed by Magic Johnson.

Ted Lloyd stepped toward the case and picked it up. Holding it close to his eyes, he squinted at the signature on the basketball. "Damn! Looks like the one and only Magic Johnson signed this bouncy ball."

A scattering of men laughed.

"Whoo-hoo! I just might bid on this myself," Ted sang out.

Suddenly, ten bidding plaques shot into the air. Emily immediately pushed the cue card up to Ted's face.

"Hold on, hold on!" Ted waved his hand at the audience. "This fetching lady wants me to tell you that the starting bid is nine hundred dollars."

Several more bidding plaques shot up.

"Okay, it's game on!" Ted roared at the audience. "I see abbbaa-dabaa-ba-dubie dubie-dada," he said waving his finger around the room until he finally pointed at the closest bidder, "I see you!"

"One thousand," the man shouted.

"We've got one thousand, but I know there's another fool out there who wants to throw away one thousand, five dollars on this pathetic orange ball!"

Three bidding plaques rose in the air and Ted whistled again. "Okie-dokie, that chump over there says he wants to throw away fifteen hundred shamolians. Anyone else more stupid than that?"

This insult did not sit well with Ted's audience and not a single plaque was elevated. Nothing but dead silence filled the ballroom.

"Oh, come on. Can't you take a joke?" Ted Lloyd geared. "I'm going to be a little reckless and bid two thousand dollars of my own war chest!"

The Calivista parents and guests stared at their auctioneer in disbelief.

"You're not allowed to bid on anything," Emily nervously whispered in Ted's ear.

"Any more bidders?" Ted taunted the crowd, completely ignoring Emily. One plaque rose from the middle of the ballroom.

"Three thousand, five hundred," shouted out an inebriated Lionel Smart. "Damned if I'll let some smart ass outsmart-ass me!"

Emily, still standing beside Ted, had been perspiring like a guilty defendant and was quite aware of the large sweat rings that had been forming under her armpits. She glued both arms tightly to her sides and stiffly walked to the back of the stage where Rachel stood.

"Don't worry," whispered Rachel. She should have mouthed *don't' worry* to the entire audience because *worry* was hanging in the air like a bad odor.

Rachel grabbed Emily's shoulders and turned her about-face. She wasn't sure what they could do to stop the actor-auctioneer, but Rachel knew they had to do something. Walking arm in arm, Rachel and Emily marched towards Ted Lloyd.

"Well, well, well," Ted Lloyd taunted Lionel Smart. "Are you crazy? Three thousand, five hundred buckaroos for a rubber ball?"

"No!" Lionel hollered. "I'm raising you to five thousand and calling your bluff."

Every guest in the room turned their attention to Valerie Smart, who, red-faced and seething with anger, tugged at Lionel's coat sleeve. Mr. V leaned close to Lionel and, with one hand on his shoulder, politely attempted to calm the excited old man.

"It's not a poker game," explained Mr. Vandee.

"I know I'm not at a poker game!" Lionel barked at Mr. V. "I want that damn basketball!"

"Going once!' Ted Lloyd yelled at the top of his lungs. All eyes darted back to the stage. "Going twice!" Ted took the gavel in his hand. "Gooooinnnngggg, going, gone!" Ted Lloyd pounded the wooden gavel on the podium and hollered, "Sold to the crazy old dude standing on his chair!"

"Oh yeah! Look who's a smart-ass now!" Lionel Smart yelled, pointing at the auctioneer, an action that caused him to wobble and nearly fall off his chair.

"Easy does it," said Mr. V, helping Lionel step off the chair.

Two exceptionally cute auction helpers, high school girls with clipboards in their hands, rushed to Lionel to get his plaque number and credit card.

"Who says you can't *rrrrrumble* at a ridiculous school auction like this one? Huh?" Ted Lloyd asked the crowd.

Up on the stage, Rachel had stepped up beside Ted on his right side, Emily on his left, and each took a gentle hold of one of his arms.

"Well, well, who do we have here?" the auctioneer first looked down at Emily and then turned to look at Rachel. "Hello, have we met before?"

Both women smiled. Rachel squeezed Ted's upper arm hoping he'd get the hint.

"Ouch, oooo, ouch!" Ted Lloyd teased loudly into the microphone. "Girls, girls, you're killing me!" Ted pulled the microphone close to his mouth and in a sexy voice whispered, "I think my two very pretty dates, well, pretty for almost over-the-hill, ha-ha-ha, want me to get to the next exciting, must-have auction item."

Every guest in the entire room had now turned their attention to the baffling auctioneer on stage. Emily was blushing bright red, even as sweat poured down her arms. Rachel reached for the cue cards, wanting to get them away from Ted who, at the same moment, reached for the cue cards himself. The two locked eyes as Ted yanked the cards away from Rachel.

"Auction item *numero dos*!" Ted yelled into the microphone. Ted held the top card high in the air, brought it to his forehead and closed his eyes. He made a humming sound, ostensibly imitating a psychic. "And the answer is, A Cabin Retreat in Whistler, British Columbia!"

The audience stared and remained silent. Emily felt another stream of sweat cascading down her arms even as Rachel felt a sudden surge of pain in her left eye, a tell-tale sign that a powerful migraine had begun.

Everyone in the ballroom silently stared at the two co-chairs with accusing eyes. Rachel knew they were all wondering how she and Emily could have hired this lewd, humorless, washed up sitcom actor. The night was a disaster and it was their fault.

Ted's eyes remained closed. "I repeat, the answer is . . . A Cabin Retreat in Whistler, British Columbia," he said as if he was a psychic expecting to *hear* more about auction item *numero dos*.

And then a small miracle happened.

"What is Auction Item Number Two?" called out a voice very familiar to Rachel.

Ted Lloyd removed the card from his head and looked toward the middle of the room, in the direction of Dr. Conrad Berger. Rachel gasped and joined everyone in the room to look directly at her husband.

"You, *mi amigo*, are right!" yelled Ted Lloyd. All heads pivoted back to Ted, like the audience at a tennis match. "But can you please answer in Spanish, *senior*?" Ted called to Conrad.

"*Que es numero dos*?" Conrad called in a lighthearted voice. Rachel's heart melted when she saw Conrad wink at her.

"You da man!" Ted said and began clapping his hands with the microphone between them. To Emily and Rachel's utter amazement the whole room began clapping and turning their heads to smile at Conrad, then to smile at Ted, and then to smile at Emily and Rachel.

"Looks like the starting bid for *numero dos*—the Canadian vacation— is four thousand dollars. Do I have a first bid?"

Because Ted seemed a little more grounded, Emily and Rachel stepped away to give him some space.

"Oh, no, no, no, don't you two lovely chickadees go anywhere," Ted said into the microphone. "I need you to help keep this higgledy-piggledy crowd from murdering me."

A few people laughed.

"You don't want to be responsible for manslaughter, do you?" Ted Lloyd asked.

Rachel and Emily looked as if they wouldn't mind killing him themselves.

"Four thousand dollars!" shouted Conrad Berger.

All heads swung around again to see Conrad holding his paddle high in the air.

"Going once," Ted shouted into the microphone.

Rachel gasped. She and Conrad didn't have four thousand dollars to spend on a mountain vacation!

"Four thousand, eight hundred," called another husky voice from the opposite side of the room.

"Five thousand," interrupted another guest.

Rachel and Emily were amazed at the rising vitality in the room. Despite Ted Lloyd's unwelcomed outbreaks of spite and malevolence aimed at Calivista School, its patrons, the good parents and everyone else, the room seemed amused. Shockingly, this equal opportunity offender had somehow charmed the audience into outbidding each other and the final bids on auction items one, two and three far surpassed Rachel and Emily's hopes and expectations. One moment, creepy Ted had been spitting insults at a room full of bemused guests, and an instant later, he had the same crowd eating out of his hand and making outrageous bids, higher and then even higher. The bids just kept coming.

Emily nodded and even smiled at Rachel, and they seemed to agree that they could leave the stage. They turned and slowly walked away.

"Girls! Ladies!" Ted Lloyd whined as he knelt on one knee. Holding the microphone with his hands in prayer mode, he sang to the tune of a famous Bob Dylan song, "Stay, ladies, stay."

Rachel and Emily froze in place, their backs to Ted.

"Stay, ladies, stay!" crooned one obnoxious guest close to the stage.

It was uncanny that more than a few other male guests joined in chorus, "Stay, ladies, stay!"

Simultaneously, Rachel and Emily turned around and with stiff smiles, walked back to their new, least-best friend, Ted Lloyd.

"That's more like it," Ted mocked as he swung his right arm around Emily's neck and his left arm around Rachel's, nearly choking both women.

"Okay you pathetic pile of parents, now that I have Tweedle Dee and Tweedle Dum back by my side, let's get this fiasco over with," yelled Ted as if leading a charge.

Grateful the evening would soon be coming to an end, Rachel turned and looked at the old travel trunk resting just off stage, Auction Item Number Four.

CHAPTER 11

UNABLE TO ENDURE much more of Ted Lloyd's antics, Conrad had taken liberty of his table during the final bidding on Auction Item Number Three and had taken sanctuary in a quiet corner of the hotel lobby.

"Pete," said Conrad into his cell phone. "The good news is, despite the evening having been an unmitigated circus, it looks like our wives managed to raise a ton of money for the school. The bad news is, my serves on the tennis court will not be forgiving. I don't know what happened to you today, but you owe me big-time, buddy, and I mean big-time. See you on the court."

Conrad tucked his cell phone into his pocket and headed back to the ballroom.

✓

*

Up on stage, Ted Lloyd had been making the most of his final moments of fame for all they were worth. "Where is our fateful finale?" Ted paused, milking the drama and looking at Rachel and Emily as if they shared a secret.

Conrad returned to the table and took his seat across from Mrs. V and Lionel Smart. He looked around the room. Everyone seemed exhausted, as if the auctioneer, like house guests and dead fish, had overstayed his welcome. Still, all eyes were focused on the stage, where Cupertino Flores and two of his helpers were dragging the large steamer trunk to the center of the stage. Conrad noticed that Rachel and Emily looked at each other as if confused.

And they were confused. Both women were trying to figure out why the trunk seemed so heavy. All it had inside was a red velvet bowtie, a ball gown, a costume tiara, plus a large envelope with the six Viking Cruise Tickets and a card detailing a luxurious two-week vacation ending in Austria at the famous Vienna New Year's Waltz. *How heavy could that be?*

Standing and watching, Rachel recalled speaking briefly with Cupertino Flores when he had arrived at the Beaumont Beach Club earlier that afternoon. He'd just come from her home with the trunk and other auction paraphernalia that had been stored in her garage. He mentioned that the trunk was '*muy* heavy,' but she'd been too frazzled to pay close attention to what Cupertino had said and, instead, hastily thanked him for delivering everything safely. She vaguely remembered asking if the dog gave him any problems and had felt relief when Cuppertino said, '*No perro*' which she was sure meant 'no problem' in Spanish. *Didn't it?*

Cupertino and his helpers dropped the trunk at the front of the stage with a thud that echoed throughout the ballroom.

"Whoa, guys, tell me there's not a couple of dead bodies in there," teased Ted Lloyd.

Most of the audience laughed.

"If it's that damn dog, it better be dead," shouted Lionel Smart.

Everyone laughed as Emily and Rachel shook their heads to assure the potential bidders that the dog was not in the trunk. Cupertino and the two assistants left the stage.

"Okee-dokee-then," Ted sing-songed. "Let's get this ohhhhh-so-mysterious Item Number Four started so we can all be done with this despicable evening of wasteful lavishness."

The atmosphere once again felt uncomfortable and edgy.

"It says here on my card that a hint will be forthcoming from Mr. Flores. Oh, goodie, we all get to suffocate the man with more applause."

Light laughter lifted the mood.

"Cupertino Flores, come on down!" Ted shouted ala *The Price is Right*.

Cupertino shuffled back on stage holding a large Lego replica of a luxury cruise ship. "That's not too heavy for you, is it Mr. Flores?" Ted taunted.

Cupertino ignored the question, walked over to Rachel and Emily, and held out the Lego ship for one of the women to take from him. Emily kindly lifted the ship from his arms and held the ship out for everyone to see.

"Aha! There you have it, ladies and gentlemen, it's your first clue to get the bidding started on mystery Item Number Four! I see here that the starting bid is for eight thousand dollars! That's a lot of moola-boola for a measly Lego ship." Ted Lloyd pretended to be beside himself.

"Ten thousand," called someone from the back.

"Eleven thousand five hundred," another person called nearby.

"Hold your horses, you drunken fools, I'm supposed to give you another clue," Ted said somewhat angrily. "Can't find it, though."

Several men playfully booed at Ted.

"Ohhhh, please, please, you're hurting my feelings," Ted said.

Emily tapped Ted's shoulder and pointed to a large red envelope sitting on the podium. It clearly read, Clue #2.

A few more friendly hecklers booed.

Ted picked up the red envelope, placed it over his heart and whined, "I don't think you like me anymore."

"Awww," several guests crooned with fake sympathy.

And then, without rhyme or reason, Ted roused the ghost of Dracula and said, "Vell, then, vhy don't vunn of our *ladies of zee night*," he paused, making lascivious gestures at Rachel and Emily, "geeve you zee next clooo." Ted whisked the envelope into Rachel's hand and then pushed the microphone close to her face.

"Oh!" Rachel was taken off guard. "Thank you, Ted." She took a deep breath. "I hope everyone has figured out that part of Auction Item Number Four includes a luxury cruise."

"Well, whoopee-duppee!" Ted mocked.

"But," Rachel glared at the auctioneer, "inside this envelope is a brochure hinting at where the cruise is headed and for how many people."

Rachel then pulled from the envelope a glossy brochure and six sleek Viking Cruise tickets and was happy to hear a fair amount of *ooing* and *ahhing*.

Ted grabbed the tickets, held them high, and spoke into the microphone. "Hey, someone just won the Super Bowl! Where are you going next?"

"I'm going to Disneyland!" someone shouted. Lots of laughter erupted which greatly helped to loosen the crowd once again.

"Wrong, you dimwit," Ted yelled. "You're going to Austria, on a Lego boat and you get to bring your nagging wife and four boring in-laws with you!"

A few guests lightly coughed.

"Twelve thousand," yelled Lionel Smart.

"Thirteen thousand," a woman from across the room countered him.

"Looks like you all just love spending time in a sardine ship with your mother-in-law!" jeered Ted.

"Better her than you!" someone heckled from the middle of the room.

"Fifteen thousand!" Lionel Smart called out.

"Now we're talking," said Ted. "Who will give me sixteen thousand?"

"Twenty thousand," Lionel shouted out.

"Lionel, you can't just go and outbid your own self," Mr. V huffed at Lionel.

"Oh, yes, I can." Lionel pushed Mr. V's hand away and stood back on his chair. "Twenty-eight thousand, because my beautiful wiff over here told me she'd kill me if I didn't take this damn Auction Number Four home."

People nervously laughed, expecting old Lionel to be standing on the table any minute.

"Come on you weaklings out there in Calivista Land," Ted yelled into the microphone. "Make this man work harder to prove his virility and love for the old bag sitting beside him."

Not one person spoke or raised a plaque.

Rachel tugged on Ted's arm, whispering into his ear while pointing to his cue card.

"Wait a minute, wait a minute," Ted called out. "This luscious little lady here tells me there is one more hint to get these bids going higher. I'm reading directly from this cue card that says, 'a once in a lifetime dream come true inside this very trunk but it won't be revealed until the final bid has been made'." Ted chuckled with disdain. "Ain't that got to be worth more than twenty-eight thousand to you bunch of cheapskates!"

"Forty thousand and that's the end of it," shouted Lionel.

The room was still.

"Going once!" egged Ted.

"Going two and three hundred final times and sold to me!" Lionel yelled. He jumped off the chair and stormed on to the stage. "Now unlock that damn trunk and let my wife see what's inside so I can finally go home and get a decent drink!"

The room full of guests stood and clapped as Lionel ran onto the stage.

"Valerie, get your hot body over here so I don't have to pretend to act all giddy on your behalf," Lionel barked at his wife.

Beaming with a big smile, Valerie Smart walked regally toward the stage. She carefully lifted her long, glittering gown as she gingerly tiptoed up the steps and stood between her husband and the steamer trunk.

Lionel bent down and attempted to unlock the latch, but it wouldn't budge. "Now what? You going to make me say Mitch-a-ca-boo-la, bibbi-ty-bobbity-boo?" yelled Lionel at Rachel and Emily. He waved his fingers at the latch, and the crowd roared with laughter.

The trunk should have opened easily but Rachel could see the latch was askew. She motioned for Cupertino to come out and help. Standing backstage, Cupertino reached into a tool box, grabbed a hammer and a large screwdriver and quickly shuffled on stage to the trunk. Lionel angrily grabbed the tools from Cupertino, bent over the trunk and furiously hammered the screwdriver through the latch. Within seconds the latch broke and fell to the floor with a loud clang, causing the waiting audience to clap and cheer.

Lionel stood to face the crowd, bowed and then turned to his wife. "There, my dear," he said in a loud, booming voice. "You may have the honor of opening the trunk."

All anyone remembered hearing was the ungodly primeval scream of Valerie Smart.

CHAPTER 12

SHORTLY AFTER MIDNIGHT, Peter Fryze was sitting in his first-class window seat, staring out at a fog-shrouded runway as his plane taxied toward the terminal at LAX. After what had happened earlier that day at Atlanta's Hartsfield Airport, he'd been loath to make eye contact with anyone on the entire flight, especially the flight attendants. He kept his eyes focused outside as he reflected on how normal his day had begun: a successful breakfast meeting; no traffic delays driving to the airport, arriving well ahead of schedule; and then an upgrade from seat 38E to 15A, an aisle seat far away from the bathrooms. Pete recalled feeling almost virtuous knowing he was on schedule to arrive at LAX in time to pick up his car in the long-term parking lot, drive to his apartment in Calivista Heights, change into his tuxedo and arrive at the Beaumont Club by five o'clock, just as he had promised Emily.

How could such a promising start to the day end up being the most miserable experience of his life? As a career cable television executive, Pete had been around some of Hollywood's most imaginative screenwriters, but he doubted anyone could have scripted the sequence of events in which he had become entangled as his plane was about to depart from Atlanta. Even by Hollywood standards, it had crossed the line from bizarre to surreal.

Was it his fault the very attractive young woman seated in 15B began talking to him even before he'd settled into seat 15A? True, he was accustomed to flirtatious advances from women. Was it his fault that he, Peter

Fryze, was by everyone's estimation including his own, strikingly hand-some, even charming as he exuded an aura of financial success with a hint of European *savoir-faire?* By his own admission, Peter was captivated by these types of casual flirtations like a moth to a flame; but not this time, he had told himself. He wasn't willing to further jeopardize his hope of restoring his wobbly marriage and moving back into the Calivista Heights home that he and Emily had been so proud to own.

The problem was three-fold. One, the woman in Seat 15B had begun making small talk even before he'd settled into his seat. Two, her glistening brown eyes, exotic long eyelashes—*fake or real*, even now, he wasn't sure which—and her long, wavy blonde hair had kept him from immediately pulling out his earphones, the universal indicator for "don't bother me, I'm going to be busy the entire flight." And three, as she continued making small talk her eyes had started to overflow with tears.

 *

"Are you okay?" Pete asked, not really wanting to engage but still drawn toward her.

The woman took a deep breath. "I'm fine, I really am. It's been a long few days, I was in Florida, well, Tampa, to visit my parents. My daugh-ter—" She paused mid-sentence, looked down, and then looked directly into Pete's eyes. "She's been so sick."

"I'm sorry to hear that," said Pete.

"It's called rhinovirus. Have you heard of it?"

"I think so," said Pete, now fully engaged. "Respiratory?"

The blond woman nodded her head as more tears spilled from her eyes.

As the LA bound airplane began to slowly back away from the gate, a flight attendant began her introductory speech from up near the galley. "Welcome aboard Flight 978 to Los Angeles."

Pete looked toward the front, where a bony flight attendant dressed in a crisp, navy-blue jacket and matching skirt was standing, her shoulders erect.

She was speaking into a handheld telephone attached to a curlicued cord that extended from inside the kitchenette. In her right hand, she was waving an information card in the air, and with practiced authority, she barked instructions into the phone. "I need all of my passengers to find the emergency information card located in the seat pocket in front of you."

As far as Pete could tell, no one, including himself, was looking for the emergency card. Or paying any attention to the flight attendant.

"Now, I'd like *all* my passengers to wave the emergency card above your head so I can be sure everyone has a card immediately available." The attendant's voice had gone from informative to didactic.

She's absurd, thought Pete. He looked at his attractive seatmate to see if she had been listening to the intercom. *Nope.*

She gazed at Pete. "Do you have children?" she asked.

"Yes, I have two." Pete smiled, then added, "But, sadly, my wife and I are separated." The moment the word "separated" tumbled out of his mouth, Pete regretted his upgrade to Seat 15A. Like the sirens of Greek mythology whose singing lured ships into dangerous waters, the eyes of seat 15B had rendered Pete powerless.

"Oh," she said as if pleasantly surprised. *Surprised he was separated or surprised he had children?* Pete assumed the former.

"FAA rules require you to turn off *all* electronic devices," the flight attendant said louder than was necessary. "And I do mean *all*."

"How old are your children?" asked 15B. They were now face to face with each other, almost as if on a love seat.

Before Pete could answer, the flight attendant's voice bellowed overhead. "Passengers, I need *all* eyes on me while I explain lifesaving, safety instructions!"

"Our son is five and our daughter is almost three," Pete answered.

"Really? *My* daughter is almost three." She smiled, happy to discover the two of them had *so* much in common.

"It is not only mandatory that *all* passengers turn off their electronic devices," the attendant's voice broke through, "but, let me repeat, it is a LAW, a requirement of the Federal Aviation Authority that *all* passengers pay close attention to me *now* as I demonstrate emergency instructions for your safety!"

Pete had heard flight safety procedures hundreds of times so, naturally, he continued to ignore the officious flight attendant standing five rows in front of him.

"Is your wife a stay-at-home mom?" asked the woman.

"She is."

"Oh, you have no idea how lucky your children are. I mean, do you think it's better for young children like *ours* to be shipped off to childcare or to be at home with their mother?" Her glistening eyes answered the question.

"Well," Pete said, trying to concentrate. "It depends." He had been trying, unsuccessfully, not to notice that this beautiful young woman was also, in fact, very well endowed. His mind now otherwise occupied, Pete was unaware that the flight attendant had suddenly focused her full attention on seats 15A and 15B, even as the plane had found its place in the runway queue line.

"I mean, everyone's situation is unique, isn't it?" said Pete, smiling at his seatmate.

"Unbelievable!" the attendant huffed loudly, staring intently at Pete and his new, very pretty friend. They both looked up and saw the flight attendant disappear into the plane's kitchenette and heard the phone slammed down.

"Does your wife want to work?" asked 15B, returning her attention to Pete.

"Ahhh, not right now," Pete faltered.

Suddenly, the attendant burst from the kitchenette holding the phone in her hand, pulling the curly cord with her, and was once again speaking to her indifferent audience. "I assume everyone can hear me *now*," her voice boomed over the intercom. Then, like a Nazi soldier, she goose-stepped down the aisle, stretching the phone cord almost to the max, nearly reaching row fifteen.

"I'm just curious to hear what *you* think because I *want* to be a stay-at-home mother, but it's just so hard, because I'm estranged from my husband and seriously contemplating divorce." The young woman lightly touched Pete's arm, causing a flutter of nervousness in his stomach.

He looked from the young woman's pretty brown eyes to the delicate hand resting on his forearm. "Boy, that's a hard one, isn't it?" said Pete.

"Emergency exits are located in the front of the plane, the middle and the back," the attendant said, thrusting her arms backward and then forward.

Pete had an inkling the flight attendant was upset . . . *but why?*

"May I ask why you and your wife are separated?" The woman spoke softly, intimately, still touching his arm.

Pete hesitated, glancing at the flight attendant then back at the woman. "Oh, gosh, that's a tough question to answer," he said, "especially after being married nine years."

The young woman's hand floated from Pete's forearm to her heart.

"That's so sad," she sighed. "I've been married just four years, and it's been such a struggle. I can't imagine being married that long and then having it all . . . end."

"Well, actually, I'm hoping my wife and I will . . ." That's as far as Pete got.

"*Discourteous!* That's what some people are! Discourteous and rude!" The flight attendant's voice blasted over the loudspeaker.

Pete looked up only to see the attendant make another about-face and march behind the confines of the kitchenette. Once again, crackling and clicking noises pierced through the intercom at their highest volume.

An older man across the aisle in 15D looked at Pete and rolled his eyes as if to say, *Can you believe this woman?*

Pete answered by rolling his own eyes.

"Is the flight attendant okay?" asked Pete's alluring seatmate.

"I think there's some kind of technical problem with the sound system," Pete answered, doubting his own words.

At that moment, the flight attendant burst out of the kitchenette holding a yellow oxygen mask in her right hand.

"She couldn't be upset that we're talking, could she?" whispered the young woman.

Because Pete had turned to answer his seatmate, he had not seen the flight attendant marching straight toward row 15.

"No way," Pete said.

"I didn't think so," she answered, once more placing her hand on Pete's forearm. "Thank you so much for listening to me. I'm just so emotional right now, I guess I needed a shoulder to lean on."

"My pleasure," Pete said, basking in the sensuality of her warm hand resting upon his arm. Pete's full attention was on the young woman and those beautiful brown eyes, so he had not seen the flight attendant pull the elastic band attached to an oxygen mask and extend it as far as it would go.

Suddenly, the flight attendant discharged the band causing a sharp snapping sound to vibrate throughout the sound system. Pete looked up to see the attendant step forward in an overly dramatic, attention-grabbing manner, stopping one inch from Pete's face.

"Ladies and gentlemen," the attendant's voice thundered throughout the plane. "In case of an emergency, an oxygen mask will drop from above, and you will need to place the mask directly over your nose and mouth." The attendant's eyes were now fixed on Peter Fryze and without warning she thrust the oxygen mask over Pete's nose and mouth.

Pete immediately jerked his head away from the mask and was now face to face with his beautiful seatmate. She began giggling . . . a cute absurdist, giggle.

"Remember to place the oxygen mask over your own nose and mouth before securing your child's oxygen mask," said the attendant, while leaning over Pete in order to whisk the mask over the nose and mouth of his stunned seatmate.

"Hey!" Pete said loudly as an involuntary reflex caused him to knock the flight attendant's arm away from his seatmate's face.

By now, most of the nearby passengers were aware something was going on in Row 15, and many craned their necks to see over their headrests.

"Help!" screamed the attendant. "I've been attacked!" She whipped the mask away from Pete's new friend and held it tightly to her chest as if to shield herself from Pete's fury.

Bewildered passengers watched the hysterical attendant scuttle toward the front of the plane and feverishly shut the curtain of the kitchenette as if protecting herself from an assault. Then every head turned to get a better view of the man in 15A who had accosted the flight attendant.

"That one's a nutcase," said the old man across the aisle.

"What a weirdo," laughed a woman leaning over the seat in front of Pete.

"I'm so embarrassed," Pete's seatmate whispered. "I guess she really was mad at us for talking during her instructions."

"Forget it," said a woman passenger from behind them. "That lady has some kind of bee in her bonnet. I noticed it the moment I got on the plane."

Additional words of support were suddenly interrupted by the sound of someone pounding on the cockpit door. The attendant's shrill voice screamed, "Stop the plane! An official of the airlines has been attacked!"

"What the—?" said the man across from Pete.

Pete and his seatmate sat stunned as muffled voices of other passengers conveyed surprise and disbelief among themselves. Moments later, the plane taxied off the runway, and passengers looked out the windows to see fire trucks, police cars and ambulances racing toward the plane. Pete felt his heart pounding through his chest the moment he saw a portable stairway rolling along the tarmac to the side of the airplane and heard the familiar sound of the airplane's engines shutting down. Seconds later, a calm, deep voice with a thick southern drawl flooded the intercom system.

"Ladies and gentlemen, this is your pilot. There's been an incident on our airplane, so I'd like y'all to remain buckled in your seats until further notice. Law enforcement officials at the terminal have been alerted and will be coming on board to assess the situation. Please remain calm until this situation is resolved, oh, and please do not leave your seats. Just until we get things settled."

Seconds later, four intense-looking FBI agents wearing blue flak jackets with the letters FBI boldly stenciled on the front and back entered the plane, followed immediately by three Atlanta Airport police officers and two paramedics.

The flight attendant greeted them by pointing down the aisle. "The man in 15A!" she screeched. "He's the one who attacked me!"

Before he could process what had happened, Pete was yanked out of his seat by two agents, handcuffed and summarily guided down the aisle like a terrorist.

"There's been a mistake," said Pete to the burly agent who was holding his right arm in a vice grip.

"Don't make this worse for yourself," said the agent.

As Pete was being escorted out the door, he was wondering how he was going to explain to Emily that he would not make it to the auction because he had been taken into federal custody. Over the years, he'd told Emily several convoluted stories to cover up a few meaningless affairs. But he knew she would never believe *this* ridiculous story or the fact that it took six hours in the Atlanta airport for the FBI to interview him, the wacko flight attendant, and all of the passengers who had witnessed "the assault."

Once the authorities had determined that the only crime to have taken place was the one the flight attendant had committed, the airline and its staff were more than accommodating in getting Pete onto the next flight to Los Angeles with a complimentary first-class seat and all the free drinks he desired.

CHAPTER 13

IT WAS JUST after midnight PST as the airplane rolled slowly toward the now quiet Terminal at Los Angeles International Airport. A very weary Peter Fryze had been staring out the window of his first-class seat, occasionally shaking his head in an effort to erase the painful, indignant memory of his brief incarceration. Anticipating angry messages from Emily, not to mention his buddy Conrad, Pete slowly reached for his cell phone and tapped the green airplane-mode button. Instantly, the phone buzzed and dinged like a pinball machine, notifying him of calls and texts that had been stored during his flight from Atlanta.

He had tried to reach Emily from Atlanta to explain his reason for the delay, but she didn't answer. Nothing new there; she led the league in unanswered calls and texts to the point where her friends, to Pete's dismay, used to contact him, not Rachel, if they needed to reach Emily. But on this night, he gave her a free pass, knowing she was swamped with auction preparations. Dressed in her evening gown, she probably wasn't even carrying her phone with her. So, instead of leaving a voice mail, he had sent Emily a short text message saying he'd be late because *there had been some complications with the airline,* which was true, and left it at that. He also knew that if he had relayed by text or voice mail the *real* reason for his delay, Emily would not have believed one word of it. Instead, she would have jumped to the conclusion that he was having another tryst, which would have been the final nail in their marital coffin. Pete decided it was better to tell her in person in order to be back in his wife's good graces.

The first text Pete read was from Conrad: *You can't be serious, bro!* A second text from Conrad simply read, *Traitor!* The third text was from Emily pleading, *Why, Pete? Another rendezvous?* This was in response to his "airline complications" text. Then another message appeared from Conrad: *Planning your demise as I sit at the dinner table with the Vandees and the Smarts.* Then came Emily's next text: *Conrad looks miserable. Says he'll never forgive you. I don't think I will either.*

Pete felt terrible. After their separation, he and Emily had worked hard to be supportive of each other, especially in front of the kids; he knew the Atlanta debacle would put their recent goodwill in jeopardy. He read the next text, another one from Conrad: *Pete, something's happened. When you leave the airport, don't go to the auction. Meet me at the West LA Police Station. Sixteenth and Pico. I'll explain later.*

Pete checked his watch. It was now 12:07 a.m. Laughing to himself, he immediately dismissed Conrad's message, thinking it was pretty lame to play a prank on him so soon.

The plane had now docked at the terminal. Pete stood up, reached for his sport coat and carry-on bag, and then slowly walked to the exit where the pilot, copilot and all five of the airline flight attendants fawned over him with apologies and well-wishes and their collective hopes to see him again real soon. Pete pushed through their line of shame as quickly as he could.

Walking through the terminal, he paused to call Emily's cell phone. He knew the auction was over, and she was probably dealing with cleanup duties—duties *he* was supposed to be helping with. He wanted to let her know it was after midnight and he was on his way, but he desperately hoped Emily would tell him not to come, that she didn't need his help with the cleanup. After one of the worst days of his life, Pete didn't feel up to anything except crawling into bed.

Weary and grumpy, Pete arrived at the curbside waiting area where a service van would drive him to a long-term parking garage. Of course, thought Pete as he stared at the thinning traffic at the terminal, there are fewer vans running at night, so it may take a while.

Pete's cell buzzed, and he pulled out his phone and read a new text message from Conrad: *I'm waiting for you in the lobby of the police station. Emily and Rachel are pretty upset. Call me as soon as you land.*

Pete grinned and wondered how long Conrad was going to keep up his stupid little charade but then thought maybe he should just play along with it. He punched in Conrad's cell number just as the courtesy van came into sight. Pete shuffled along with a cluster of other road warriors, one of whom was flagging down the same van. Pete kept his phone to his ear.

"Pete," said Conrad in an angry tone of voice.

"Con, before you continue this little prank of yours, you have to know that—"

"Pete! Pete," said Conrad, even angrier now. "Vickie Mack is dead, and our wives are suspected of . . . *murder*."

"That's great, Con," said Pete, laughing as he stepped into the van.

"It's not a joke, man. Where are you now?"

"Just landed. I'm on my way to the parking garage," Pete answered, smiling as he took a seat in the van.

"Pete, you've got to believe me. Just get to the police station on Pico and I'll explain everything. This is not a joke," Conrad whispered before hanging up.

"Got it," said Pete, fully believing that it was, in fact, an elaborate joke. Pete shook his head, smiling to himself. He decided to try calling Emily one more time, knowing she would admit the hoax.

"Oh, Pete, I'm so glad you called. Did you talk to Conrad?" Emily's voice warbled as if she'd been crying.

"Yes, I just spoke to him. Em, please don't make me drive to the police station. I know you and Con want to get back at me for not making it to the auction, but I've had a really, really bad—"

"Pete! Stop! You've got to come here! Please believe me! I need you here. I really do," Emily sobbed.

Pete thought she was overdoing the distress and doing an incredible job of acting.

"Okay," Pete sighed heavily. "I'll go along with your prank, and I'll drive all the way over to the police station, but when I get there and don't find you or Conrad or Rachel, I'm driving to my apartment and going to bed."

"I've got to go. Detective Aroma is waiting for me," Emily sobbed again before hanging up.

The van had reached the next terminal, and a dozen more passengers were jostling into the seating area. Now squeezed between two large men, he wondered if ten years from now he'd be able to laugh at this practical joke of theirs. He also wondered if he should just drive to his apartment and tell Emily that he'd gone to the station and the police didn't know what he was talking about.

But then he tried to recall. *Had he heard sirens in the background while talking with Emily . . . and maybe even with Conrad?*

"Geeeeze," Pete sighed in defeat.

Conrad and Emily would not be giving him any slack for missing the auction so he might as well drive to the police station and get it over with. And once they heard about *his* day, they were going to be very sorry. Pete would make sure of that.

It was almost one thirty in the morning when Pete finally pulled up in front of the Police Station on Pico. He was tired and weary but resigned to go along with whatever Conrad, Emily and Rachel had cooked up. He left his suit coat, briefcase and laptop in the backseat, feeling certain no one would dare break into a car parked right in front of a police station. But after the day he'd had, Pete wondered if his confidence was misplaced. Shaking off his doubts, he walked slowly to the front steps of the one-story red brick building.

Before he reached the steps, the front door swung open. Conrad rushed out and grabbed Pete's right arm. "Glad you're here," Conrad said somberly.

Pete thought Con's exaggerated performance was comical. "Okay, I'm here," Pete scoffed. "Can I go home now?"

"No, you can't go home now!" Conrad was taken aback at Pete's demeanor. "Rachel and Emily are inside there." Conrad thrust his arm in the direction of the building, "And they're about to be accused of murder. This is not a joke, Pete!"

"Right," Pete scoffed. "I get it. Vickie Mack is dead, and our wives did it. The world is a better place now. So, what's next in this pathetic ruse?"

"What's next is we go inside and see if we can get our wives out of here!" Conrad's voice squealed much too high for a grown man, let alone a respected doctor.

As tired as he was, Pete could not help but laugh at Conrad's absurd performance. "Okay, let's go rescue our damsels in handcuffs."

Pete stormed through the front door and into the police lobby. The brightness of the room startled Pete's senses. He stopped to allow his eyes to adjust even as he looked at the front desk with its bulletproof window.

Conrad stepped up to the window. "This is Peter Fryze, Mrs. Fryze's husband. Officer Selby wanted to be notified when he arrived."

The desk clerk looked at Pete.

"Actually, I am the *estranged husband* of the murderess, Emily Fryze," Pete said with as much sarcasm as he could muster.

Conrad stared hard at Pete, incredulous at his friend's behavior.

The officer looked at Pete with a blank expression. "I need your driver's license and I need you to sign in." The officer pushed a ledger through an opening at the bottom of the bulletproof window.

Pete looked at Conrad. "You really are making me do this? Some other time this might have been funny but not tonight."

"License, sir," the officer demanded.

Pete glared at the officer and then at Conrad. Shaking his head, Pete spoke condescendingly to the officer. "Okay. Fine!" He reached for his wallet, angrily pulled out his driver's license and shoved it under the window. "Are we done now?" he snapped at both Conrad and the officer.

"Pete, are you okay?" Conrad asked.

"You still need to sign the ledger," the officer barked at him.

The force with which Pete grabbed the pen caused the ledger to crash to the floor. Pete glared at Conrad.

"Sir," said the officer. "You want to pick that up?"

Conrad reached down for the ledger, then pushed it into Pete's chest. Pete huffed loudly and then angrily scribbled his name on the piece of paper.

The officer raised his eyebrows and lowered his head to see over his reading glasses. He fixed his eyes on Pete while reaching for the buzzer that unlocked the door to another area of the station.

Conrad angrily motioned for Pete to follow him.

Pete shook his head with disbelief but continued to follow Conrad into a large room with numerous metal filing cabinets and desks, all piled high with folders. Police officers in various stages of busyness hovered over computers.

Two men, both dressed in civilian clothes, seemingly in deep discussion, looked at Conrad and Pete, then stepped towards them.

"Detective Selby," said Conrad stoically, "this is Peter Fryze, Emily's husband."

Detective Selby nodded at Pete and reached to shake his hand, but Pete stuck his fist in the officer's direction.

"I prefer the pound to the much-too-formal handshake, don't' you?" said Pete still thinking he was being pranked.

"Uh, not really," said the detective coolly.

"Oh, too bad," chided Pete.

Roma, Selby and Conrad stood in silence while trying to understand why Pete was acting so carelessly.

"Ah, Mr. Fryze, this is Detective Roma," said Selby gesturing to his partner. Roma nodded, but did not extend his hand. "Please follow us to the interrogation room." Mick Selby pointed down the hallway.

"Only if you say *pretty please*," Pete said before being shoved forward by Conrad.

Officer Roma led the way into a square, cold room with metal chairs and a metal table. Detective Selby motioned for Conrad and Pete to take a seat. Conrad immediately sat down and motioned for Pete to do the same. Pete shook his head in disgust, then angrily pulled the metal chair away from the table and reluctantly sat down beside him. The two detectives sat across the table from the two husbands.

Selby looked directly at Pete and began the interrogation. "Detective Roma and I have spoken with your wife and Mrs. Berger, and we have written statements from each of them. Understandably, they are both pretty shaken. We aren't going to charge them with anything at this time, but you need to know that they are considered prime suspects in what appears to be the murder of Mrs. Vickie Mack."

"Enough already," Pete interrupted. "Con, what do I have to do to stop this little farce of yours? I know you think I chickened out of my end of our deal, and I'm truly sorry you had to do this thing all on your own but—"

"Pete!" Conrad squealed loudly. "Would you just stop? Please!"

Roma and Selby looked at each other in a knowing kind of way before Detective Roma stood up to close the door to the room.

"Mr. Fryze, I'd like to hear about the *deal* you made with Dr. Berger. And I know my partner over here," Selby pointed at Roma, "is curious to know what it was that you chickened out of?" Detective Selby spoke in a different tone than before. It had a darker quality that immediately startled Pete.

Instantly, the mood in the room felt very tense. Pete looked at both officers and his friend with a stunned deer-in-the-headlights expression on his face.

"In fact, we're so interested that I'm going to ask you and Mr. Berger to write about the deal you two made, why you chickened out, and every other little thing you know about the Calivista auction."

Officer Roma reached for the top drawer of the metal filing cabinet, pulled out two writing tablets and silently placed one in front of Pete and one in front of Conrad.

"Dr. Berger, why don't you come with me to the next room." Roma gestured for Conrad to follow him.

But before Conrad stood, Selby asked him, "One other thing, Dr. Berger, have you ever been arrested?"

"No, sir, I have not," Conrad said solemnly.

"Mr. Fryze, have you ever been arrested?" Roma asked.

Pete looked at Roma's badge and nametag. "What's it to you, Detective Aroma?"

"We're going to run a criminal history on both of you, so you might as well help us out here," said Roma. "And, it's Detective *Roma*."

"Well, as a matter of fact, I was arrested just this morning," Pete said carelessly.

"Pete! Cut it out!" Conrad shouted angrily. "What do I have to do to make you see this is not a prank." Conrad looked at the officers and added angrily, "He's never been arrested. He thinks we're all acting here."

Selby ignored Conrad and looked directly at Pete. "Mr. Fryze, why don't you tell us about this morning's arrest," said Selby in full command of the room.

"Ah, geeze." Pete took a deep breath, then heaved with a sigh.

"Oh, please tell us," mocked Roma. "We'll even say 'pretty please' if you like."

Pete gave up trying to stop Conrad's ridiculous prank from continuing, because at that moment the first glimmer of doubt entered his mind. Cautiously, he gave the officers and Conrad an account of the day's earlier events that led to his arrest. "But I wasn't charged with assault on an employee or any official of the airlines," Pete said when he finished telling his story. "Or anyone else!"

"Fascinating story," Selby said somewhat dubiously. "Sounds like you got unlucky today."

"I was certain Conrad here and our wives were angry at me for not showing up at the auction. Frankly, I'm still not completely convinced you two jokers aren't friends of Conrad's and are just helping him get back at me." Pete mustered a half-smile directed at Detective Selby, but Selby didn't so much as blink.

In fact, Selby was actually feeling a little sorry for the guy. "Okay," Selby tapped the table twice with his pen. "So, here's what's going to happen. While both of you write down your statements, Detective Roma will get to work on your background checks. If everything looks clean, we'll let you and your wives go home and get some rest."

CHAPTER 14

THE CLOCK ABOVE the filing cabinet in the interrogation room ticked its way towards 4:15 a.m. Detective Selby, his arms crossed over his chest, leaned against the filing cabinet and stared at the folders scattered across the metal table.

A few feet away, Detective Roma sat on a metal chair reading aloud from one of the hundred or so handwritten accounts produced by witnesses earlier that evening. He stopped mid-sentence and looked up at his partner. "Who was this Vickie Mack? I mean, not a single person has said anything nice about her or even how sad or sorry they were that she died."

"What about Vickie Mack's mother?" asked Selby.

"Sheesh!" said Roma. "That woman didn't stop wailing even after taking two Valiums." Roma shook his head. "You want to know what's really weird? The old bag seemed more upset about her daughter not getting to wear some especially designed red, white and blue dress!"

"She was pretty weird, but how about that Dr. Conrad Berger?" Detective Selby interrupted. "The guy had a Tampon apparatus stuck inside the pocket of his tuxedo. And when I told him I'd have to confiscate it, he seemed all defensive and tried to convince me it wasn't his," said Selby, rolling his eyes. "I just took it and asked him if it was that time of the month."

Aaron Roma guffawed, then added, "And don't forget Peter Fryze . . . detained by the FBI in Atlanta, *yesterday!*"

Selby shook his head, pushed several of the files to one side of the table and pulled his note tablet over to review the case. "Here's what we know. Vickie Mack was divorced and had a seven-year old stepdaughter who lived with the ex-husband. A girl named Juliette. The child still attends Calivista Elementary School even though the ex-husband, *did we get his name,* refused to attend the event because Vickie Mack would be in attendance." Selby paused to look at Roma who was reviewing his own tablet.

"I felt sorry for that school custodian," said Roma. "He was shaking the whole time I was with him. He kept saying, 'Trunk es heavy, *muy, muy* heavy.'"

"What about Vickie Mack's stepfather?" Selby flipped to a page in his notepad. "Mr. Lionel Smart. Here's what he said. *I can't lie to you, sergeant general, my dear wife's daughter was the meanest snake-woman I ever came across, so you can see why this kinda thing was gonna happen sometime. That's* what the old guy said. Then he winked at me." Selby raised his eyebrows in amazement.

"What I don't get is how ninety percent of the people interviewed were convinced Rachel Berger and Emily Fryze had murdered Vickie Mack, with the caveat that they were surprised Rachel and Emily hadn't done her in sooner," said Roma.

Flipping through the pages of his notepad, Detective Selby paused, and then looked up. "You should have heard Rachel Berger when I met with her. She sounded like a coke addict, a *Diet* Coke addict," he laughed.

"At least she didn't hiccup throughout her entire interrogation," Roma sighed. "I mean those were the loudest, grossest hiccups I've ever heard. How could someone so pretty produce such monster burps?"

Selby laughed.

Detective Roma added, "I have to tell you, Mick, I just don't see how either one of them, Mrs. Fryze or Mrs. Berger, could be capable of murder . . . especially Mrs. Fryze. I've never questioned anyone, not even my own grandmother, who seemed so above suspicion and . . . and . . . well, so wholesome."

"Ya' just never know," cautioned Detective Selby. "I've seen stranger things, that's for sure. As far as I'm concerned, Calivista Heights is just the type of place where someone would stuff a body in a trunk, leave 'em for dead, then present the body to a room full of people as some sort of . . . sick joke."

Detective Roma sat up as if struck by a bolt of lightning. "I know this sounds crazy, but what if everyone at that gala aided and abetted in the murder of Mrs. Mack? And then tried to plant the blame on two unknowing women like Mrs. Berger and Mrs., ah, Emily Fryze? Huh?"

Selby and Roma stared at each other with raised eyebrows.

"I think we're getting punch drunk," said Selby as he scratched his head. "Go home. Get some sleep and we'll start over around eleven tomorrow morning. We won't get anything from the lab until mid-afternoon anyway."

CHAPTER 15

THE CELL PHONE next to Rachel's bed rang, waking up both Rachel and Conrad.

Rachel reached for her phone and smiled meekly at her husband. He looked at the clock, frowned, then climbed out of bed and walked to the bathroom.

"Hello?" mumbled Rachel.

"Do you realize what day and time it is?" Emily asked, sounding like she'd been up for hours.

"I'd rather not," Rachel said with dread in her voice. Instantly, the vision of Vickie Mack scrunched inside the travel trunk flashed before her.

"This was to be the day and hour, exactly fifty-six hours after the auction, when we were going to celebrate. We thought it would all be behind us," Emily reminded her best friend.

"I'm so happy you woke me up to tell me this," groaned Rachel.

"Is Conrad at work already?" asked Emily.

"No. He's going in late today. We're still pretty wonky after all the, well, you know."

"I know. Sorry I woke you up," said Emily.

"Actually, I was going to get up soon to get Robbie ready for school. Are you taking Max and Molly today?" asked Rachel.

The night before, she and Emily had discussed whether or not their children should even go to school today, given all the attention surrounding their alleged involvement in Vickie Mack's death.

"I am," said Emily. "But listen, um, I really called to tell you to go look outside at your front yard."

"Right now?"

"Yes, right now."

Rachel suddenly felt wary. "Well, okay," said Rachel, holding her cell phone to her ear as she walked out the bedroom and down the stairs to the front of her home.

"I'll just stay on the phone if you don't mind," added Emily.

Rachel pressed her cell phone between her right cheek and shoulder leaving both hands free to unlock the front door and open it wide. Her eyes blinked against the bright sunlight, and as she stepped barefooted onto the welcome mat just outside the door, she hugged her waist tightly as if guarding herself from the morning chill.

"Holy Moley!" squealed Rachel.

"I thought so." Emily's voice vibrated through the phone. "There are two in my front yard. How many do you have?"

Rachel stood staring at the backside of two hulking posters amateurishly secured to five-foot rods with gray tape. Someone had hammered the poles into Rachel's thick, green lawn. Quite aware that she was wearing only her nightshirt, actually Conrad's Vikings T-shirt that came just to the middle of her thighs, she threw caution to the wind and brazenly tiptoed across the wet, dewy grass so she could see what was written on the front of the two signs. "Ohhhhhh, no, no, no, no, no," Rachel whimpered.

Free Berger and Fryze! Now! read one poster in thick black letters. As if possessed, Rachel dropped the cell phone, and her hands flew to cover her mouth. Her eyes darted to the second sign, and she groaned again. In bold black letters, she read the following words: **Berger and Fryze R Victims!** A bright red heart surrounded the words.

"Rachel!" Emily's muffled voice called from between long blades of grass.

Rachel bent her knees and reached for the phone without taking her eyes off the two signs. She wiped the dew from the face of the phone, then held it to her ear with her left hand while tugging at the first sign, the one that read **Free Berger and Fryze!**

"Don't even try to remove the signs from your yard," warned Emily as if she could see Rachel. "Take a look up and down the street." Feeling numb, Rachel looked next door, gasped, then looked a little farther down the street and gasped again.

"I know," Emily sighed with empathy. "I went to get the paper this morning and found the same thing in my front yard."

"Ohhhhhhhh!" Rachel ran tiptoe over the cold wet grass, stumbled up the three front steps and into the house, and slammed the front door.

"Rachel. Rachel. Listen, after we take the kids to school let's meet at that coffee shop. You know the one where no self-respecting VCH woman would ever be seen in?"

"The Beanery?" asked Rachel leaning against the inside of the front door.

"Yeah. Nobody will bother us there and we can just kind of . . . chill."

"Okay, but they'd better have Diet Coke, or we'll have to go some-where else."

"I'll bring a whole six-pack from my refrigerator just in case," said Emily before hanging up.

Rachel rushed upstairs to her bathroom, looked at the clock and real-ized it was too late for her to take a shower and still get Robbie to school on time. She jumped into her go-to gray sweatpants, pulled on her go-to black sweatshirt, brushed her teeth, then rushed into Robbie's bedroom. He was sound asleep, totally content and completely unaware that Captain's hairy head and two hairy paws were draped over Robbie's legs. This was the only time of day when Captain seemed to be mellow and the only time of day when Rachel felt happy Conrad had convinced her to keep the dog. "For Robbie's sake," Rachel repeated over and over as if it were her mantra.

Captain acknowledged Rachel's entry into the bedroom with one open eye that followed her every move. With a quiet, unthreatening, guttural groan, he let her know he did not like to be disturbed when he and his best buddy were resting on the bed together.

"Good morning to you, too, Captain, sir," whispered Rachel. She slowly stroked the top of Captain's head, and he let out a softer, almost grateful groan.

Sleepily, Robbie opened his eyes and bent forward to wrap his arms around Captain's neck. "Isn't he the very best dog in the whole world, Mommy?" said Robbie in a foggy voice.

Rachel did not like to lie, but there was no one on earth except Robbie who could honestly describe Captain as the very best dog in the world.

"He sure loves you," Rachel said stroking the heads of her son and his dog. "Robbie, sweetie, think you can get your school clothes on while I get breakfast ready for you?"

"Okay, but can me and Captain have peanut butter and jelly on toast today?"

"Probably not Mr. Captain, but you can, for sure. I'll meet you in the kitchen when you're all dressed. And Bubbie, we're running a little late, so you need to hurry."

While sprinting downstairs Rachel could hear the heavy thumps of Robbie and Captain jumping off the bed, which made her smile and forget that this was not like any other school day. It also made her forget that Conrad had finished his shower and was working in his upstairs office because of what had happened at the auction.

Rachel hastily toasted a piece of bread, spread peanut butter and jelly on it, and slapped the toast onto a small plate. But in her rush to pour milk into a juice glass the milk bounced into the glass and then out onto the counter and kitchen floor. At the very same moment Captain and Robbie bounded into the kitchen, and Captain, spying the milk on the floor, happily lapped up every drop.

"Look Mom, Captain's cleaning the floor for you," Robbie giggled. He was dressed in his school uniform with the green polo shirt hanging over his khaki shorts.

"Well, thank you, Captain," said Rachel.

Her kind words encouraged the dog to jump up, put both paws on the counter and attempt to lick the inside of the cap of the peanut butter jar.

"No, no, no," Rachel said to no avail.

Captain seized the cap between his teeth and raced into the family room.

"He loves peanut butter, you know," Robbie said with his mouth full of toast.

Rachel squeezed her eyes shut for a second, silently cursing Captain and yet managing to regain her composure. "He sure does."

Robbie wolfed down his toast and wiped his mouth with his arm. "Can Captain ride in the car with us on the way to school? Please, Mommy?"

"Only if you go upstairs and brush your teeth and get your backpack," said Rachel and then teasingly added, "In sixty seconds . . . starting right now!" Robbie would do almost anything if it meant winning some kind of a contest. "Fifty-nine, fifty-eight . . ." Rachel called out.

Robbie raced out of the kitchen, through the living room and up the stairs. Captain, who loved any activity that looked like playtime, dropped the peanut butter cap and bounded behind Robbie, his teeth tugging at the tail of Robbie's shirt. Robbie's giggling laughter melted Rachel's heart. *Captain,* she thought, *you may not be the world's best dog, but you might be the best dog in the world for Robbie.* Basking in a moment of pure happiness, Rachel took a deep, peaceful breath and then . . . Robbie and Captain stampeded down the stairway, dashed through the living room and careened down the hallway to the door leading to the garage. A torn swath of Robbie's green shirt flapped from Captain's mouth as he chased Robbie out the door.

"Noooooo," Rachel whined. She snatched her purse from the kitchen counter and hurried to disentangle the barking chaos she now heard coming from the garage.

CHAPTER 16

SHOCKINGLY, IT WASN'T bedlam that Rachel found when she opened the garage door. Instead, it was a miracle! Robbie and Captain had seated themselves in the back of her white Jeep Cherokee. Robbie's seatbelt was buckled, and Captain was sitting beside him with his mouth open, tongue hanging out the side, and a long pull of saliva dripping onto the car seat. He was smiling the smile of a happy, innocent dog.

"We won, Mommy!" Robbie shouted through the passenger window, which encouraged Captain to bark over and over again.

"You did win, didn't you?" Rachel said competing with the dog's dissonant woofing. "Captain! Stop barking, pleeeease!"

Rachel opened the front door, slid into the driver's seat and instantly felt something cold and wet on her bottom.

"*Ooofta!*" Rachel sat up just enough to find that Captain had left her a present . . . the torn piece of Robbie's shirt, soggy with Captain's slobber. The throbbing beginnings of a migraine caused Rachel to remember with dread that she hadn't had her standard and very vital morning Diet Coke. For a moment, she considered running back into the house to grab a can from the refrigerator. Any other day she definitely would have, but she didn't want to risk arriving late to school, not the first school day back after Vickie Mack's murder. More importantly, she didn't want to give Captain another reason to begin barking. But the instant she started the engine Rachel regretted her decision as the sound of the motor only intensified the accelerating pain of the migraine. Nonetheless, she buckled her seatbelt and mindlessly reached for the garage door opener.

"Mommy, Captain loves taking me to school," said Robbie.

Rachel turned to smile back at her son but was immediately smacked on her cheek with Captain's wet snout and slimy tongue.

"See, he's saying thank you," Robbie laughed.

"Yuck, Captain!" Rachel spitted, while trying to shove Captain back into his seat. "Stay, Captain!" she yelled even though the dog had never stayed *anywhere* on command. Rachel rubbed at her cheek to wipe Captain's drool from her face and then put the car into reverse. The car had not been backing out of the garage for more than a few seconds before the sound of an unfamiliar *screech* registered in Rachel's mind, coming from her rear bumper. She instantly slammed on the brakes.

"What is that?" Rachel twisted to look out the back window. "Oh, my God! Oh, my God!" Rachel saw Conrad's car in the driveway, not directly behind her, but close enough for her to have sideswiped it. She had completely forgotten Conrad had been working at home that morning.

"Mommy, you just said *Oh, my God,* and we aren't allowed to say that," Robbie said, sounding horrified and appalled.

"Robbie, sweetie," Rachel breathed heavily. "That was a real prayer to God." She put the car in park, then added, "I'm just going to check Daddy's car. Okay?"

"Okay."

Rachel opened her door, jumped out of the Jeep and rushed over to Conrad's beloved forest green Audi convertible. His pride and joy. The side-view mirror was bent backward, and the front side was scratched all the way to the driver's front door—a long, nasty, paint-streaked scratch. Rachel nervously assessed the damage, got into her car and gingerly drove it forward, hearing the same horrible scrapping sound she'd heard moments before. Once the Jeep had rolled back inside the garage, she stepped on both the brake and the emergency brake, dashed out of the car, ran over to the workbench, grabbed an old rag and darted back to the Audi.

"Mommy, what are you doing?"

"I just want to see if I can make this better," Rachel whispered guiltily.

Robbie and Captain watched Rachel rub the rag over the long, snake-like scratches. Captain thought it was a new game, so he pounced onto Robbie's lap and tried to climb out the half-opened back window. Rachel was much too focused on trying to erase the scratches to notice that Captain was stuck halfway out the passenger window, swinging his front legs as if he were doing a dogpaddle.

"Mommy, look, Captain's swimming!" Robbie was giggling at the sight.

Rachel dropped the rag and darted over to the Jeep to push the crazy dog back inside. "Stay!" she whispered with supreme authority, hoping Conrad, upstairs in his office, had not heard all the commotion.

She turned to assess the damage to the Audi and was slightly relieved to see that the white scratches, paint streaks from her Jeep, looked almost like scuffmarks that sort of blended in with the car's forest green paint. Carefully, Rachel took hold of the sideview mirror, successfully snapped it back into its proper position, and for some reason, felt downright buoyed by her success. Quite aware of the time, Rachel stepped away from the Audi to assess the damage one more time. *Maybe,* she thought, *Conrad will be so preoccupied and harried while talking on his cell phone and getting into his car that he won't notice the scrapes and tiny little dents.* Feeling only a little bit guilty for her deceitful plan, Rachel jumped into the driver's seat of the Jeep, buckled herself in, and started once again to back out of the garage.

"Mommy, aren't you going to go tell Daddy?" Robbie sounded alarmed and bewildered.

"Oh, yes, Robbie. After I drop you off at school. I just don't want you to be any later than you are already. Is that okay with you?" said Rachel, ever so contritely. *Of course she would tell Conrad, but it would have to be under the right circumstances, preferably with some wine and music while Robbie slept.*

"Oh," Robbie paused to think. "Okay, but I don't think Daddy's going to be happy."

Rachel slowly backed the Jeep out of their driveway and onto their street.

"Whoa, look at everybody's front yard! It's just like Christmas decorations!" said Robbie, excited to see so many signs.

Rachel pushed hard on the gas pedal and the car lurched forward with a loud screeching of the tires.

"Is it Christmas already?" Robbie asked.

"No, it's not." Rachel furiously tried to think of something to distract her son.

"Fffrrreee, oh, that word's *free*," Robbie said attempting to decipher the words on the signs. "One sign says free . . . Berger—"

"Oh, my gosh, Robbie! Look at the fire up on that hill," Rachel yelled and pointed her right hand toward the empty knoll on the opposite side of the street. Nothing could steal Robbie's attention faster than sightings of fire trucks, fires, policemen, police cars and ambulances.

"Where?" Robbie shouted.

Robbie's sudden excitement to locate the fire triggered Captain to think that another new game had begun. For the first time ever, Rachel was actually grateful for the dog's unruly barking and jumping since his over-zealousness prevented Robbie from noticing the 'Free Berger and Fryze' signs along the next two streets.

Minutes later when Rachel turned the Jeep into the school's driveway, she was comforted to see three cars ahead of her in the drop-off lane. The drop-off teacher was still assisting students out of their cars. Though Robbie might be one of the last to arrive, on this particular morning, Rachel was so very grateful he'd made it on time . . . sort of.

"Good morning, Robbie," sang Miss Diamond as she opened the back door for Robbie to exit. She was the music teacher and spoke in a super sweet, singsong way. "Better hurry to your class or you'll be late."

"Okeydokey," said Robbie as he climbed out.

Captain anxiously barked and once again tried to jump out of the backseat's half-open window. Robbie turned around and shouted, "Bye, Captain. See you after school."

"How are you doing?" Miss Diamond asked Rachel, again super sweetly.

"Okeydokey," said Rachel, mimicking Robbie. She knew the music teacher meant well.

"Everyone is rooting for you and Emily. You two were so *abused* by that woman . . . what I mean . . . I hate to say it, but Mrs. Mack deserved much worse."

Miss Diamond's patronizing, sympathetic tone made Rachel want to scream: *We did not kill Vickie Mack, so don't feel sorry for Emily and me!* But, of course, Rachel didn't say that. Instead, she smiled at Miss Diamond. "Hmm, thanks," she said through her teeth. Then she slowly drove to the end of the drop-off lane.

Dreading the thought of telling Conrad about his Audi, Rachel eased her car through the parking lot toward the exit lane, then reluctantly turned on the left-turn signal to head straight home. Suddenly, she heard another car honking behind her. Rachel glanced at the rearview mirror and saw Emily motioning for her to turn right, not left.

"Oops, I forgot. Okay, okay." Rachel had forgotten about the plan to meet Emily at the Beanery. She obediently flipped the turn signal to the right, waved back at Emily and drove in the direction of the coffee shop, the one that didn't have that certain Calivista recherché appeal. Driving along Pacific Coast Highway, Rachel caught a glimpse of Captain stretching his head out the back window, ears flopping in the wind, his mouth snapping at the airstream blowing in his face. The sight of him through her rearview mirror triggered the memory of the first time she'd taken him for a ride. He was just nine weeks old and so cute and so calm and so big for such a young puppy.

"How in the world did I let you into my life?" Rachel asked Captain who cocked his head between ferocious air-chomps as if wondering why all his biting and snapping had not provided him with a reward. He responded with a bark.

"Oh, yeah, our dear friend, Vickie Mack," said Rachel with contempt. *How could I forget?* The surprise donation, given to the auction committee by "an anonymous donor" had arrived six weeks ago at her front door.

CHAPTER 17

ORIGINALLY, NO ONE on the school's auction committee knew that Vickie Mack and the nameless donor of the dog were secret lovers. Nor did they know that Vickie Mack had surreptitiously badgered certain school trustees, namely her mother and stepfather, Valerie and Lionel Smart, into accepting the "puppy donation" on behalf of the auction committee.

"Who wouldn't be willing to pay thousands for such a pedigree puppy?" Vickie had asked the thirty-three moms on the auction committee.

Rachel and Emily both allowed that *they* wouldn't, but almost every other member of the committee voted to accept the so-called "generous donation," not because any one of them would pay thousands for the puppy, but because for some odd, inexplicable reason, the committee members found Vickie believable when she had pronounced with remarkable authority, "You know, they say puppies *always* bring in the highest bids at live auctions."

"And just who are *they*?" Rachel had whispered to Emily, who just rolled her eyes.

Vickie had failed to divulge to the auction committee that the anonymous donor, her latest secret lover, a married but soon-to-be-divorced dog breeder from somewhere deep in the San Bernardino Valley, had abruptly left for a business trip and could not care for the eight-week old puppy. Apparently, he was being unfairly harassed by a local TV station, whose irksome investigative reporter had called his breeding operation an "illegal puppy mill." Vickie saw no need to reveal these *minor details* to her mother, stepfather, Rachel, Emily or any of the auction committee members. So, two mornings after the auction committee had voted to accept Vickie's *windfall* donation, the doorbell at the home of Conrad and Rachel Berger rang repeatedly.

Robbie had been seated cross-legged on the family room floor a few feet away from the television, watching Captain Hermit, his favorite cartoon show, while spooning Captain Crunch, his preferred breakfast cereal, into his mouth.

"Now where did I put my key this time?" Captain Hermit asked his tv audience.

Robbie was so entranced by the question posed to him by Captain Hermit that he didn't hear the initial chiming of the doorbell. "It's in the drawer!" Robbie shouted at the television.

At the same time, Rachel was in the upstairs master bathroom enjoying the luxurious pulsations of shower water falling over her head. For the moment, she was only mildly conscious of how much time she had left to dry off, throw on some clothes and drive Robbie to school—before he'd be late, *again*.

The doorbell rang along with a round of knocks at the front door.

Robbie looked in the direction of the door, decided to ignore it, and turned his attention back to the television. "Look in the drawer!" he shouted at the befuddled Captain Hermit.

The doorbell sounded again along with louder knocking.

"Mommy!" Robbie hollered toward the upstairs bedrooms. "The door-bell's ringing,"

"Where, oh, where did I leave my magic key?" Captain Hermit asked his TV audience. "Can you please help me find my key?"

A mesmerized Robbie nodded his head and thrust his pointer finger forward so the Captain would finally realize the magic key was hiding in a desk drawer. But another round of door-knocking and the unrelenting ringing of the doorbell distracted Robbie enough to turn his attention away from helping poor Captain Hermit.

Reluctantly, Robbie left his bowl of cereal and the TV Captain and walked to the front door. He put his ear against the door and with hesitancy asked, "Hello?"

"Robbie, it's Mrs. Mack," Vickie urgently had called from the other side of the door.

"Uh, my mom is in the shower," Robbie answered.

"That's just fine. Please open the door," Vickie Mack demanded.

"Uh," Robbie thought hard before cupping his hands to his mouth and calling out, "I'm not allowed to open the door without one of my parents with me."

"Then please tell your father to come to the door," Vickie said irritably.

"Wellllll, uh," Robbie wavered, knowing that under no circumstances was he to ever open the door without mom or dad being present. "Uh, my dad's in the shower, too." Robbie knew full well that his father was at work and not in the shower with his mom, but he felt he wasn't at liberty to say so.

"Well, go get one of your parents, please," ordered Vickie Mack.

"Wellllll," Robbie hesitated again. "I can't because they are kind of busy in there together," Robbie said. "And I can hear they are *really* busy." He was sure this information would cause Mrs. Mack to go away and come back another time.

"Good Lord!" gasped Vickie.

"Maybe you should talk to them later when they're done in the shower," Robbie suggested.

Vickie was not one to be deprived, not even by a small child. "Robbie, do you know what I have with me?" said Vickie ever so sweetly.

"No," answered Robbie honestly.

"I have a little puppy dog right here beside me," sang Vickie with even more sugar in her voice.

"A real puppy dog?" Robbie inhaled with sudden wonder and amazement.

"Yes, a real, live puppy dog, and he wants to meet you right now," said Vickie, further seducing the innocent boy.

Robbie wasn't sure he believed Mrs. Mack had a real puppy dog, so he asked, "Is he yours?"

"Ugh, of course he's not my dog," snarled Vickie with disgust.

"Well, whose dog is he?" asked Robbie.

"He's nobody's dog, yet." Vickie had never shown any warmth towards Robbie Berger; in fact, she did not like the boy, nor any children for that matter, but Vickie desperately wanted Robbie to open the front door. So, she cleared her throat and lured him with something much better than candy. "Robbie, this doggy needs someone to take care of him for a short time. Would *you* like to take care of him?"

The temptation was just too much for a boy who'd been begging to have a dog of his own. Putting the rules that had been drilled into him by his mother and father, Robbie swiftly unlocked the door and opened it.

"Huh!" Robbie gasped, then exhaled with sincere compassion. "Awwwwww."

Robbie barely noticed Vickie Mack, because his eyes and open hands were focused on the all-black, curly haired puppy that was passionately licking Robbie's face.

"Robbie, you know that your mother is keeping some of our donations at your house until our school auction, don't you?" asked Vickie, leading him on.

"Uh-huh," Robbie giggled as the puppy jumped up on his chest.

"Well, this puppy is the newest donation that your mother has to keep at your house until the auction. "

"Uh-huh," said Robbie.

"Well, here is his leash," Vickie said, hurriedly grabbing Robbie's right arm and placing the red vinyl leash into his hand.

"I better go get my mom."

"No. No. I don't have time to wait for your parents to finish . . . whatever they're doing upstairs."

"But. . ." Robbie was sure he should run upstairs and get his mother.

"No. No, no! Your mother knows all about this puppy, so—" Vickie paused to push the dog's bottom from the front porch through the doorway and into the foyer. She then pushed Robbie inside the entryway just enough to be able to close the front door. "*Goodbye!*"

The ecstatic six-year-old boy and the yippy, playful, eight-week old puppy remained in the foyer happily rolling all over each other for at least five minutes before Rachel, towel wrapped around her body, her hair soaking wet, came out of the bedroom to see what was causing the strange noises downstairs.

While it took a few seconds for Rachel to comprehend that the floppy black mop jumping all over her son was a puppy, she instantly realized where the dog had come from and who had brought it to her house.

"Mommy, Mrs. Mack said you have to keep this donation at our house with all the other donations," Robbie said innocently. "Oh, and she told me to give you this note." He pointed to a bright yellow envelope taped to the dog's leash.

"Arrrrr!" Rachel ran down the stairs and flung the front door wide open, knowing it was futile to think Vickie would still be on the front porch or in the driveway standing by her car. But Rachel couldn't stop herself from racing to the front yard, still holding the bath towel barely above her breasts, to look in every direction for the wretched Vickie Mack. Not even noticing the catcalls coming from a passing car or the stunned look on old Mr. Peterson walking along the sidewalk, Rachel ran back into the house. She stared numbly at her very happy son with his arms around the rambunctious puppy, then bent down to tear the note from the dog's leash.

Rachel,

As I told you at the committee meeting, the donor of the dog is out of the country for several months. Obviously, we can't keep this donation in the school storage room with the other donations, it just wouldn't be legal or humane. And, since you, as the head of this year's auction, have accepted the responsibility of storing the remaining incoming donations in your garage, I'm delivering this item to be in your care until auction night.

I only wish I could take care of this darling puppy, but everyone knows I am deathly allergic to all animals with fur. Just so you know, a situation has suddenly occurred causing me to be out of town until tomorrow evening.

For some reason my cell phone isn't taking calls, but I will try my best to contact you when I get to my hotel in San Diego.

Hugs and kisses, Vickie

Rachel scrunched the note into a tight ball before throwing it onto the floor. Then, storming upstairs to get dressed, she called out, "Robbie, please take the dog out to the backyard to pee before we leave for school!"

"Okay, but Mommy?" Robbie looked at his mother.

"Yes?" Rachel stopped at the top step to hear Robbie's question.

"Don't you just love this puppy, Mommy?" Robbie asked wistfully.

"No, Robbie, I don't," said Rachel very soberly. But then just as soberly she added, "But if you do, I am happy."

"I *really* love him!"

"Sweetie, did Mrs. Mack explain to you that this puppy is for the auction, and that he's not ours?"

"Not yet." Robbie had repeated the most important two words Mrs. Mack had said to him that morning.

"Not yet?" asked Rachel.

"And guess what?" Robbie called up to Rachel. "I'm going to call him Captain after Captain Hermit." Leaving not a second for Rachel to respond, Robbie and Captain sprinted toward the backyard.

CHAPTER 18

RACHEL HAD ACTUALLY felt encouraged that morning six weeks ago, even though she and Robbie had been running late and then were stalled in the long carpool lane for several minutes. Curious and adoring students had kept running over to get a glimpse of the cute puppy whose head was dangling out the window, his tongue hanging to one side. Parents who had been dragged over to her car by their children seemed to express an abundance of affection, even heartfelt longings, for such a cute doggy. So, when Rachel drove away from the school that morning, she convinced herself that bringing Captain along on the drive to school had actually been a brilliant idea. If she did this each day, more and more students and their parents would meet and fall in love with him and, well, *come auction night. . .* Foolishly, Rachel had allowed herself to wonder if maybe Vickie Mack had been right after all about the potential of this puppy generating very high, competing bids.

Just two days later, Rachel was still feeling enthusiastic about having Captain as a passenger in the backseat of her car as she left the school drop-off area and drove along Vista del Mar to make a quick stop at the grocery store. She hadn't been on the road more than three minutes before she heard light but rapid honks coming from the car in the next lane. She glanced to her left and saw two young children in the backseat of a green SUV waving and laughing. Captain had been providing an entertaining sideshow by sticking his head out the back window and barking. Rachel couldn't help but feel a little giddy that Captain was such a fun attraction. She had to admit, he was adorable.

At the next stoplight, a second car pulled up beside Rachel and tooted its horn. The driver enthusiastically waved at Rachel, who, with a smile and a merry wave of her hand, acknowledged that she knew there was a loveable puppy in her backseat.

"Captain, you're a hit!" she called back to him.

Rachel became increasingly hopeful, even buoyant, as several other cars drove past and more drivers and passengers waved, honked, and even tried to mouth their delight at seeing Captain in the back seat. To each one, Rachel happily tooted her horn in return. But like a dark storm cloud covering the sun, Rachel's joy faded the moment she had spied a red Mercedes Benz convertible in her rear-view mirror.

"She's ba-ack," moaned Rachel.

Vickie's red Mercedes pulled up behind Rachel's vehicle and began honking, but not with the light and friendly beeps of the previous cars. No, the long blasts from the Mercedes were angry, ear-splitting honks designed to intimidate. Annoyed by the noise, Rachel looked in the mirror and watched Vickie's car zip from behind and into the next lane. Staring straight ahead, Rachel hoped Vickie would just drive on by. Wrong. Two more ear-splitting honks forced Rachel to turn and look, and even though Vickie's face bore a look of exaggerated distress, Rachel felt obliged to give a light wave of her left hand and a great big smile, hoping this would encourage Vickie to move along. Instead, Vickie continued to drive beside Rachel, blasting her horn non-stop, nudging her car toward Rachel's. Upset over the noise, Captain had begun to moan which quickly morphed into full-scale barking.

Rachel stepped on the gas pedal to move ahead of the Mercedes. Vickie did the same. Rachel's foot jumped from the gas pedal to the brake pedal, but Vickie matched every change of speed, like a crazed racecar driver. Defeated, Rachel slowed down, then turned to give Vickie another fake, happy-face-smile, provoking even more anger from Vickie.

"Well, what's her problem, Captain?" Rachel glanced over her left shoulder to give the puppy an approving smile. But Captain could not return the smile because his head was stuck between the window and the roof of the car; his back paws frantically hopped up and down on the window button and each of Captain's desperate jumps caused the window to move up or down against his throat.

"Ohhhh, no, no, nooooo!" Frantic, Rachel fumbled with the control buttons on her armrest, but when she realized it wasn't forcing Captain's window to go down, she swung the car to the side of the road, put it in park, and in one fell swoop, hurled her body into the backseat, lifted Captain's back paws, pressed the window button with her elbow and heaved a sigh of relief when Captain began barking and whimpering. As Rachel hugged and kissed the agitated puppy, Vickie Mack, who had parked her car ahead of Rachel's, stormed toward the open door.

"You're the most heartless, calloused human being in the world!" shouted Vickie. "I'm reporting you to every authority I can find! You'll never drive again! I'll have your license revoked! You should leave this town before it's too late!"

"I must have forgotten to reset the window lock when I was in the carpool lane," said Rachel with a sob as she hugged and cuddled the very responsive and forgiving dog.

"You're a cruel, heartless fool!" shouted Vickie from close range. "I've never seen anything so irresponsible! You could have killed him!" Vickie's bloodshot eyes bulged, and her angry face flushed crimson red, matching her hair and her car. Rachel's tears and sincere remorse had done nothing to calm Vickie down. "It's true, Vickie," said Rachel. "I was irresponsible, and I have no right to be caring for this sweet puppy. I'm terrible at this. Vickie, I think you need to return him to the breeder or take him home with you until auction night."

In seconds, Vickie grasped the consequences of Rachel's proposal. "Okay, I'll forgive you *this one time* for your terrible, *terrible* and nearly unforgiveable lapse of judgment," said Vickie. She turned and was about to leave, then stopped and faced Rachel one more time. "Just be more attentive with puppies—and children, too!" Then she turned and pompously marched back to her red Mercedes and sped away.

In the ensuing days, as the auction grew closer and Vickie Mack had not attempted to contact Rachel with a single complaint or suggestion, Rachel could not help but feel an undertow of suspicion, a sick sense that this just might be the calm before the proverbial, horrific storm. Rachel had tried to shake off the foreboding feeling but could not escape the premonition that something terrible was about to happen.

A week after the car window incident, Rachel walked to her mailbox without noticing the rolled-up newspaper laying on the driveway. Instead, she unlocked the letterbox, pulled out a stack of mail and the weekly coupon magazine that she never bothered to read, and began walking back to the house. That's when she spied the *Calivista Post*. She reached down, picked it up, and added it to the stack of mail.

Most respectable Calivista residents would rather die than admit that the real reason, maybe the *only* reason, they paid the hefty annual *Calivista Post* subscription fee was because of the "Penny for Your Thoughts" column; it certainly was not because of the drab reporting on local citizens. But the "Penny for Your Thoughts" column was anything but drab, for it was where any resident could submit a public complaint about anything. Without exception, the penny grievances were petty, trivial and sometimes mean-spirited. But, oh boy, they were more entertaining to read than a juicy gossip column.

That is why on the sixth day after Captain's car window incident and a few minutes before Rachel needed to pick Robbie up from school, Rachel had hurriedly tossed the mail onto the kitchen table and sat down so she could quickly scan the latest "Penny for Your Thoughts." She knew she'd be able to reread the column to Conrad that evening after Robbie went to bed. It was their favorite Thursday night entertainment, which usually left them rolling with laughter. "Who needs Colbert," Conrad would say, "when you have Thursday's 'Penny for Your Thoughts'." There was no comparison.

Rachel rolled the rubber band off the newspaper before glancing at the wall clock to be sure she had a few minutes more before she had to leave for school. When both sides of the newspaper started to curl toward the center Rachel swept both hands to flatten them, and in doing so, the following headline came into view:

Animal Cruelty on the Rise in Calivista!
See Penny for Your Thoughts, page 2

Below the headline was a large black and white photo of a helpless puppy in great distress. Rachel read the headline again while squinting her eyes to reexamine the photo of the dog. Then she screamed involuntarily but so loud that she startled Captain who began barking with the ferocity of a ten-week old puppy. Rachel rubbed the corners of the pages together three times before successfully flipping to page two. There it was:

Animal Cruelty on the Rise in Calivista

This week's headline-grabbing "Penny for Your Thoughts" item was not just *the leading complaint,* Rachel quickly noted; it was this week's *only* complaint. As if possessed by fear, Rachel began to read the following story:

Calivista Heights has a new and serious problem, usually associated with our inner cities, and it is on the rise!! Too many of God's wondrous creatures are taken in as family pets but are NOT treated as God would want them to be treated. I recently was driving along our beautiful Calivista Drive when in the lane beside me I saw an absolutely charming puppy in the backseat of an older white Jeep Cherokee. I was charmed by the sight until I looked closer and saw the adorable puppy's tongue hanging out. HE WAS CHOKING!!! All because the cruel, heartless driver of the older white Jeep Cherokee was not paying attention!! The neck of the poor, sweet, innocent puppy was trapped between the backseat window and the roof of the car. Obviously, the calloused, uncaring driver had not bothered to secure the window safety locks!!!

Most shocking of all, after extensive investigation, I discovered that the driver of the older white Cherokee is the parent of a child enrolled at a local school, and that child is under the age of seven!!! What if this very same window had been choking this woman's own son?!!!

I took my own life into my hands by forcing the unnamed, reckless driver of the white Jeep to pull over to the side of the road, where she brazenly admitted she had never even thought to engage the backseat window locks. Citizens of Calivista, this is shocking!! Please! Please!! Be certain that your window locks are engaged, if not for the sake of your trusting animal passengers, then at least for the sake of your helpless, innocent and trusting children riding in the back seat.

Signed, Miz Anonymous

Rachel didn't have time to read the entry again. Instead, she slapped her hands to the sides of her head and tried to calculate how many mothers she would encounter in that day's school pick-up lane who would have already read today's "Penny for Your Thoughts"? *Lots.* And how many older, white Jeep Cherokees drove through the streets of Calivista? Rachel knew the answer. *One.*

CHAPTER 19

RACHEL HAD DRIVEN her car into the tiny lot behind The Beanery and was searching for a parking spot while trying to suppress her memories of Vickie Mack's letters to the local paper. Finding a slot, she pulled into the space, put the car in park and turned off the engine. "Okay, Captain boy," she said, turning to the back seat. "You get to come sit outside with us, but no barking. Okay?"

She had just gotten out of the car and had opened the back door for Captain to jump out when Emily approached. She reached out to pet Captain's fluffy head and he jumped up on his back legs and lunged forward, nearly knocking Emily off her feet.

"Oooo, Captain. You are such a good boy, yes, you are," cooed Emily. "And you're not going to bark, are you? We don't want any more noise complaints, do we?" said Emily.

*

Emily had not meant to trigger Rachel's memory of the 'Official Noise Complaint' Vickie Mack had sent to the Berger's home several weeks before, written "on behalf of the Calivista Heights Neighborhood Association." The letter, handwritten by Vickie, had accused Rachel and Conrad Berger of "noise pollution from an incessantly barking dog."

Rachel and Conrad knew they had better do something about Captain or Vickie would not let up on her attacks. So, they sought the advice of a local veterinarian who suggested they purchase a specific dog collar made for howling dogs. On the collar was a small device filled with a liquid that proved to be putrid smelling to all dogs. When the dog barked, the device was instantly ignited and the putrid liquid would spray upwards into the animal's nose, the theory being that the dog would associate his barking with the discharging of the foul smell and would, therefore, cease barking all together. "It's one hundred percent effective," both the vet and the salesperson at the pet store had assured Rachel and Conrad.

They bought the ballyhooed device but quickly discovered the special collar was not only one hundred percent expensive, but also *one hundred percent ineffective.* When Captain's first bark ignited the initial burst of rancid spray into his nose, he was understandably startled, voicing his objection with a high-pitched whine. But after the second or third time the spray shot through his nose, Captain had decided he had discovered a new game where he would be instantly rewarded with a delicious treat each time he barked. He even discovered that when he barked rapidly, he'd be rewarded with the same rapid number of yumminess.

Just two weeks into temporarily housing Live Auction Item Number Four, otherwise known as Captain, Rachel had no choice other than to take the puppy with her everywhere she went. She was not going to give Vickie Mack any further cause to muscle the Association into imposing a noise pollution fine on the Berger property.

Vickie may have been finished, but Miz Anonymous was not. A week after the Association's letter had been sent, a new "Penny for Your Thoughts" headline appeared:

Noise Pollution on the Rise in Quiet Calivista!
See Penny for Your Thoughts, page 2

This time, Rachel refused to read the column, choosing instead to throw the entire issue into the garbage.

Rachel had taken to giving Captain large, meaty bones purchased from the butcher each time she had to leave him alone in the car. It didn't matter that her car smelled as if an animal had died under the car seat, because the bones usually kept Captain occupied and happy until she returned. But then one fine morning, Rachel opted to shop at the more upscale Calivista grocery store with the higher priced items—and where one never had to wait in a checkout line.

She'd given Captain a fresh uncooked bone and left him happily gnawing on it in the backseat of her car. Rachel had not been inside the store more than five minutes when the voice of the store manager called out over the intercom.

"Would the owner of a white Jeep Grand Cherokee please check on your dog? It appears he is in great distress. I repeat, would the owner of a white Jeep Grand Cherokee please check on the dog in your car. He is very distressed, and we will need to call Animal Control if he is not rescued in the next few minutes."

Rachel did not immediately comprehend what was being announced over the intercom until she looked up the aisle toward the manager's desk and saw Vickie Mack standing beside the store manager.

A week later the headline for the "Penny for Your Thoughts" read:

Animal Cruelty Still on the Rise in Quiet Calivista
See page 2

Miz Anonymous had struck again.

*

Emily, Rachel, and Captain found a table in the small area of the outdoor café. It was chilly outside, and neither of the women had jackets on.

"Sorry we have to sit outside," Rachel said. "I'm just afraid Vickie Mack is going to show up and accuse me of leaving Captain in the car or alone at home." But then Emily looked at her, tilting her head to one side and Rachel suddenly remembered that Vickie Mack was dead. "Oops, sorry," whispered Rachel.

"Don't worry about it." Emily wrapped her arm around Rachel's shoulder.

"I honestly forgot for a second," Rachel said.

Emily took a deep breath, as if reinforcing her own inner fortitude. "It's such a big relief knowing that Miz Anonymous can no longer harm us or anyone else."

Both Emily and Rachel were aware of patrons at two other tables staring at them.

"Do you think those people know who we are?" Emily whispered just as Rachel's cell phone rang.

Rachel stared at her phone for a second, looked up at Emily with alarm written all over her face, then held the phone to her ear.

"Hello?" Rachel said with a very jittery voice.

Emily could hear most of what the caller was saying, but she mouthed the word, *Detective?* to her friend.

Rachel nodded. "That's fine, Detective. We'll see you then," said Rachel before hanging up.

"Was that the handsome detective?" Emily whispered.

"That was Detective Roma. He and Detective Selby are coming to my house around five tonight to review a few things," whispered Rachel. "Emily, you don't think they have any evidence against you or me, do you?"

"Of course not." Emily hesitated and then wondered out loud, "Could they?"

"Well, why are they coming to my house tonight? You don't think they're going to arrest me?" whispered Rachel.

"Well, whatever happens, don't you dare give me up, you hear?" Emily said grim-faced.

Rachel stared at Emily and then looked at the tables surrounding theirs. It was obvious that she and Emily were being scrutinized by several other café patrons.

"Um," Rachel hesitated. She looked as restless as Captain who kept pulling on his leash. "You know, I think I need to go home if that's okay with you. I just feel kind of . . . weird being out."

Emily covertly scanned their surroundings. "I guess coming here was a bad idea," she said with more than a hint of worry in her voice.

The two friends left the table together, and as they walked to their cars, Emily put her arm around Rachel's shoulders. "We're going to be okay. I promise," said Emily.

Driving home, Rachel's mind was so focused on the impending meeting with the detectives that she'd all but forgotten the incident with Conrad's car. This was partly because Conrad's car was not in the driveway when she got home. In fact, she had forgotten Conrad had even been working at home that morning until she noticed the yellow post-it stuck on the refrigerator.

Rachel, I had to stop by the office for a couple of hours. I'll leave early and be home for dinner. Promise. Con

Despite the note from Conrad, any memory of having swiped the side of Conrad's car had vanished into the cosmos.

The phone rang all morning and all afternoon, calls from friends leaving messages of undying support for Rachel and Emily *no matter what.* Rachel knew that kind of loyalty was flimsy, but she kept herself busy with household chores until it was time to pick up Robbie. Rachel was intent on arriving at the carpool lane thirty minutes early in order to be the first in the carpool lane. That way, no one could corner her with questions and innuendos about last Friday night's auction. As luck would have it, Robbie's class was the first to march into the carpool lane, and Robbie's teacher quickly brought him to the car. Mrs. Harvey graciously greeted Rachel, then opened the backseat door and helped Robbie into the car with a cheery smile. "Have a good rest of the day, Mrs. Berger."

There was nothing in the teacher's tone to suggest she was even aware of the auction night's events. So, on the drive home Rachel quizzed Robbie about his day and was encouraged that he had not been confronted with any issues pertaining to Vickie Mack.

As the next two hours dragged by, Rachel could not stop wondering what it was the detectives wanted to show her, or tell her, or . . . ask her.

CHAPTER 20

DETECTIVE SELBY PULLED the black, unmarked sedan close to the curb on Monte Carlo Drive, a residential street in the hills above Calivista. He shifted into park and waited as Detective Roma finished a phone call.

"Okay, we're set to meet Mrs. Berger at five p.m. She'll call her husband and ask him to be there, too." Roma looked out the window and pointed. "This the dead lady's house?"

"Yup," said Selby.

The detectives exited the car and stopped to stare at the odd, two-story home that was glaringly inconsistent with all the Neo-Mediterranean style houses throughout the neighborhood. Vickie Mack's stark white house was an odd mix of southern plantation and Beaux Arts architecture. Bright purple shutters at each of the front windows stood out against the glaring white walls. Six twenty-foot pillars, also painted purple, lined the lengthy front porch.

Selby lingered a little longer at the front steps to take note of a ceramic statue wearing a jockey's helmet and painted in purple and white jockey attire, holding a purple lantern as if to light the way to the front door, which, at that very moment, opened.

"Nice touch, huh?" Detective Joe Miller, a bulky, seasoned veteran of the LAPD forensic team with a penchant for details, wore a smirk on his fleshy face and sweat on his forehead. Miller's sleeves were rolled up, and it was obvious he had been at Vickie's house for several hours. "C'mon upstairs," said Miller.

Roma patted the jockey on the head and followed Selby and Miller up the winding staircase to the second story. When they reached the top of the stairway, the three men turned to the right and entered a cavernous master bedroom. Despite floor to ceiling windows offering breathtaking views of the Pacific Ocean, everyone's attention was instantly drawn to a colossal, four-poster bed on the opposite side of the room. What at first glance looked like a shocking red, white and blue coverlet spread across the bed turned out to be, upon closer inspection, an ostentatiously patriotic, red, white and blue, floor length, formal evening gown. Someone had very carefully draped the gown across the bed.

"Good golly Miss Molly!" said Selby appraising the dress.

Standing at attention, Roma put his hand on his heart. "I pledge allegiance, to the flag—"

"So, we took fingerprints throughout the house," interrupted Detective Miller, "but so far there's nothing to suggest anyone broke into the place and kidnapped the deceased."

"Okay," sighed Selby.

"So, if the deceased *was* kidnapped before being stuffed into that trunk," said Miller, "it was probably by someone she knew well enough to let into her house. I'm thinking like those two housewives you interviewed."

"Maybe," said Selby. "But supposedly there was a lot of tension between the two ladies and the deceased. From what I hear, the two housewives hated her. I doubt Mrs. Mack would have even let them inside."

"You kidding?" said Miller. "There's a couple of pictures on the bathroom counter with the three ladies all smiley-smiley and huggy-huggy."

Pleased with his discovery, Detective Miller walked into the master bathroom and returned holding a framed photo in his gloved hand, an eight-by-ten glossy of Vickie Mack standing between Rachel Berger and Emily Fryze, their arms wrapped around each other's waists, their smiles so exaggerated they looked posed for comedic effect.

Roma took the photo from Miller and held it in his hands. He scarcely looked at the faces of Vickie Mack and Rachel Berger but found it hard to take his eyes off the beautiful Emily Fryze. *Yes,* he thought, *her smile looks slightly exaggerated, like the other two women, but there's something about her . . . something more than a little captivating.*

Detective Selby glanced once more at the photo, then continued his perusal of the room. "Maybe our two suspects and the deceased didn't hate each other after all."

CHAPTER 21

✓

SELBY COULD NOT have known that Vickie Mack loathed Rachel and Emily from the moment the two women had moved into the neighborhood and hated them even more when they were chosen to be co-chairwomen of the school's annual auction . . . over her. Concerned about her own "spotless" reputation, Vickie did not want the public at large to know the extent of her animosity towards the two women, so as a cover, she opted to shadow Rachel and Emily at every school function making sure she was seen and photographed with her two "adversaries" at every opportunity. This would certainly prove to the world that she harbored no hurt feelings over not being named Auction Chairwoman.

Until Rachel and Emily had moved into the neighborhood, Vickie had assumed that her sprawling, custom-built hillside estate overlooking the Pacific Ocean, courtesy of husband number three, a blue-blood trust-funder from Connecticut, had transformed Vickie Mack into *a very important woman.* In her twisted mind, her newfound status meant that being Vickie's loyal friend and ally *in all things social, political and otherwise* would be *a very wise move for anyone, but especially those two upstarts.*

Mr. Mack's family inheritance, a large trickle-down from the founder of a Wall Street hedge fund, allowed Vickie the luxury of fighting the City of Calivista Heights over a developer's plans to build smaller, *under one point five million dollar track homes* on the vacant lots on Calle Verde, just one street level below Vickie's. After spending staggering amounts of money in legal fees, Vickie lost the battle with City Hall, but that didn't stop her from secretly taking revenge on every unsuspecting family that dared to move into the smaller homes below hers.

Within a year of losing her legal battle with the city, the new homes were completed and the Frost family, one of the first buyers of a new house on Calle Verde, had become Vickie's first victim. A few weeks after they took possession of their dream home, Mr. Frost set up a portable basketball hoop in the middle of his driveway. Unbeknownst to the Frost family, Vickie considered this an act of neighborhood sabotage comparable to setting up a meth lab or a crack house, such would be the damage to the community. *Not in my lifetime,* vowed Vickie. She was not about to let *her* neighborhood become the kind where children played in their front yards and left wagons, bicycles and basketballs on front lawns and driveways.

Having studied the CC&Rs to the point of memorizing certain sections, Vickie knew that homeowners were prohibited from placing *stationary* basketball hoops in their front yards. However, each homeowner was allowed to have one *portable* basketball hoop in their driveway with the stipulation that all basketball hoops would be rolled out of sight or placed inside garages when not in use.

As the one and only member of the Neighborhood Beautification Committee, Vickie relentlessly badgered the Homeowners Architectural Committee into adding an amendment to the CC&Rs warning that any violation of the rules concerning basketball hoops would force the Association to take immediate possession of the offender's hoop. Then without being asked, Vickie had appointed herself the *official basketball hoop beautification enforcer.* Within months of the Frost family's arrival on Calle Verde, they had forgotten to remove their basketball hoop from their front yard on three different occasions. Mr. Frost did not think much about the first two semi-official-looking notices warning of "serious consequences" for CC&R violations. But the day after receiving a third violation notice, the young Frost boys woke up to find that their basketball hoop had vanished into thin air.

Vickie felt no remorse when the *offending* Frost family had put their house up for sale and moved far away from the neighborhood. To the contrary, convinced that every neighbor viewed her as champion and hero, Vickie had felt not only victorious but powerful . . . until the Berger family and the Fryze family moved onto Calle Verde. That was when Vickie sensed she was about to lose her self-imagined power base that, in her deranged mind, had given her prior control over almost everyone in Calivista Heights.

Just weeks after the Frost family had packed up their belongings and relocated to another town, Rachel and Emily had moved onto Calle Verde, and with only a few houses between them, they had quickly bonded as best friends. Almost immediately, Emily and Rachel started a routine of daily walks around the neighborhood with Emily's then two-year-old daughter and three-year-old son sitting in a double stroller while Rachel's then three-year-old son rode on a tricycle guided by a long safety handle held by Rachel.

Vickie had made a habit of hiding in the far corner of her backyard, high-powered binoculars in hand, to clandestinely spy on all the families on the street below, especially on Rachel and Emily, who appeared to be *so* nice and to have *so* much fun together, stirring deep envy within Vickie, envy bordering on hatred that was exacerbated every day as the two women walked by Vickie's home.

From her upstairs guestroom, Vickie had often observed the two women as they paused in front of her house. *Obviously, they were commenting on its magnificence . . .* Vickie was certain, which stirred within them their own sense of inferiority and jealousy.

One day, Vickie had decided she had to connect with the two women as they approached her house . . . to better understand these new rivals to her throne.

"Hello, hello, hello," Vickie called out to them. Her "hellos" sounded like the yelps from a puppy desperate for attention.

Had Rachel and Emily not been such new arrivals to the neighborhood, that is to say, had they been forewarned about the infamous redhead of Monte Carlo Drive, they would never have returned Vickie Mack's greeting and would have made an about-face and walked in the opposite direction, *fast*.

But on that day, Rachel and Emily were just being neighborly as they crossed the street to meet this vivacious woman wearing a loud, flouncy, pink-flowered blouse and fire engine red short-shorts that matched *to a tee* the color of her blazing red hair.

"Well, it's about time we met. I'm Vickie Mack, and you are . . .?" She thrust her hand toward Rachel, then flashed an enormous, red lipstick-accented smile, a smile so unnaturally large that it caused her upper lip to shoot above the line where the teeth and the gums met, exposing a shocking expanse of pink gums.

"I'm Rachel Berger." Rachel shook Vickie's hand.

"And I'm Emily Fryze. We live on—"

"Oh, I know where you live," said Vickie with an air of pomposity. "You moved into the tract homes below my street. Honestly, those tiny houses were built so close together they might as well have been attached like condos. Of course, condos and townhouses will never be allowed here."

Rachel was so stunned by Vickie's audacity that she was momentarily rendered speechless. Then she mumbled, "Ah ha."

"They might be a *little* close together," Emily offered, sounding wimpy and defensive.

Vickie ignored them both, then proceeded with her mission. "Forgive me, but I couldn't help noticing that the two of you have been admiring my manor," said Vickie.

"Oh, yes, it's quite unique," Emily offered politely, but actually wanting to say that her house bordered on the absurd with its massive purple columns and shutters.

"I know," said Vickie. "I fired the architect and took over the architectural design myself. Sometimes I think I missed my calling, don't you?" Vickie spoke with a pronounced, phony New York accent.

"Impressive," said Rachel with more than a hint of disingenuousness.

"Yes, well, very nice to meet you both." Vickie flashed another grand smile, once again revealing her ample gums, and then, as if she had been lying in wait for this moment, she began a series of rapid-fire ramblings about all the *vitally important things* they should know about the neighborhood.

"You've probably noticed some people park their cars in their driveways overnight. *Well*, the Association and I are working on an amendment to force all homeowners to park their cars in their garages. I know you both have just moved into the neighborhood, and your garages are still filled with moving boxes and such, but you'll want to make room for your cars very soon. *Won't you?*"

Rachel and Emily nodded in unison like two mute bobbleheads.

"Oh, and I'm so happy to see that neither of you has placed a basketball hoop in your front yards," said Vickie, leaning in conspiratorially, as if sharing fresh and juicy gossip. "They do *not* belong in an exclusive neighborhood like ours. Don't you agree!"

More bobble-heading nods ensued from Rachel and Emily, gestures that could have meant yes or no or both. Rachel would clearly not share with this odd woman the fact that she and Conrad were planning to buy an adjustable basketball hoop for Robbie.

"The CC&Rs won't allow it," Vickie snapped with total authority.

Vickie continued to hold Rachel and Emily captive, quoting paragraphs from the CC&Rs, until Robbie and Max had begun picking up little rocks from Vickie's garden and throwing them into the street. This was a welcome excuse for Rachel and Emily to say goodbye to Vickie Mack and walk away.

After they had put enough distance between Vickie and themselves, Emily looked at Rachel and murmured, "Well, she seems, umm . . . friendly."

"Mmm-hmm." Rachel checked over her shoulder to be sure Vickie was not following them. "Maybe just a little over-the-top."

"What*ever* do you *mean*?" said Emily, mimicking Vickie's faux accent, then offering a toothy, donkey-like smile. Both women giggled but instantly felt guilty for making fun of their new acquaintance. The very last thing either Rachel or Emily wanted was to be cruel to someone else. But then, Rachel and Emily had not yet learned the meaning of the word *cruel,* and they had absolutely no idea of the level of cruelty Vickie Mack would be capable of reaching.

They were about to find out.

CHAPTER 22

MICK SELBY LOOKED at his watch before closing the door to Vickie Mack's house. 4:55 p.m. He and Detective Roma were about to drive to the Berger house on Calle Verde, the next street down the hill.

"What the–?" said Roma, staring in the direction of their car.

A skinny teenager wearing skinny black jeans and a tight, pink T-shirt was sitting on the hood of the unmarked police car. To the boy's left, a frumpy, middle-aged woman wearing a baggy housedress was leaning against the side of the car, her arms folded against her ample chest. It was obvious she was not wearing a bra.

"You're detectives, right?" the woman called out in a horsey voice.

"Ma'am?" enquired Mick Selby.

"How about you jump off the car," Roma called out to the boy in a firm, no-nonsense voice.

The boy looked around as if Roma were addressing someone else, then skittered off the car's hood, shaking his head at the inconvenience.

"Heartbroken, just heartbroken about our dear Vickie," the woman lamented somewhat heavy-handedly.

"Oh yeah?" Roma watched as the teen leaned against the car's hood. "Are you heartbroken too?"

"Well, yeah," said the boy, thrusting his hands into the front pockets of his skinny jeans.

"And you are—?" asked Selby.

"He's Lawrence and I'm his Aunt Ruthie," interrupted the stocky woman with the voice of a dedicated smoker. "Lawrence lives with me."

The boy slowly withdrew his hands from his pockets and casually placed them on his hips.

"And your relationship with Vickie Mack is—?" asked Selby.

"Dear friends. Just dear, dear friends ever since we moved here," answered the woman, as if speaking for both of them.

"Well, *Aunt Ruthie*, my partner and I are on our way to an appointment right now, but since you were dear friends with Mrs. Mack, I know you won't mind if we take down your name, address and phone number. I gather you live nearby."

"Nine-ninety-nine Calle Verde," answered Ruthie. "The street below this one."

"Okay," said Selby as Roma handed the woman a pocket tablet and a pen. "Please write down your names, address and phone numbers."

"Sure," the woman said, scribbling her name. "Lawrence and I might be of some help in your investigation of the two auction ladies." She handed him the tablet. "We know them, too, don't we, Lawrence?" The teenager nodded, then crossed and uncrossed his arms over his chest and tilted his head to the side like a puppy.

"Okay, then. We'll be in touch with you," said Mick.

Ruthie looked pleased as she and Lawrence watched the detectives enter their car.

"Strange pair," Selby commented as they drove away.

"Ya think?" grinned Roma.

Five minutes later, the detectives parked on Calle Verde and walked up the steps leading to the front porch of the Berger home. At the top step, Roma reached out to push the doorbell.

BAMM!

Something heavy rammed against the front door from inside, causing Roma and Selby to step back. Instinctively, the detectives reached under their blazers toward their handguns. They paused long enough to hear three more vicious blows against the door—BAMM! BAMM! BAMM! Then they heard the frenzied whining and scratching of a dog.

"What the—?" said Roma, ready to pull out his gun.

"Sit, Captain! Sit!" commanded a woman's voice from inside. The door opened halfway, and Rachel peaked around the corner. She was bent over and holding onto the collar of a mid-sized, black, wire-haired dog.

"Sorry," Rachel apologized. "He's hard to control." Just behind the jumping dog stood a dark haired, brown-eyed boy of six, clearly in awe of the detectives.

The detectives relaxed.

"Hi!" Robbie waved at the detectives. "Captain won't hurt you. He just wants you to pet him."

"Oh yeah? Guess I'd better pet him then," Roma said kindly. He bent down and attempted to pat the dog's jerking head.

"Detective Selby, Detective Aroma, please come in," Rachel said while struggling to hook a brown leather leash onto the dog's collar. "He'll calm down in a minute."

Aaron Roma flinched but did not correct Rachel's mispronunciation of his name. Instead, he and Selby watched, somewhat dumbfounded, as Rachel pulled the overly excited dog into the living room and wound the end of the leash around the leg of a bulky wooden coffee table.

"I know this looks weird, but it's the only way to keep Captain from jumping on you," said Rachel, looking apologetic.

"Ah ha," Selby answered.

As Rachel watched Detective Selby take a seat on the sofa as far away from the dog as he could get, she silently prayed for Captain to stop whining and biting at his leash.

Robbie sat down next to the dog, patting his back. "Captain doesn't think you're a real policeman," said Robbie.

"Why is that?" asked Roma.

"Well, you aren't wearing police uniforms," answered Robbie with a child's logic.

Rachel was about to offer both men a glass of water but was stopped by the sound of Conrad storming through the back door. He entered the family room and angrily tossed his briefcase onto the nearest chair before noticing the detectives sitting in the living room.

He took a deep breath and then walked towards the living room. "Hello, detectives. Sorry I'm late." Conrad reached across the coffee table to shake hands with the detectives.

At that exact moment, Captain, wanting Conrad's attention, lunged forward pulling the coffee table with him, causing Conrad to tumble on top of the table.

"Captain! Sit!" yelled Conrad as he pulled himself up.

"I'm so sorry," said Rachel, apologizing to the detectives for the chaos.

Selby looked at Conrad then at Rachel. "No problem."

Sensing he was more agitated than usual, Rachel then turned to her husband, who had taken a seat on the ottoman. "Is everything okay?" she asked.

"No," Conrad snapped at her. "Everything is *not* okay." Then he looked at the detectives. "You won't believe it! Someone backed into my car today and didn't bother to leave a note or anything. You should see the scratch marks on the whole left side of my car," Conrad said angrily.

Rachel gasped loudly, for until that very moment she had forgotten that she'd run into her husband's beloved convertible that morning.

"Nothing I can do about it, right?" Conrad angrily asked the detectives. "I'll probably never find out who did it."

Before Selby or Roma could respond, Robbie shouted, "She did it!" He pointed his finger directly at Rachel and stared at her with impunity.

Involuntarily, Rachel screamed and threw both hands up to her mouth. Everyone in the room looked at Rachel, accused of yet another crime.

"What?" Conrad had a confused look on his face. He quickly turned to look at Rachel and then back again at his son.

"Connie, I was going to tell you later tonight. I really was," cried Rachel. She was mortified at having been outed by her very own son. But she was more than mortified that the detectives witnessed Robbie's accusation, knowing it was true.

"Oh, great," Conrad groaned. "Would have been nice if you'd just told me."

Rachel could tell the detectives were intrigued with the exchange between her and Conrad, and she worried immediately that they would now distrust *anything* she might say. They probably were wondering if she'd withheld evidence from them, too.

"Conrad, you weren't home after I took Robbie to school, and I'm just so anxious about, well, you know, after what happened the other night I . . . I truly forgot until you just now mentioned it." Rachel tried to make her words heard above the sound of Captain chewing on the coffee table leg to which he was tied.

"Ma'am," Roma said with some hesitancy while pointing at Captain.

"Captain, stop!" Rachel and Conrad shouted.

"Robbie, would you please take Captain to the backyard while Mommy and I talk with the detectives?" said Conrad. He carefully loosened the leash from the coffee table leg and handed it to Robbie.

"Come on Captain," Robbie sang as he tugged at the dog's collar. The dog happily followed the boy out of the room and through a sliding glass door. Robbie carefully closed the screen door behind him.

"You've got your hands full with that dog," Selby commented.

"He's the curse of Vickie Mack," Rachel sighed. She then proceeded to tell the detectives how Captain had come into their lives. She told the whole story: how Vickie forced the puppy on the auction committee, how Vickie left Captain at her front door with Robbie, and how Robbie fell in love with the dog. She even told the detectives about the "Penny for Your Thoughts" columns written under the guise of Miz. Anonymous, which caused the fast-growing puppy to become a liability to the auction committee and how, at the last minute, it was decided that Captain would no longer be offered as Auction Item Number Four, given all the bad publicity.

Both detectives listened with interest to her long, rambling story. They also noted the intermittent comments by Conrad that supported Rachel's summary of events. It was obvious to the detectives that Mr. Berger liked the dog enough to keep him for their son, but they weren't so sure Mrs. Berger felt the same way.

"Well," said Mick Selby. "Sounds to me like you had some fairly good reasons *not* to like Vickie Mack."

"She was no friend of mine," sighed Rachel. "That's for sure."

"Interesting you should say that," said Roma. He took a breath, looked at Selby, then continued. "While we were at Vickie Mack's house today, we saw several photographs of you and Mrs. Fryze with Mrs. Mack." Detective Roma again looked at his partner for corroboration.

"You three women looked pretty happy to be together. You know, kinda like you three were all best friends," added Selby.

Rachel groaned. "Vickie had a camera with her at every school function and made sure she had several pictures taken with Emily and me. She wanted everyone to see that she just loved us, which she didn't. It was such a farce, but we couldn't refuse to take a picture with her, because she'd be sure to cause a big scene in front of everyone."

"Interesting," said Mick Selby. "Why do you think she had so many pictures of the three of you framed and placed on her nightstand, in her living room, and even in her master bathroom?"

"Really? Ugh, I, I, I don't know why. Maybe she threw darts at them," said Rachel, shuttering.

Selby paused to look at his notepad. "That was some trunk you had on stage." He was tempted to say it could have easily held two dead bodies, but he thought better of it. "Isn't there a special name for that kind of thing?"

"It's called a steamer trunk. You know, the kind people used to take with them on long voyages across the ocean. We borrowed it from the high school theatre department, because the original plan was to have a puppy sitting in it. The puppy was supposed to be the last item auctioned off." Rachel heard Captain and Robbie playing outside. "But you can see how *that* worked out. When the cruise ship tickets were donated, Emily and I decided to keep the steamer trunk to kind of go with the theme of traveling across the ocean to Europe. We thought it was kind of fun and would help out with the bidding."

The questioning by the detectives continued, covering a few other concerns related to auction night until they were interrupted by the sound of the doorbell. In an instant, Captain burst through the closed screen door, knocking its frame to the floor. Unfazed by what he'd just done, the dog sprinted to the foyer and hurled himself against the door. BAMM!

Rachel dashed to the foyer, grabbed Captain's collar, and then carefully opened the door.

"Oh, hi, Rachel," said Ruthie, standing on the front porch next to her nephew. "Lawrence and I were all the way up the street and heard

Captain barking. We saw the detectives' car and figured they were here to interrogate you, so we thought we'd offer to take the dog on a walk. That way you can be interrogated in peace and quiet."

Aunt Ruthie nudged Rachel and Captain aside, looked into the living room, and waved. "Hello, detectives. We just want to help as much as we can."

Both Selby and Roma nodded at Ruthie as she peeked around the half-opened front door.

"Thank you, Ruthie," Rachel answered icily as Captain whined and jumped. "But no thanks. We're fine." Captain jumped onto Rachel's back as she spoke.

"You sure?" asked Ruthie.

"We're almost finished here," said Detective Roma from the living room.

Without saying goodbye, Rachel pushed the door closed, which forced Ruthie to retreat.

"Nice neighbors, huh?" added Roma.

"Not really. They're just snooping around. That's what they do," said Rachel, instantly regretting her words. "I'm sorry but they are the world's biggest gossips and would never offer to help except for some nosy reason."

"We know the kind," said Roma, making Rachel feel a little better.

"I'll just take him to the garage," said Conrad as he walked over to Rachel and pulled on Captain's dog collar.

"That's not necessary," said Selby. "I'm sure we'll have more questions as the investigation continues, but we're done for today."

As the detectives stood up and walked towards the door, Captain lurched in their way, causing both men to flinch. Together, Conrad and Rachel held Captain's leash as tightly as they could.

"No need to see us out," said Roma. "You've got your hands full."

CHAPTER 23

GRATEFUL TO BE leaving the chaos behind them, the detectives stopped and paused on the Berger's front steps and exchanged looks of dismay.

"Not those knuckleheads again," Roma said under his breath.

Selby shook his head in disbelief, then headed down the porch steps toward their unmarked car where Ruthie and Lawrence stood side by side, leaning against the vehicle's trunk.

"I'm sure you don't need *me* to tell you that the black BMW over there belongs to Vickie's boyfriend," said Ruthie with supreme authority. Lawrence pointed to the only car parked across the street.

"Oh, yeah?" said Mick Selby. "How do you know it's the boy-friend's car?"

"The license plates," said Aunt Ruthie. "D-O-G-O-N-I-T," Ruthie spelled out the letters. "The boyfriend is a dog breeder."

"I think we'll go have a look," Roma said.

Ruthie and Lawrence followed the detectives over to the BMW.

"You have any idea how long it's been parked here?" asked Selby.

"Since the day of the auction. Just ask Lawrence," said Aunt Ruthie.

"Me?" asked Lawrence, his voice cracking.

"That's our house, the one next door to the Berger's. Lawrence was watering the grass on the side yard between our houses that afternoon, and he saw Vickie park the boyfriend's car right here," said Aunt Ruthie.

"What time would that have been?" Roma asked the boy.

"Four o'clock," answered Ruthie for her nephew.

"So, Lawrence, is that about right?" asked Selby. "You saw Mrs. Mack park this car right in this spot around four o'clock on Friday afternoon?"

"Well, I, I, I don't know if it was this exact spot or exactly at four o'clock," said Lawrence. He began the nervous crossing and uncrossing of his arms again.

"I don't need exact, Lawrence," said Selby.

"But you saw Mrs. Mack park the car right here, is that correct?" Roma added.

"Yes, but that's all I saw."

"Was the boyfriend with Mrs. Mack?" asked Roma.

"No. She was alone," the teenager said. "But that's all I saw."

"He saw Vickie knock on Rachel's front door," added Ruthie.

"Well, yeah, I saw that, too," Lawrence said defensively. "But that's all I saw."

"Did anyone answer the door?" asked Mick.

"No," Lawrence said much too quickly.

"Did Mrs. Mack return to the boyfriend's car?" asked Roma.

"No. She walked around to the side door of Rachel's garage, near where I was watering the grass." The teen paused. "But that's all I saw, except I told her that Rachel wasn't home."

"What did Mrs. Mack say?" Roma prodded the boy.

"She said she knew where Rachel was."

"Where was that?" asked Roma.

"At the beach club getting things ready for the big hoo-ha," Ruthie interrupted, implying the detectives were total dimwits.

"Then did Mrs. Mack return to the car?" asked Selby.

"No, she told me she was going to check on Captain to be sure Mrs. Berger hadn't tied him up and left him alone in the garage again." Lawrence crossed and then uncrossed his arms, finally placing his hands on his hips. "But that's all I know."

"The crazy dog tears things up if Rachel doesn't tie him down," Ruthie interjected. "I don't know why she bothers—that dog chews through every rope she ties him up with. He runs away a lot but always comes back."

"Okay," said Selby. He took a deep breath and directed his next question to Lawrence. "So, did you see Vickie Mack go into the garage?"

"Yes, but that's all I know!" Lawrence's arms were now tightly crossed over his chest, no longer trying to uncross them.

"Did you see Mrs. Mack leave the garage?" Roma asked.

"No. I'm telling you that's all I saw," Lawrence squealed.

"That's all you saw," Selby repeated.

"Well. . ." Lawrence hesitated. "Yes."

"Okay," Selby said with irritation as he wrote down a few notes. "So, Lawrence, I just want to be clear about a few things." Mick tried to sound casual, hoping to relax the skinny teen. "You saw Mrs. Mack walk into the garage."

"Yes." Lawrence hesitated, unfolding his arms again. "I told you she said she was checking on Captain. He was barking a lot."

"Oh, you didn't mention the barking," Roma commented.

"Well, yeah." Lawrence seemed agitated.

"So, Mrs. Mack opened the side door and walked into the garage," said Selby.

"Yes."

"Did you see her come out of the garage?" Selby continued.

"No, I told you, I saw her go in, and that's all I saw!" The pitch of Lawrence's voice rose a little higher with each word.

"So, Mrs. Mack went into the Berger's garage and you kept watering the grass?" asked Selby.

"Yes! Well, until a pickup truck drove into Mrs. Berger's driveway, but that's all I saw."

"Oh? You saw a pickup truck drive into the Berger driveway while Vickie Mack was still in the garage and you were still watering the side yard?"

"Wellll, yeah . . . but, that's—"

"Did you see who was driving the truck?" Roma interrupted, preventing Lawrence from completing his mantra.

"Kind of. He was a short Mexican guy. He said he was picking up some things for Mrs. Berger to take to the auction."

"He told you all that?"

"Well, yeah, but that's *all* he told me."

"Anything else about him that could help us out?" Selby asked.

"Not really. He wasn't very talkative. He just went in the side door of the garage."

"The same door Mrs. Mack had gone into but had not yet come out of, is that right?" asked Roma.

"Yes. And that's all I know."

"Had you ever seen the short Mexican man before?" Selby asked.

"Maybe, I mean, I think he's a janitor at Calivista Elementary. You should go talk to him, because—"

"That's all you saw and all you know," said Roma, finishing Lawrence's chant.

Mick Selby figured that was not all Lawrence saw or knew, but years of experience told him to hold off further questioning for another time.

"Thank you, Lawrence. You've been very helpful," said Detective Selby.

"It's our civic duty, you know," Ruthie said.

"Civic duty?" Roma cocked his head to the side.

"To help you out with your investigation." Aunt Ruthie lifted her chin looking quite sanctimonious.

"Well, we can see that you are both civic minded, and I probably don't need to tell you this, but I will anyway. You are not to discuss this case with anyone other than Detective Roma and myself." Selby looked Lawrence in the eye and then turned his gaze directly at Ruthie. "And I would also request that you both stay in town for the near future. Understand?"

Ruthie regarded Detective Selby's words as praise, almost equal to having been granted a badge of, of . . . *camaraderie,* or even *solidarity,* so she straightened her neck and shoulders and acknowledged the detective's words. "Of course, anything for our men in blue and for the good of our city!"

CHAPTER 24

LATER THAT EVENING, dinner time at the Berger house turned into a disaster. While Robbie was setting the table and Rachel was preparing a salad, Captain managed to reach the top of the kitchen counter and grab the roast that Rachel had removed from the oven just five minutes earlier.

"No, no, no, no!" Rachel yelled as she watched Captain run through the recently installed doggie door into the backyard with the entire roast locked between his teeth. Conrad chased after him and was able to reclaim most of the grassy, gummed-up roast, but it was not salvageable. So, the family of three sat at their kitchen table and enjoyed a dinner consisting of steamed broccoli, lettuce salad and overcooked mashed potatoes.

"You know what my health teacher says?" Robbie's elbow rested on the table with a broccoli spear in his hand.

"Hm?" Rachel muttered, still smarting from the *she did it* incident. Would this apparent deception on her part cause her young son to become a pathological liar? Never mind the fact that his mother was a suspect in a criminal investigation who could one day be put on trial *and possibly be found guilty of murder.*

"Well, Miss Sandy says that we shouldn't eat red meat, because it's bad for us." Robbie bit off the top of the broccoli. "That's why Captain took the roast," he added while chewing broccoli with his mouth open.

"Oh, really?" Rachel coolly regarded the wiry-haired canine now tied to the backyard tree.

"Yep. Captain wants us to be very healthy and not eat red meat."

"So, I guess it's okay with you and Captain, and of course Miss Sandy, if we all become vegetarians." Rachel stabbed one of her broccoli spears with her fork and held it up for Robbie to inspect.

"What's a *vegenarian*?" Robbie asked.

"*A vegetarian* is someone who never eats red meat, not even hot dogs or hamburgers, and definitely never eats pepperoni pizza," said Rachel.

"Welllll," Robbie paused to carefully contemplate what his mother had just told him, "I think maybe Captain doesn't really want us to be one of those *batarians* because he likes it when I give him pieces of my hot dogs."

Conrad knew from Rachel's body language that it would be best to get *the dog* as far away from her as possible and for as long as possible.

"You know what I think?" Conrad winked at Robbie.

Robbie shook his head.

"I think we'd better take Captain to the park before your mom turns him into a hot dog." Conrad stood up and tousled Robbie's hair. "Want to come with me, champ?"

Within minutes, the Audi convertible was headed into town with Robbie and Captain happily sharing the windswept backseat. Conrad pushed a few buttons on the dashboard and placed a call. Something had been nagging at him ever since the detectives had left their house, and he wanted Pete's take on it.

"I'd love to meet up with you and Robbie," said Pete into his cell phone. "I'll meet you at the park in five minutes." Pete was grateful for the excuse to leave his cramped apartment and walk the two blocks to Calivista Park . . . how many months had he lived there? *Too many.* Up until last week, he had been optimistic that things between Emily and him had improved to the point where she might soon let him move back home. But then auction night happened, along with his ill-fated return flight from Atlanta, and now the tension between Emily and him was worse than ever. Emily didn't say it out loud, but Pete knew she didn't believe his excuse for missing the auction and probably thought he had been involved with another fling. As he walked to the park, Pete once again blamed his entire predicament on Vickie Mack . . . *well, maybe it wasn't entirely her fault. . . .*

Pete entered the park and saw Captain and Robbie zigzagging between trees and bushes looking for the tennis ball Conrad had purposely thrown into a patch of ivy.

"Captain is one crazy dog," said Pete stepping beside Conrad. He would never have kept a dog like Captain. Too much hassle.

"You're right," Conrad chuckled. "But Robbie loves him. To tell you the truth, his craziness is nothing compared with all the craziness of last year."

"Tell me about it," said Pete, nodding his head in agreement.

"But you want to hear what bothers me more than all the insane things that have happened?"

To Pete, Conrad's voice sounded so unlike himself, almost tortured. "Sure," Pete laughed.

"This morning Rachel rammed her car into the side of mine and had all morning and all afternoon to call and tell me about it. But she didn't."

"So, how'd you find out? I mean, are you sure Rachel did it?"

"Listen to this, when I got home today those two detectives were in my living room talking to Rachel and Robbie. So, the first thing I said to the detectives was that my car had been hit and no one left a note."

"Why did you even bring it up to them?"

"I guess I thought that since they were already at our house, they could also investigate who damaged my car."

"So, did they say they'd do that for you?"

"They didn't have to. After Rachel acted all surprised about the car and didn't say anything, Robbie jumped up and pointed at Rachel and said *she did it.*"

"In front of the detectives?"

"Yep. Which makes me think she was never going to tell me and that she was going to let me think someone else had hit my car."

"Yeah, well, we both know I'm probably not in a position to pass judgement on someone in regard to holding back information."

Conrad looked at Pete knowingly and sighed. "Sorry, bro. It's just . . . I never thought Rachel would ever lie or hide something from me, but it's pretty clear she did. I mean, it makes me wonder how many other crazy things she's done and hasn't told me."

"Like what?" Pete asked.

"I'm glad you asked," Conrad paused to gather his thoughts. "Here's a question for you. Remember the night you and Emily and Rachel and I went out for dinner at that Tex-Mex restaurant? I think it was a few months before you and Emily separated."

"You mean before . . . umm—" Pete paused, gathering his thoughts. "That was before the photos of me surfaced . . . on Facebook."

"Right." Conrad was sorry he'd brought it up but felt the need to continue. "And do you remember during dinner and after a few too many margaritas, Rachel and Emily started telling all sorts of horror stories about Vickie Mack?"

"Yeah, I remember." Pete shook his head. Just the thought of Vickie Mack and all the grief she had caused their two families was extremely painful.

"It probably doesn't mean anything, but do you also remember when Rachel said she wished Vickie Mack had never been born?"

"Ahh, yeah . . . and it was Emily, I think, who said something about contemplating hiring a hit man to get rid of Vickie," Pete said very cautiously.

"Right!" Conrad pointed his index finger at Pete. "It was funny at the time. Rachel said finding a hit man would be no problem!" Conrad's eyes widened to emphasize his anxiety, then he spoke again. "Rachel's toast went something like . . . *Here's to the demise of the horrible, awful, deplorable, no good Vickie Mack!*"

Pete and Conrad silently stared at each other wide-eyed for a very long moment.

"Oh, come on, Conrad. No one in their right mind would hire a hit man to knock off a person and dump the dead body in a voyage trunk that they knew would be opened in front of an audience at an auction." Pete wanted to laugh but couldn't.

"You're right. Of course, you're right."

"I mean, Connie, there's no way Rachel or Emily could come up with such a cockamamie idea without telling us first . . . right?" Despite his confidence, Pete's voice had a slightly desperate ring to it.

"That's what's been gnawing at me since Rachel lied about the car accident," said Conrad, looking down at his toes.

The two men stood quietly for a moment as they watched Captain chase a squirrel around a tree. Captain stood on his hind legs, his front paws planted firmly on the trunk of an oak tree, his eyes focused on the squirrel that stared back at him from the safety of a sturdy branch. Captain's frustrated barks echoed throughout the park.

Finally, Pete broke their silence. "You know, the other night I walked over to Ron's Grocery Store from my apartment. I was going there to get a few TV dinners."

"Gourmet, I assume," Conrad chided.

"Right!" Pete scoffed. "As I entered the store, I walked past the newspaper rack and noticed the *Calivista Post*. It was unbelievable! Plastered on the front page of a **SPECIAL EDITION** was a picture of Emily and Rachel, and guess what my first thought was?"

"What?" Conrad asked.

"Thank goodness that's not *my* picture in the paper."

"Geesh!"

"So, out of the blue this strange little man shouts from behind me, 'WELCOME TO RON'S!' It totally shattered my composure."

"Ha! I know who you're talking about. I bet he shouted that at you a few more times," said Conrad.

"Yes! He shouted, 'WELCOME TO RON'S!' again, and all of a sudden I realized everyone in the store was looking at me."

"Rachel calls him The Greeter," said Conrad. "She told me that the store has a policy of hiring people with learning disabilities to bag the groceries."

Pete seemed to ignore Conrad's explanation. "Yeah, well, as if that wasn't bad enough, a woman I don't know from Adam, comes up to me, points to the newspaper, then tells me she recognized me as Emily's husband."

"Oh, man," Conrad said sympathetically.

"Wait 'til you hear this," said Pete as he rubbed the back of his neck. "She said something like . . . *it must have been so terrible to see that poor woman's body all mangled in the steamer trunk, of all places.*'"

"Just what you needed," said Conrad.

"Right. Well, I told her I had not been at the auction and therefore hadn't seen the body in the trunk."

"I hope that stopped her," Conrad empathized.

"What do you think?" Pete asked rhetorically and annoyed. "She said, *Well, no matter what anyone says we all are behind your two wives.*"

"What did you say?"

"I told her I have only one wife," smiled Pete. "She laughed . . . something more like a condemning twitter. And then she told me how dreadful and bizarre it must feel to be married to someone who's a murder suspect."

"Geeze!" Conrad shook his head.

"I told the woman to have a good day and left the store without the TV dinners."

"That's too bad."

"Yeah, well, to tell the truth, as I walked back to my apartment, I realized that it did—*and still does*—feel dreadful and bizarre to be married to a murder suspect."

"I know what you mean," Conrad agreed.

"Wanna hear what's even more dreadfully bizarre?"

"What?"

"Being the husband of the murder suspect *and* the man who had an affair with the woman who was murdered."

CHAPTER 25

IT HAD BEEN a long day for Detectives Selby and Roma. They'd spent a few hours at Vickie Mack's house going over evidence with Detective Miller and the forensic crew, followed by an impromptu encounter with Ruthie and Lawrence and then a meeting with Rachel and Conrad Berger along with their son and their very crazy dog. They had skipped lunch, a particularly irksome omission for Selby, who complained of headaches and even fatigue if he didn't keep a regular diet. It was now past 6:00 p.m. and after another unexpected yet curiously informative encounter with Ruthie and Lawrence, Selby and Roma had pulled to a stop in front of Juliet's Café.

"Hey," said Roma pointing through the car window. "Look who's over there handing out a parking ticket."

Mick looked across the street and saw Officer Mew writing out a ticket while ignoring a visibly irate woman. Neither Selby nor Roma could make out the exact words being blasted at Officer Mew, but it wasn't hard to understand the essence.

"I have no idea how he does that," said Roma, shaking his head.

"Does what?" Mick asked.

"Just keeps on writing, ignoring that woman yelling in his face." Roma smiled, shaking his head.

Mick parked the car across the street from Officer Mew, and before either he or Roma got out of the car, they watched Officer Mew turn his back on the expensively coiffed, forty-something woman and officiously place a parking ticket under the windshield wiper of her car. He then turned to the woman, tipped his hat at her, and walked ahead to check the next parking meter.

"Nice touch," said Roma as he opened the car door.

Selby and Roma were still laughing at poor Office Mew as they walked toward the Café. They were about to enter when they were distracted by the newspaper rack stationed at the entrance.

"Well, who do we have here?" said Roma.

One lone issue of the *Calivista Post* sat inside the news rack with a front-page headline that read **SPECIAL EDITION** in large block letters. Splashed below the heading were the faces of Rachel and Emily with a teaser asking, *What Do These Two Women Know About the Murder of Vickie Mack?* In the lower right-hand corner of the front page was a small photo of Aunt Ruthie and Lawrence, with another teaser: *Ms. Ruthie Hershey and nephew Lawrence Hershey Will Miss Their Dear Friend.*

Got any change on you?" said Mick to his partner. "I've got three quarters in my pocket and need one more."

Roma reached into his pocket. "Here," he said, flipping the coin to Selby.

Just as Selby pulled the *Calivista Post* from the news rack, Officer Mew walked toward the parking meter directly in front of the café.

"Hey, Mew, wait up!" Mick called out.

Officer Mew looked at the two detectives and casually walked over to them.

"Looks like you're not winning any friends here in Calivista," said Roma.

"You got that right," Mew answered with no hint of humor in his voice. He glanced down at the newspaper Selby was holding. "At least no one's tried to drag me down the street like her." Officer Mew was pointing at the picture of Aunt Ruthie in the bottom right corner of the paper. "Not yet anyway."

"What do you mean?" Selby asked.

"See that lady right there?" he said, pointing again at the picture of Aunt Ruthie.

"Yeah," both detectives said.

"I was writing out a parking ticket for her not more than a week ago, well, less than two weeks ago, right over there." Mew pointed to a parking spot across the street. "She was begging me to tear the ticket up when this black BMW pulls up right beside where we were standing. The lady in the BMW rolls down her passenger window and starts yelling. I kind'a figured she was mouthing off at me, so I ignored her. But then the lady I was giving the ticket to started yelling back at the BMW lady."

"You're sure she wasn't yelling at you," asked Roma?

"Positive. Those two women started mouthing off to each other, and people on the sidewalk started paying attention," said Mew.

"What were they yelling about?" asked Roma.

"The BMW female told the other female to 'bleep-bleeping stay away from her bleep-bleeping boyfriend.' So, this lady," said Officer Mew, pointing again to Aunt Ruthie's photo. "She charges up to the BMW, thrusts her arm through the front passenger window and starts waving her finger in the BMW lady's face. She had a pretty good mouth full of bleeps too."

Officer Mew paused for a moment to look at the newspaper.

"So, get this," said Officer Mew. "I'm about to go over and tell both women to take their argument somewhere else when a driver behind the BMW starts honking his horn, I mean really honking, 'cause the BMW is blocking the road. So, you know what the BMW lady does?"

"Nope," Roma answered.

"BMW lady rolls up the front passenger window."

"Okay." Roma was trying to picture the scene.

"The problem was, that lady," Mew pointed to Ruthie's picture once more. "She still had her arm halfway through the window." Officer Mew nodded his head at the detectives. "It looked to me like the BMW lady deliberately rolled up the window to chain in the other lady's arm. "Guess what happened next."

"No clue," Selby answered.

"With the one lady's arm trapped in the window, the BMW gal puts her foot on the gas and bolts forward, dragging the other woman down the street!"

"Whoa!" Roma did not expect this.

Mew nodded his head to acknowledge Roma's surprise, then pointed once again to the picture of Ruthie. "This one here ends up looking like a human flag with her legs waving along the side of the car. I ran after her and I'll tell ya, her legs were flailing all over the place until the BMW reached the corner way down there." Mew pointed toward the end of the street. "That's where she suddenly stopped. Then I see the window roll down and BMW lady yells for the other lady to get bleeping off her car. The lady in the picture falls to the ground, and the BMW chick screeches her tires and drives away."

"Unbelievable!" Roma said.

"What's more unbelievable is that the lady from the picture wasn't hurt, not one bit. She wouldn't let me call for an EMT or anything. She just kept screaming about how she was going to kill BMW lady."

"Did you get the BMW's license number?" asked Roma.

"Yep. It was one of those fancy plates," Mew answered.

"Any chance, you remember any of it?" Roma asked.

"Sure do. D-O-G-O-N-I-T." Mew spoke each letter very carefully then added, "*Dogonit*. Get it?"

Selby and Roma looked at each other. Then Selby picked up the questioning. "Did you follow up on the case?"

"No, I didn't." Mew slowly shook his head. "I wrote up a report, though. I'm thinkin' . . . let the big guys at the precinct follow up."

"Did you find out who the BMW driver was?" Selby asked.

"I heard it was registered to some guy living out of the country. Maybe it was a stolen car. I don't know."

"Mew, I'm pretty sure the person driving the BMW was Vickie Mack," Selby said.

"Oh yeah? Who's that?"

"You know, the woman they found dead in that steamer trunk last Friday night," said Roma.

"Ya' don't say." Officer Mew sighed.

"Yep, seems like she was pretty much the most hated person in town. But hey, Officer Mew, that would make you only the *second* most hated person in Calivista."

Mew chuckled. "Guess I'll stay clear of those big steamer trunks." Mew winked at the detectives, then turned his attention to the row of parking meters.

"Be safe out there, Officer Mew," Mick Selby said with a smile while opening the door to the café.

Roma followed his partner inside, where they sat down at a table next to the window overlooking the street.

A waitress appeared almost instantly, putting a fresh coffee pot and two menus on the table. "I'll be right back to get your order," she said as Selby opened the *Calivista Post*.

"Take a look at our Aunt Ruthie . . . and Lawrence." Mick pushed the newspaper across the table.

Aaron looked at the title of the article below Ruthie's photo: *Best Friend of Murder Victim in Mourning*. He looked up at Selby then read out loud, *"I just don't know why anyone would do this to dear Vickie," said Ruth Hershey, a local resident. "She was my dearest friend in all the world."* Asked if she knew whether the murder victim had any enemies, Ms. Hershey was at a loss for words and could only shake her head. *"She was loved by everyone."*"

Aaron Roma raised his eyebrows.

"According to Officer Mew, the car dragging incident happened just a few days before the murder," Selby said.

Roma took a sip of his coffee. "You think Aunt Ruthie forgave Vickie Mack that quickly for dragging her down the street?"

"She'd have to be a saint to do that. Did she seem like a Mother Teresa to you?" asked Selby.

Roma shook his head. "Funny how Aunt Ruthie never mentioned to us that her *dearest friend in all the world* almost killed her by dragging her down the street."

"Time to pay Aunt Ruthie and Lawrence another visit."

CHAPTER 26

"HE'S NOT RIGHT you know," said Aunt Ruthie matter-of-factly.

Detectives Selby and Roma had just sat down in chairs across from Aunt Ruthie, who was seated in her pink, Pepto-Bismol hued couch.

"I beg your pardon," said Mick, instantly assuming that Ruthie was referring to her nephew, who was seated beside her on the sofa.

"I said he's not right, you know, *wacko*. It's obvious, and don't say you haven't noticed," said Ruthie without hesitation.

Selby and Roma looked at Lawrence.

Lawrence nodded his head to confirm his aunt's claim.

"Ah, well, no, I haven't noticed," said Aaron Roma, shifting positions in his chair. He turned to his partner. "Have you?"

"Nope," said Selby.

"I never met his mom and dad," continued Ruthie. "But if you want to know what I think, they must have been wacko too."

Both detectives stared at Ruthie.

"Okay," Selby said. "What does this have to with anything?"

"That's why he gave him up for free," Ruthie added.

"Who?" asked Roma.

"The dog breeder," said Ruthie.

"The dog breeder is wacko?" asked Roma.

"No! I'm saying the dog breeder, Vickie's boyfriend, must have known the dog was wacko. That's why he donated it to the auction in the first place."

Selby and Roma stared at Ruthie.

"Let me get this straight," said Selby, clearing his throat. "You're telling us that the Berger's dog, the one called Captain, is a wacko dog. Is that right?"

"Well, it's obvious if you know what to look for," Ruthie said. "Isn't that right, Lawrence?"

Lawrence nodded his head.

"Most wacko dogs come from wacko parents," added Ruthie.

"Huh. Did you know that, Detective Roma?" Mick looked matter-of-factly at his partner.

"Learn something new every day," Roma deadpanned.

"So, tell me, Ruthie, ahh, how did you become so knowledgeable about dogs?" asked Selby.

"A dog breeder told me," said Ruthie.

"Oh, yeah? What dog breeder would that be?" Selby asked.

"Jerry Andino, the guy Vickie was dating," Ruthie said, as if it were common knowledge.

"Okay. And how did you come to know Mr. Andino?" asked Selby.

"How do you think? Vickie and I were dear friends, and she introduced us to him. Lawrence and I were always at Vickie's house—Vickie loved Lawrence." Ruthie patted Lawrence's knee. "She was like a second aunt to him."

Lawrence solemnly nodded in agreement. "Very close," he whispered.

"Vickie used to . . . to—" Ruthie choked on her words as if emotionally taxed. "She used to call Lawrence her little CIA agent."

"Impressive," said Roma. He cocked his head in Lawrence's direction. "Why did she call you that?"

"I don't know," Lawrence whined, shrugging his shoulders.

"Lawrence is just being bashful. He has a knack for knowing about things around town before anyone else does, and Vickie, being a bit of a gossip, liked chatting-up with him."

Ruthie spoke as if she were proud of this piece of information. Selby and Roma glanced at each other.

"That true?" Roma looked at Lawrence.

"Maybe," Lawrence whined, clearly covering something up.

"Well, since you were so close to Mrs. Mack, what did you think of this Jerry Andino . . . Mrs. Mack's boyfriend?" asked Roma.

"Nothing," Lawrence whined again.

"Ach," Aunt Ruthie barked at the detectives. "It's a waste of your time if you're looking into the boyfriend."

"Why is that, Ruthie?" asked Selby.

"The man's been out of the country," explained Ruthie. "He wasn't even in town when the murder took place. He, umm, got into some kind of legal trouble with his dog business, so he left the country."

"For selling . . . disturbed dogs?" Roma quipped, eliciting a glare from Selby.

"Nah! For tax reasons," said Ruthie, oblivious to Roma's dig.

"How do you know this?" Roma asked.

"Lawrence told me," responded Ruthie.

Lawrence jumped up from his seat. "No, I didn't. *You* told *me!* Remember?"

"Ach, I don't remember who told who." Ruthie waved her hand as if waving off a fly. "Jerry may have mentioned it to me first."

"Wow. Jerry confided in you that he was leaving the country? You and Jerry must have been close." Selby let that hang in the air for a moment.

Aunt Ruthie's face flushed bright pink. "We were friends . . . that's all."

"Any chance Vickie was suspicious about your friendship with Jerry?" continued Selby.

"Ach, Vickie was suspicious of everything and everyone, wasn't she?" Ruthie looked directly at Lawrence.

Lawrence winced. "I guess so?"

The detectives looked at each other, then Roma took over. "So, Lawrence, since you had such a close relationship with Mrs. Mack, did she ever mention she suspected Mr. Andino was two-timing her?"

"Mmmmm, maybe."

"I don't understand *maybe*," Roma pressed.

"Well, she may have mentioned it once or twice."

"Like what?"

"Well, mainly she asked if I'd ever seen her boyfriend hanging out with any other women."

"I guess that's because, like your aunt said, you have a knack for knowing what's going on before anyone else," said Roma.

Lawrence recoiled further into the pink couch. "I guess."

"What did you tell her?" asked Selby.

"I might have mentioned that sometimes when I got off the school bus, I noticed Jerry's car parked in front of Aunt Ruthie's house."

"His car was never parked *in front* of my house!" Aunt Ruthie interrupted, furious.

"Well, maybe not *right* in front of our house—" Lawrence backpedaled.

Roma held up his hand to calm Ruthie. "Lawrence, did you ever see Jerry Andino at your aunt's house?"

"Noooo, but I might have seen him leaving our house a few times."

Ruthie gasped and placed her hand over her heart.

"How many times would you say?" pushed Roma.

"Maybe two or three times."

"Was this something you might have told Vickie Mack? I mean, you were her little CIA agent." Roma was closing in on the jugular.

Lawrence looked like a trapped squirrel.

Aunt Ruthie's eyes were about to pop out of their sockets.

Selby picked up the questioning. "Lawrence, was there anything else you might have mentioned to Vickie Mack that would make her think another woman, someone like your aunt, was after her boyfriend?"

Lawrence suddenly looked at Ruthie. "I didn't mean to tell her, Aunt Ruthie! It just popped out of my mouth one day when Vickie and I were talking."

"What popped out of your mouth?" Ruthie screeched.

"I told her how you said Jerry was sexy and hot and that if she didn't watch out you were going to make a play for him." Lawrence was now hunched over and staring at the floor.

Ruthie gasped. "How dare you tell her that!"

"Well, that's what you told me," said Lawrence with his whiny voice.

Ruthie glared at her nephew. "You are such an idiot!"

"You know I've got to ask you, Ruthie, was there something going on between you and Mrs. Mack's hot and sexy boyfriend?" Detective Selby's voice was soft, almost compassionate. "Not that there was anything wrong with that."

Ruthie huffed. "Vickie and I were very close, very dear friends, and I would never *try* to steal her boyfriend," said Ruthie as she wiped sweat beads from her upper lip. "But was it my fault that Jerry had lost interest in *her*? Besides, who was *she* to get so huffy and jealous? It's a known fact that Vickie had numerous affairs with all sorts of married men, even while she dated Jerry. You'd be surprised to know who some of them were."

"I'm sure I would, but let's hold off on that for a second." Selby paused and looked at Ruthie. "What I'd really like to talk about is a recent altercation that happened in town."

The room became as quiet as a morgue as Aunt Ruthie stared at Detective Selby. "I heard it was between you and Vickie Mack," continued the detective.

Ruthie stiffened her back and looked as if she didn't know what he was talking about.

"Sounded like you got your arm stuck in the boyfriend's car window, and you were dragged along the street by your *dear friend* Vickie Mack."

"Oh, that! That wasn't anything," said Ruthie waving her hand in the air again.

"That's really interesting," said Selby cocking his head sideways. "You know, if a *dear* friend of mine dragged me down the street like that, well . . . I'd be pretty mad, and I sure wouldn't keep telling people we were dear friends." Selby stared at Aunt Ruthie, who didn't say a word.

Roma stepped in. "If that had happened to me with a lot of towns-people watching, man, I'd probably be thinking of all kinds of ways to get back at that friend."

Ruthie remained stone faced.

"I mean, I'd be so angry I'd want to get revenge," Roma sounded more sympathetic than accusatory. "How about you, Lawrence, wouldn't you be angry enough to want revenge?"

"Me? No!" Lawrence looked directly at his aunt.

"I'm just wondering if you and Aunt Ruthie ever talked about some kind of retribution," said Roma.

"Well," Lawrence looked pleadingly at his aunt. "Aunt Ruthie, you did say that you'd find a way to get back at Vickie. Remember?"

Ruthie clutched her heart and gasped loudly.

"Is that true?" Selby looked at Aunt Ruthie.

"Well, it's just like you just said. Who wouldn't want revenge after being humiliated like that?"

"Especially by someone who was your *dear friend*," added Selby.

"Yes, my dear friend, who at times could be a very evil woman!"

All eyes focused on Aunt Ruthie. An internal alarm rang in her head. "Okay! Okay! Now I get it! You two smart-assed detectives think I killed Vickie, my dearest friend, and then stuffed her into a steamer trunk? Well, that's absurd!" Ruthie stood up to leave the room but then thought better of it and sat back down.

"I agree it does sound absurd," began Roma, "except for the fact that the last time we spoke, neither you nor Lawrence mentioned the car dragging episode or the fact that Mrs. Mack might have suspected you and Jerry Andino were having an affair."

Unprompted, Lawrence pointed an accusing finger at his aunt. "She said she'd kill me if I told you about the car thing!"

Ruthie shot up from her seat and pointed at Lawrence. "How dare you! I did not say I'd *kill* you!" Ruthie shot daggers at her nephew, then glowered at the detectives as if wanting to shout at them, too. Instead she collapsed into her downy pink sofa.

"So, Ruthie, can you tell us why you didn't mention the incident to us the last time we spoke with you?" asked Roma.

"I, I, I," Ruthie stuttered. "I was afraid of how it might look to you."

"What do you mean?" Selby asked.

"Oh, pa-*leeze*! Don't play me like a fool. It probably looks like I had a good reason . . . a, a, a motive to murder Vickie."

"You might have a point there," Roma said.

"Lawrence, tell them I did not murder Vickie Mack!"

Lawrence looked at his aunt but kept his mouth shut.

"You're kind of quiet over there, Lawrence," said Mick Selby. "Your aunt just asked you to tell us she didn't kill Mrs. Mack. Do you have any reason to suspect her?"

"No, he does not!" shouted Ruthie.

"Lawrence?" nudged Selby.

"All I know is what I already told you." Lawrence again crisscrossed his gangly arms.

"Do you think your aunt was serious about getting back at Mrs. Mack?" asked Selby.

"Yes . . . no . . . how should I know?" Lawrence whined feebly.

"Maybe you *know-it-all detectives* should be looking a little harder into *dear, sweet Emily Fryze*. She's the one who had a motive to kill Vickie!" Ruthie yelled.

"Why do you say that?" Roma felt a twinge in his stomach.

"Ack! It's common knowledge that Peter Fryze had a fling with Vickie Mack!"

"Common knowledge, huh. I don't recall anyone ever mentioning it to me." Selby looked at his partner. "Detective Roma, anyone ever tell you that Mr. Fryze had a fling with Vickie Mack?"

"Nope." Roma felt another spasm in his stomach.

"How about you, Lawrence, did you know about a *fling* between Mrs. Mack and Mr. Fryze?" Selby asked.

"Well, duh! Everyone knew about it!" Lawrence rolled his eyes and wrinkled his face, as if casting aspersions on two dimwitted detectives.

At this point, Selby wondered if Ruthie and Lawrence were trying to throw out a preplanned smoke bomb.

"The affair didn't last long," said Ruthie. She had regained her confidence.

"And how do you know that?" Selby gave a quick glance towards Roma, sensing his partner was slightly on edge.

"Vickie told me! Like I said, we are—*were*—dear, dear friends. She told me everything." Ruthie felt she had regained the upper hand and was enjoying it.

"So, tell us what you know about Mr. Fryze and Vickie Mack's affair," continued Selby.

"All I can tell you is . . . the day Emily and Rachel were named co-chairs of the Auction, Vickie was hell-bent on destroying those two women in any way she could."

"Why was that?" asked Roma. He was thinking about Emily Fryze and couldn't imagine why anyone on God's green earth would want to harm her.

"Because being named auction chairperson is such a prestigious job."

"How so?" Roma asked.

"Duh, the whole parent association expects the auction chairs to bring in tons of money for the school. And when they do, they're like heroes. That's what Vickie wanted—to be a hero to the whole Calivista Elementary School community."

"So, how does Peter Fryze fit into all this?" asked Selby.

Ruthie sighed as if fielding *another stupid question*. "Sooo, whenever Pete Fryze showed up at the neighborhood pool or at the park with his kids . . . without Emily . . . because she was at a school auction meeting, well, you figure it out." Ruthie waved her hand in the air and said, "*La-dee-dah.*"

"Hmm. I guess I'm not so good at figuring these things out," deadpanned Selby. He looked at Roma. "Can you figure it out?"

"I'm not so good at it either."

"Okay, I'll spell it out for you two," Ruthie said sarcastically. "Everyone knows Pete has a past. Now do you get it?"

"What kind of past?" Roma seemed genuinely interested.

Ruthie looked at Roma as if he were a cretin. "Ack! Everyone knows Pete's a big flirt. I heard he'd had at least two affairs under his belt," Ruthie guffawed, "and probably a whole lot more!"

The detectives' lack of rejoinder caused Ruthie to further explain. "Soooo, Vickie figured with Pete's past and Emily being gone so much of the time because of all the auction duties, he was an easy mark."

"And—" Roma probed, wanting more dirt.

"And?" Ruthie threw her hands in the air. "So, Vickie started showing up at the pool wearing a bikini and carrying a flask in her beach bag. Then she started bringing prepared dinners to Pete on the nights she knew Emily was at an auction meeting. *Aaaand,* one thing led to another. It's the law of nature and, well, there you have it. La-dee-da, la-dee-da."

Roma cleared his throat, then asked, "When would you say the affair between Mrs. Mack and Mr. Fryze began?" *The Emily Fryze he'd interrogated would have been deeply hurt by this information, so hurt that her marriage might be . . . over? He wondered.*

"I just told you. Months ago." Ruthie was feeling her oats.

"How long would you say it lasted?" Selby asked.

"Ack, a month or two. Maybe three," Ruthie said.

"Did Vickie Mack tell you that?" Selby asked.

"Of course, she did! Vickie wasn't *really* interested in Pete Fryze. He wasn't her type, if you know what I mean. Besides, she was already dating Jerry Andino, the dog breeder from San Bernardino. She just wanted to get some evidence, you know, some pictures of her and Pete together so she could send them to Emily."

"What kinds of pictures?" Selby asked.

"What do ya' think?" Ruthie asked rhetorically, annoyed by the detective's question. "Pictures of Vickie in the pool and in the hot tub rubbing against Pete. Vickie at the park with her arms around Pete's neck while the kids played on the jungle gym. That kind of thing."

"Were these selfies?" Roma wanted to know.

Ruthie slowly turned to look at Lawrence.

"What?" Lawrence jumped out of his seat.

Detectives Selby and Roma stared at Aunt Ruthie's nephew.

"Okay. . . so what! I took the pictures but only because Vickie paid me."

"How much did Vickie Mack pay you to take pictures of her with Peter Fryze?" Roma asked.

"Enough." Lawrence shrugged his shoulders as if his price was top secret.

"Did Mr. Fryze ever see you taking pictures of him and Vickie together?" asked Roma.

"No, I mean . . . I don't think so. But I do know he eventually saw the pictures."

"What makes you say that?" Roma was drilling down.

"Well, it's kind of obvious. I mean, the day after Vickie put the pictures in the Fryze's mailbox Pete moved to an apartment in town." Lawrence looked almost pleased with himself.

"When was this?" asked Selby.

"Well before the auction," Ruthie chimed in.

Mick Selby exhaled, looked at Aaron Roma, then at Lawrence and Ruthie. "Well, you've both been really helpful. I think we're done for now, but I'm sure we'll need to speak with you again." Selby narrowed his focus and gave them a stern warning. "Once again, neither of you should discuss any of this information or anything regarding the auction murder with anyone, including each other. Do I make myself clear?"

Aunt Ruthie and Lawrence nodded in unison.

CHAPTER 27

IN A COMMUNITY of multimillion-dollar homes, Peter Fryze's apartment, a few short blocks from Calivista Village, was decidedly downscale, a major setback, and an embarrassing discomfiture for him. But after Emily had asked him, in no uncertain terms, to leave their spacious ocean view home, Pete had no choice but to lease one of the Ocean Breeze apartments on Alan Street, a depressing one-bedroom on the ground floor.

"He's the clown who thought it was all a big joke," said Detective Roma as he and Selby walked toward the apartment complex. Roma had built up a considerable antipathy toward Peter Fryze, and he knew exactly why, too.

"Yep," said Selby, shaking his head. He rang the doorbell, and a few moments later, the door opened.

"Hello, detectives." Pete's tone was decidedly different than at their last encounter as he stood in his doorway barefooted, dressed in jeans and a bright orange Polo shirt.

"Our apologies for the short notice," said Selby as he shook Pete's hand.

"No problem, I was working from home today." After an unsettling handshake with Detective Roma, Pete gestured for the two detectives to come inside and closed the door.

The apartment looked like someone had started to move in but then gave up. A row of half-opened moving boxes had been pushed against a wall, and a long metal desk cluttered with folders and a matching rolling desk chair had been pushed against a sliding glass door that led to a tiny enclosed cement patio. Sitting on the floor beside a faux fireplace was a flat screen TV, a cable box and an opened suitcase revealing three starched and folded white dress shirts.

Roma pointed to the lime green bean bag chair in the center of the room. "I'd love to get the name of your decorator," said Roma, less for its comedic value than for taking a jab at the man who had hurt the lovely Emily Fryze.

"Nothing like Staples and Goodwill to give a house a homey feel," said Pete. He smiled, hoping to loosen the conversation, but instinct told him not to engage in needless humor and niceties with these two men.

"As you might have guessed, we've got a few questions," responded Selby.

"Okay then." Pete moved a few steps to a counter that separated the living room from the kitchenette. He picked up a four-legged bar stool and placed it next to the desk chair and then dragged the lime green beanbag to face the stool and desk chair.

"Please, make yourselves comfortable," Pete said as he flopped onto the beanbag.

Selby reached for the chair, Roma sat on the bar stool, and for a moment, the three men just stared at each other.

"So, how long have you lived here?" Detective Selby asked.

"Too long," Pete answered.

"I hear you, but really, I want to know how long you've lived here in this apartment. Is it months, years?"

"Almost five months." Pete shook his head. "But I'm pretty sure I'll be moving back home soon," he added.

Aaron Roma felt a slight pinch in the pit of his stomach, then looked Pete in the eye. "Mr. Fryze, do you mind telling us why you and Mrs. Fryze are separated."

"Geeesch." Pete wiped his hand across his mouth. "I had a totally— and I mean *totally*—meaningless fling with another woman." His words and the arrogance with which Pete presented them hung in the air for a few moments.

Selby cleared his throat. "And whom was that *fling* with?"

"I'm guessing you're here because you already know." Pete had a look of defiance on his face.

The detectives stared at Pete, and for a moment, nobody said a word. Roma stared at him in a way that made Pete squirm.

"Alright! Vickie Mack," Pete raised both hands as if to say *you got me*. "Let me guess. Emily told you about my meaningless fling." There was no hint of contrition.

Roma's disdain for this man was growing by the second. *How could a woman as sweet as Emily have married someone so full of himself?*

"Actually, Mr. Fryze, it was not your wife who informed us of your *fling* with Vickie Mack," said Roma. He had no intention of revealing his source. His only goal was to push the man's buttons.

For the second time that day, Mick Selby observed a change in his partner's approach, now taking the tone of prosecutor rather than investigator. With a quick glance at Roma, who knew exactly what that look meant, Selby took over the questioning.

"Mr. Fryze," Mick Selby interjected, "I'm a little curious as to why, on the night of the murder of Vickie Mack, the same night we spoke with you at the precinct, why you never mentioned any kind of connection between yourself and the deceased."

"Why would I? I was out of town when Vickie was killed." Pete hunched his shoulders and lifted both hands in the air. "Look, fellas, my little fling with Vickie, which ended several months before her . . . *demise*, had no connection to what happened that night. None."

"Mr. Fryze, were you aware there were photos taken of you and Mrs. Mack in some compromising positions?" Selby stared at him wearing a game face.

"Yes." Pete used both hands to push himself out of the beanbag, groaning as he stood up. "I need a bottle of water. You guys want one?" Pete walked toward his compact kitchen and opened the skinny refrigerator door.

"I'm good," Selby said.

"Nope." Roma chimed in with a surly one-syllable response.

Pete returned to the living room and, before sitting down, lifted the water bottle in the air as if offering a toast. "So, yes, there were some photos of Vickie and me."

The two officers waited for him to continue.

"And . . . I regret that Emily found them."

"Tell me," Selby continued. "How did those photos and the revelation of your relationship with Ms. Mack affect your marriage?"

Pete Fryze spread both arms to show the vastness of his tiny apartment. "Behold, you are looking at the result of those pictures."

"I assume your wife asked you to move out of your house," continued Selby.

"Yup." Pete took a swig of his water.

"That's kind of harsh," said Roma with an air of sympathy, *hombre a hombre*. "I mean, especially since, as you said, your *fling* with Vickie Mack was so insignificant."

Pete looked at Roma as if, finally, someone understood. "You've got *that* right."

"Especially since it was your first and *only* fling." Roma remembered Ruthie's claim that Peter Fryze was known for having had several previous affairs, but the detective wanted confirmation from Mr. Fryze and, maybe, just maybe, Roma wanted to rub it in a little bit. Actually, he wanted to rub it in a whole lot.

Pete looked at Roma, baffled as to why the detective sounded defensive on behalf of Emily. Pete's first instinct said, *Nahhh;* but his primal intuition said, *Huh.* "Look, you guys, my wife loves me, and she's come to terms with the fact that for some inexplicable reason, women have always been attracted to me. They come out of nowhere. I don't even have to go looking. So, yeah, I've had a few other affairs, and, yeah, it's been a minor problem in our marriage, but Emily has always known that all the other women mean nothing to me."

Detective Selby noticed Roma's jaw muscles constricting.

"I gather your wife did not interpret your fling with Mrs. Mack as meaningless, since, as you've said, she sent you packing. Have I got that right?" said Roma trying, with little success, to conceal his contempt for the husband of the beautiful Emily Fryze.

"Bingo." Pete winked and pointed his index finger at the detective. "But you have to understand, Emily was hardly ever around for the last year and a half."

"How so?" Roma asked.

"There were a whole lot of nights and weekends when Emily was busy with all her auction responsibilities, all the meetings and school politics, so I was forced to take over with our kids, the meals, get them ready for bed, and all the other stuff of raising a family."

"I hear you," said Selby in solidarity. "I've got three kids of my own. Sometimes an eighteen-hour workday seems easier than just one hour of taking care of the kids." Mick did not really feel this way. He valued every minute he had with his children.

"You've got that right," said Pete reaching out to fist-bump with Selby. "I mean, when Vickie started showing up and offering to help out with cooking dinners, stuff like that, it was hard for me to turn her down. And then one night just after I'd put the kids to bed, Vickie showed up at the front door. She said she'd been dining out with friends and, knowing Emily would still be at a committee meeting, decided to order a real dinner for me . . . along with a bottle of wine. She said she couldn't stay long but would love a glass of the wine. One glass led to another and another, and we ended up getting too cozy on the couch of our living room."

"Was that the first time you and Vickie got . . . cozy?" Selby asked.

"That was the *only* time we got that cozy. I mean, yeah, there had been a few times at the pool and maybe at the park when we'd flirted with each other."

"Any idea who took the pictures of you and Vickie Mack," asked Selby.

"No, but I'm pretty sure it was her one and only friend, that weirdo Ruthie, or else she hired someone."

"Any proof that Vickie had someone take the pictures?" continued Selby.

"Not exactly." Pete shook his head. "But the day after Emily kicked me out of the house, I called Vickie and asked if she was aware of the pictures. She said she'd seen them and thought they were pretty good of the both of us. She even laughed and asked me what Emily thought of them."

"Whoa!" said Selby.

"I know, unbelievable!" Pete looked at both detectives. "At that moment, I hated Vickie Mack more than anyone in the world."

"What did you say to her?" asked Roma.

"I told her I hoped she'd burn in hell."

"Do you have the photos?" Roma probed.

"No. Emily destroyed them. I'd be willing to bet there are some at Vickie's house, but I don't know." Pete swiped his hand over his mouth. "I should have known what Vickie's real motives were."

"Her real motives?" asked Selby.

"Well, the sex, for sure, but obviously, Vickie also wanted to hurt Emily. I get that now. Vickie was a witchy kind of woman . . . you know the type."

Selby paused for a moment to let that sink in.

"Mr. Fryze, you've got to admit that from our point of view," Selby looked at Roma who was sitting stone-faced on the wooden stool, "you and/or your wife seem to have had reasons, you know what I mean, *motives*, to want Vickie Mack dead." Selby looked Peter Fryze in the eyes.

"What? No way!" Pete swiped his hand over his mouth again. "I'll be honest with you, I'm not sad Vickie's dead but I didn't do it."

"And what about your wife?" asked Selby.

"You've met my wife," Pete stretched his arms wide. "Sheesch, Emily doesn't have an angry or mean bone in her body! She forgives everyone and anyone of every offense."

"Including her husband's adultery?" Roma stared at Pete.

"Yes, including my . . . *trivial flings*." Peter Fryze spoke as if challenging Detective Roma to a duel.

Detective Selby interrupted the exchange. "Mr. Fryze, you're obviously a bright man, so I don't need to tell you that from the beginning of time, hurting someone you love, like being unfaithful, or, as you put it, having *trivial flings*, can ignite emotions of rage and revenge in the one who's been hurt, enough rage to cause a normally sane and forgiving person like your wife to . . . commit murder."

The moment Detective Selby said this, Pete flashed upon his conversation with Conrad at the park. His gaze made him look like the proverbial deer in headlights.

"Anything you want to tell us?" Selby asked.

Pete hesitated for several long seconds. Roma felt his heart stop.

"Okay, okay. So, here's kind of a weird thing," Pete said hesitantly, as if he were having second thoughts.

"Go on," said Selby.

"There was this night before the auction, before Emily knew about me and Vickie, when Emily and I had dinner with Conrad and Rachel at the local Tex-Mex restaurant. By the time we'd all had a few Margaritas, Emily and Rachel kind of started joking about hiring a hit man to kill Vickie Mack. It just was so out of character for both of our wives to bring up something like *knocking off* anyone . . . you know? Even joking about hiring some kind of hit man was so out of line. Man, this is really freaking me out." Pete took a swig from his water bottle.

"What is?" Roma's jaws were clenched tight and several veins running up his neck popped out.

"Well, you know, that Emily could even consider the insane idea of trying to find someone like a hit man . . . you know what I mean? It's not like there's enough money in our bank account to pay someone to do that."

Roma's eyes were drilling into Peter Fryze's.

"Actually, that's a good point Mr. Fryze," said Selby. "It's not unusual for people who don't have a lot of cash to find underlings or people who are dependent upon them for one reason or another to commit the act of murder."

"Oh, yeah?" Pete looked confused.

"Do you know of anyone like that . . . in relation to your wife or Mrs. Berger?" asked Selby.

"Good God, no! I mean, well—" Pete hesitated and scratched the back of his head. "Of course, it's crazy to think this, but there's this janitor at the school who thinks Emily walks on water. Emily mentioned him all the time—he helped with the auction . . . *a lot!* I mean like every day."

"Did you ever meet him?" Selby probed.

"Only once or twice when Emily dragged me to a school event, a school play or a musical. After one or two of the events, she'd made a big deal of introducing me to the guy."

"Wow! He must be pretty important to your wife," replied Selby.

"Geesch!" Pete shook his head. "That janitor acted like the heavens and earth opened up for Emily."

"Can you describe him?" asked Selby.

"He was kind of short and sturdy. A Latino. I think he had a mustache, thick black hair."

"Do you know his name?" Selby asked while Roma listened intently.

"Actually, I do, because Emily was always mentioning him and telling me about his hard life before he came to America. Come to think of it, he might be an illegal."

"His name?" asked Roma.

"Cupertino Flores. How do you forget a name like that?"

Without revealing any recognition of the name Cupertino Flores, Roma continued his questioning. "Mr. Fryze, did your wife personally know any of the other *insignificant* women in your life besides Mrs. Mack?"

"No, all the other *incidents* took place out of town."

"Are any of those other women with whom you had *incidental flings* . . . are any of them dead?" Roma was wearing his anger on his sleeve.

"Good God, no! They're all alive and well." Pete looked at his watch. "Look, I've got a plane to catch, and I haven't finished packing, so if you don't mind, can we wrap this up?

"Sure," Selby interjected, "but before we go, you need to write down names, addresses, phone numbers of the various women with whom you've had extramarital affairs."

"Really?" Pete felt trapped and weary. "I might have phone numbers, but addresses?"

"And hotels."

"Geesch, you're killing me."

CHAPTER 28

"DETECTIVES?" EMILY WORE an innocent look of surprise when she opened the door and saw the detectives standing on the front porch.

Detective Aaron Roma smiled, completely charmed by her. "Sorry to show up unexpectedly, Mrs. Fryze," Roma said with true sincerity. "Detective Selby and I were wondering if we could take a few minutes of your time to ask some questions."

"Ahh, well, Molly and I were just playing 'tea party' and—" Emily looked over her shoulder toward the family room, where Molly was engaged in serving cookies to two teddy bears, then turned back to the detectives, looking directly into the intoxicating eyes of Detective Roma. "Of course. Please come in."

Roma held the door open for Selby to follow Emily into the foyer, which allowed him to note the tight-fitting, white t-shirt Emily was wearing over even tighter fitting blue jeans. She was barefoot with light rose-colored polish on her toenails. Roma took a deep breath and followed Selby and Emily through the foyer, past the living room and into the family room.

Apparently, the Fryze house was the exact floorplan of the Berger's house—same first floor layout with the foyer leading into a living room that flowed into a family room that was connected to a kitchen. The only differences between the two houses were the lighter-stained hardwood floors, the cream-colored paint on the walls and the furniture, which was less formal than the Berger's. To Roma, this home was warm and welcoming . . . very much like Emily.

"Molly and I were having a little tea party," Emily repeated as she led the detectives into the family room. Kneeling at the square coffee table, Molly was going through the motions of pouring water from a miniature porcelain teapot covered with dainty, red ladybugs.

Molly looked up as the detectives walked into the room. "You want thomme tea?"

Selby tilted his head as if considering her offer.

"Oh, no, sweetie," Emily smiled. "This is—"

"I would love some tea," Roma interrupted. He stepped toward Molly, bent down and carefully accepted the teacup and saucer she held out to him.

"Carefwul," Molly warned him. "Hot."

"Thank you," Roma said, then softly blew over the top of his teacup.

Molly was delighted to have a new guest at her tea party. "You want thugar?"

"Yes, please." Roma waited patiently as Molly reached for a miniature sugar bowl from which she daintily scooped real granules of sugar. He was quite taken with this little girl who looked very much like her mother.

"Queem?" Molly held up a miniature creamer.

"Oh, I shouldn't but maybe just a little."

An unexpected feeling of gratitude filled Emily's heart as she watched the short interaction between her daughter and Detective Roma. Pete rarely took the time to *really* interact with Molly, and when he did, he was always distracted by his cellphone, the newspaper or the TV.

"Detective Roma, it's obvious you have children of your own," Emily said.

Aaron Roma looked at Emily. "Ah, no I don't. I thought I'd wait until I got married."

Emily smiled and offered a warm nod of her head.

Detective Selby, now fully aware of the somewhat out-of-bounds dance of emotions taking place between his partner and a suspect, favored getting down to business over scrutinizing the unstated dynamics between the two other adults in the room. Mick cleared his throat and began. "Mrs. Fryze—"

As if startled out of a trance, Emily and Aaron looked at Mick. "Hmm?" asked Emily.

"Detective Roma and I met with your husband, earlier today."

"I see," Emily said quickly turning her attention to her child. "Molly, sweetie, how would you and your teddy bears like to watch a cartoon while I talk with these nice men in the living room?" Molly jumped from her tea set as Emily reached for the TV remote control.

Moments later, Selby, Roma and Emily sat in the adjacent room while cartoon animals chirped in the background.

"I'll get right to the point," said Selby. "We understand there were photographs taken of your husband and Mrs. Mack."

Emily looked down at her lap. "Yes, there were pictures," she said softly. She didn't mention how devastated she had felt when she'd first seen the pictures of Vickie and Pete in compromising positions.

"Do you mind showing them to us?" Selby asked.

"I burned them."

"Understandably. I know this must be difficult for you," Selby said.

"No." Emily interrupted. "No, it *was* difficult but not so much anymore. The thing with Vickie wasn't the first time my husband was unfaithful."

"How many times would you say your husband has had an affair?" Selby asked.

"Three that I know of, not including Vickie. But the thing with Vickie was the last straw for me."

Selby and Roma had heard similar words spoken by suspects before they confessed to murder. "The last straw?" asked Selby.

"I just mean that I am in the process of divorcing Pete."

"Your husband is under the impression that he'll be moving back home in the near future," Roma said, then waited intently for her answer,

"Pete told you that?" Emily looked repulsed. "He's delusional. He knows I've retained an attorney. I just wanted to wait until after the auction to file the papers." Emily said this while looking only at Detective Selby, but Selby sensed that her words had been uttered for Detective Roma's benefit.

"I see," Selby said.

"Look, Pete's not a bad guy, it's just that there will always be other women he won't be able to resist. But just for your information, I don't blame him for the thing with Vickie Mack."

"Why is that?" Selby asked.

"Vickie wanted to hurt me," Emily swallowed. "And, well, obviously, she succeeded."

"It seems Mrs. Mack took pleasure in hurting Rachel Berger, too," said Selby, hoping to generate a response from Emily.

She remained quiet for a moment, as if preparing to choose her words carefully. Emily assumed the detective was referring to the "Penny for Your Thoughts" entries by *Miz Anonymous*. "Nobody was safe from Vickie's wrath, not even someone as kind and harmless as Rachel or as, well, as Cupertino Flores, our school custodian."

"That's interesting that you mention Mr. Flores," said Selby. "His name has come up a few times. I understand that you and Mrs. Berger liked him."

"Oh, yes. Cupertino is a lovely man."

"What was Mrs. Mack's relationship with Mr. Flores?" asked Selby.

"Not a good one. Vickie threatened to look into his and his family's citizenship, and she took every opportunity to order him around and humiliate him, even in front of the students."

"That must have made Mr. Flores pretty angry," added Selby.

"You'd never know it."

"You like him?" continued Selby.

"Oh, I do, very much. Rachel and I could never have pulled off the auction event without Cupertino's help. He worked after hours and sometimes on the weekends. Of course, the school wouldn't pay him for all the overtime, so Rachel and I did. Cupertino would do anything we asked of him."

"Boy," Selby said as he blew out a gust of air. "It must be nice to know someone like that, someone who would do anything you ask of them." Selby had put away a few people who were willing to do anything for someone else.

At that moment, Detective Selby decided that it was time to pay a visit to Mr. Cupertino Flores.

CHAPTER 29

THE NEXT MORNING Detectives Selby and Roma drove to Calivista Elementary School, where they found Cupertino Flores waiting for them at the entrance to the school parking lot. He was wearing charcoal grey janitorial slacks and a work shirt with the name *Flores* embroidered on the left pocket. Even from the car, the detectives could tell the short, stocky man was as nervous as a prisoner on the way to trial. He timidly directed Selby to a parking spot labeled Visitor.

"Cupertino Flores?" said Aaron Roma as he closed the passenger door and reached out to shake the janitor's hand.

"Si, yes, *Señor* Detective," answered Cupertino, his head bobbing up and down as he returned the handshake.

"Thank you for meeting with us this morning. We don't want to take too much of your time," said Roma calmly. *"Habla les preguntas en Espanol?"*

"No," came Cupertino's response. "In English *es* okay." He looked at Selby, assuming that would be better for him.

"Detective Selby," said Mick as he reached out to shake Cupertino's hand. "We have a few questions about the night of Vickie Mack's murder."

"Of course, *señor*. But I tell you everything I know when I see you on Friday night," stammered Cupertino.

"One thing we weren't so clear about," said Mick.

"Si, Señor Detective?"

"Mr. Flores, how well did you know Mrs. Mack?" asked Selby.

"Ohhhh, not too good. She come here almost every day and talk to lots of people but not too much with me. She just tell me if I need to do something better." Cupertino looked very solemn.

Selby continued. "Oh, yeah? Was she your boss?"

"Ohhh, no. The principal *es* my boss, but Miss Vickie Mack is *muy importante* at this school, and I do what she tell me to do. Sometimes she is *sustituir*. . .ah, how you say? *Substitoo-tay* teacher, and I clean extra her classroom, because she no like chalk here and there and children papers here and there."

"Sounds like she was picky about those things. More picky than the other teachers?" asked Mick.

"Ohhhh, *si, señor. Mucho mas.* Other teachers not so much picky."

"You liked Mrs. Mack, though, right?" It was Roma's turn to ask.

"Ohhh, *señor*. I am very sorry, but Miss Mack very hard for me to like too much."

Both detectives nodded as if agreeing with the prevailing opinion. "So, Cupertino, we weren't aware that Mrs. Mack was a substitute teacher at the school. Would you say she was well liked by the students and the other parents?" added Mick.

"Ohhh, no, señor, not very much. Sometime I see *los niños,* they cry if they know Miss Vickie must be their substitute teacher. I not know about all the parents, but I tell you Miss Vickie was very mean to Miss Rachel's son not so long ago." Cupertino furrowed his brow and slowly shook his head.

"Really? I bet that didn't make Mrs. Berger very happy," prodded Mick further.

"Miss Rachel is very nice lady, but Miss Vickie, she not so nice to Miss Rachel's little boy. I think Miss Rachel was not very happy with how Miss Vickie talk about little Robbie." Cupertino continued to shake his head.

"So, how do you know this?" asked Mick.

"Oh! Miss Vickie call me to her classroom at recess to put in new ceiling light bulb, and I hear Miss Vickie call Miss Rachel. She say to Miss Rachel come to school right away. She say Robbie is very bad boy."

"Do you know why the boy was in trouble?" asked Mick.

"Ohhh, please. I cannot tell you." Cupertino was visibly distraught. "Maybe you ask Miss Rachel. She can tell you everything."

"I can tell you like Mrs. Berger," Roma interjected.

"*Ohhh, si!* Miss Rachel and Miss Emily, they very nice ladies. I help them a lot. They very important ladies for the auction. I carry donations to Miss Emily's and Miss Rachel's garages, then take the things to the auction place. I do anything they ask me."

Selby silently wondered if the janitor had been willing to stuff a dead body into a trunk to help out the nice Mrs. Berger and Mrs. Fryze.

"Mr. Flores, we're aware that you went to Mrs. Berger's house the day of the auction," Mick said calmly.

"*Si!* Yes, I go to Miss Rachel's house to get the big trunk for the auction. It is too big for Miss Rachel's car. Miss Rachel tell me to go to her house, and she leave the side door open for me. She say not to worry *porque el perro*, forgive me, because her dog *es* in the garage on a rope. She say the trunk not too heavy for me and Pedro to put into my truck."

"Who is Pedro?" asked Roma.

"Pedro is my helper. He no speak English. Do you want to talk to him?"

"Not right now, maybe later," answered Mick.

"So, Cupertino, what time would you say you and Pedro arrived at Rachel Berger's house?" asked Roma.

"I think maybe four o'clock, maybe sooner. We have to get trunk to auction club before five o'clock before people start to come to party."

"Mr. Flores tell us what happened when you parked in Mrs. Berger's driveway," said Mick.

"Ohhh, we, me and Pedro, go to the door on the side of Miss Rachel's garage."

"Was there anyone else around?" asked Mick.

"*Si.* A boy. I do not know his name."

"What did he look like?" asked Roma.

"Ohhh, very skinny. He say, 'Hello' and I say 'Hello' to him. And he come to side door with me and Pedro, but he no go inside. He stay at door and watch us."

"He stayed outside the garage?" asked Mick.

"*Si.* He just watch me and Pedro go inside."

"Was the dog in the garage?" wondered Mick.

"*No, señor. No perro.* Just the rope. No dog in garage like Miss Rachel say he would be."

"Where do you think the dog was?" asked Roma.

"When I see no dog, I think maybe Miss Rachel leave him inside her house. And I ask the skinny boy at the door if he see the dog, and he say maybe the dog run away. I not know for sure where is the dog, but I think that it is very good for me and Pedro. The dog *es muy loco en la cabeza*," said Cupertino drawing an imaginary circle next to his temple.

"I know what you mean," Selby agreed.

"So, there's no dog in the garage when you arrived . . . was the trunk in the garage?" Roma asked.

"*Si senor.* I see the big trunk. It is closed. Pedro and I try to pick it up, but it is *muy* heavy. I think, 'Why did Miss Rachel say it not too heavy?'"

"That is odd, isn't it?" said Roma.

"Then I think maybe she put more auction things inside it. I tell Pedro first we will open the trunk and take out all the heavy things, then we will carry the trunk onto the pickup truck. I tell Pedro we will put heavy things back into the trunk when we get to the auction place."

"What did you find in the trunk that was so heavy?" asked Roma.

"The trunk was locked, *señor.* I cannot open it. Pedro cannot open it. We have no key for the lock."

"But Mrs. Berger told you it would not be too heavy, is that right?" asked Mick.

"*Si, Señor* Detective. Maybe she think not too heavy for me and Pedro."

"So, Mr. Flores, tell me, if the trunk was so heavy, how did you get it into your truck?" Roma asked.

"Ohhh, we begin to push the trunk to the side door. That is where the skinny boy is standing. He *es muy bien* and say to me he will help take the trunk to the truck. He tell me and Pedro we must be very careful with trunk. He say he worry for us to drop the trunk."

"So, let me get this straight. You and Pedro *and* the skinny boy carried the heavy trunk to your truck? Is that right?" asked Mick.

"*Si, Señor* Detective. All the time Pedro make joke of trunk. Pedro no speak English, but he say to me *en Espanol*, 'What is in this thing?' Pedro then say, 'Maybe a dead body.' And we laugh. I tell skinny boy what Pedro say, but the skinny boy no laugh. He no smile. He say we are bad to make joke."

"So, you and Pedro and the boy were able to lift the trunk onto the bed of your truck?" continued Roma.

"Ohhh, *si*. And I say *gracias* to the boy, then me and Pedro drive the truck to the auction club place. When we are there, we get a man to help us carry the trunk to the back of stage. When I find Miss Rachel and Miss Emily, I tell them the trunk es *muy* heavy and I cannot open it *por que el cerradura*, oh sorry, the lock *es trabarse*."

"The lock was jammed," Roma translated for his partner.

"*Si! Muy trabarse.*" Cupertino concurred.

"What did Mrs. Berger and Mrs. Fryze say when you told them this?" asked Roma.

"Ohh, they so very busy with auction, but Miss Rachel say, 'Okay and thank you' to me and Pedro. Miss Rachel say she have a key for the trunk to unlock. Miss Rachel say she will need me and Pedro to carry the trunk on the stage after all the people no more eating the dinner."

"So, you and Pedro stayed at the Beaumont Beach Club all night?" asked Mick.

"No, *señor*. Pedro go home, but I stay until you and this other Mr. Detective tell me I can go home. And now here I talk to you again," said Cupertino Flores as earnest as a judge.

"Well, we thank you very much for your time, Mr. Flores. Please do not talk to anyone about the day or the night of the auction," Mick cautioned the janitor.

"Ohhh, *si Señor* Detectives. I talk to nobody. I just stay to my work here at the school."

Selby and Roma got into their car and watched Cupertino Flores walk toward the school office.

"I think we need to talk with Rachel Berger again," said Selby. "I'm a little curious about the day Vickie Mack called her to the classroom."

"And maybe we should revisit our friend Lawrence," Roma added. "It's kind of remarkable that he never mentioned that there was a second janitor at the Berger house the day of the murder."

Selby nodded his head in agreement. "He also never mentioned helping the two janitors with the trunk."

CHAPTER 30

WHEN SHE HEARD the doorbell ring, Rachel was grateful Captain was across the street inside the dog grooming van getting a bath, because whoever was at the door would be spared an assault by her maniac dog.

At the same time, Detectives Selby and Roma, remembering the last time they had arrived at the Berger's front porch, braced themselves for the dog's assault from inside. Rachel opened the door wide, and both detectives looked past her, certain the dog would come bounding at them any second.

"Detectives?" Rachel wondered why they hadn't called to let her know they were coming.

"Sorry to bother you again, Mrs. Berger," said Mick Selby. "We were nearby, speaking with Cupertino Flores at the school and thought we'd take a chance that you might be at home."

"Of course, would you like to come inside?" Rachel noticed both detectives looking behind her.

"Is the dog in the backyard or something?" Roma asked.

Rachel laughed and pointed across the street. "You're lucky. He's locked inside the van with the words *Bubbles and Best Buds* in pink and blue lettering." Pink and blue dogs surrounded by far too many bubbles had been professionally painted on every inch of the van. "Captain chased a skunk last night, and the skunk had the last word."

"Ah, well then, that's good for us, isn't it?" Mick Selby said with a smile.

Rachel gestured for the detectives to follow her into the living room.

"We won't take up too much of your time," said Selby, pausing as he took a seat on the couch. "Here's the thing. We understand there was an occasion when Mrs. Mack called and asked you to come to your son's classroom a few days before the auction and . . . uh . . . and that there was a lot of tension between you and Mrs. Mack. Is that true?"

"Yes . . . that's true," said Rachel. A queasy sensation sped through her veins. She did not like where this was headed and wondered if she should have an attorney present. "I think it was Wednesday or Thursday."

"So, that would have been just a day or two before the auction took place. Is that correct?" Selby asked.

"Yes." Rachel spoke quietly, afraid of her own words. At that moment, she had an odd sensation, like she had channeled into an alternate universe in which she, Rachel Berger, was in an episode of NYPD Blue with Detective Selby in the lead role. Ohhh, if only Selby looked like Tom Selleck, she, Rachel Berger, would willingly tell him anything and everything he wanted to know no matter the consequences. But he was no Tom Selleck.

"We're very interested in knowing about the specific exchange that took place between the two of you that day," Selby said.

At that moment, Rachel would have given anything *not* to have to tell the detectives about that afternoon when she and Vickie had met at Calivista Elementary School.

"In fact, we understand Mrs. Mack called you and insisted that you come to the school immediately to discuss something about your son," Selby added. "Were you at home when she called?"

"No. I was at the nail salon in town." Rachel looked down at her bare feet—*would her toes become evidence against her?* She quickly looked back up at the detectives, embarrassed they might be judging her to be just another pampered Calivista housewife with nothing better to do during the day than to have manicures and pedicures.

"What nail salon would that be?" Selby asked.

Did she really have to tell them that she had been sitting in a cushy, spa-massage chair at Madam Na Na's Nail Nation? Would they even believe her if she told them that this was not her *thing* and that she had felt sinfully decadent that day as her feet luxuriated in a small tub of warm, swirling water? Rachel knew how pointless it would be if she were to tell the detectives that she had only been complying with Emily's recommendation that, since she planned on wearing open-toed shoes to the auction, she *owed* it to the world to make the toenails on her size ten feet more presentable.

As wonderful as it was to have an occasional pedicure, Rachel always worried someone from school would discover her whiling away the day at Madam Na Na's. But on that particular late morning, knowing Robbie was happily ensconced in Mrs. Harvey's first-grade classroom, Rachel thought it would be okay to lean her head back, close her eyes and relax for a while. Sadly, she was only seconds into willfully allowing a feeling of calm to envelop her when the song, *Yes, Sir, that's my baby! No Sir, I don't mean maybe,* burst forth full throttle from Rachel's lap. Immediately, every head in Na Na's Nation fired looks of scorn in Rachel's direction. Embarrassed, she bolted from her lounging position and reached for her cell phone that was in the side pocket of the purse. Her sudden jolt caused her purse to slip from her lap and into the bucket of warm water where her feet had been soaking.

Seeing what had happened, one of Madam Na's assistants expertly pulled the purse from the water as Rachel's cell warbled its grand finale of *Yes, sir, that's my baby now-owww.* Quick as a cat, another Na Na assistant reached inside the wet purse and thrust the cell into Rachel's hands.

"Rachel!" a shrill voice screamed from the cell phone. Rachel fumbled the dripping wet phone, her fingers accidentally tapping the speaker icon. The two Na Nas were now toweling off the purse, the floor and Rachel's wet lap.

"Hello?" whispered Rachel.

"Rachel Berger!" screeched the voice on the phone.

"This is she," Rachel said trying to wave off the Madam's Na Nas from dabbing at her thighs and crotch.

"Rachel, this is Vickie Mack!" the voice screamed for all to hear.

The Na Nas kept bowing their heads at Rachel. "All better now. Cell no broken. Ha! All better, yes!" said a Na Na as she gingerly placed the purse in Rachel's lap.

"Yes, yes. All better. Thank you so much." Rachel bowed twice to the two Na Na girls.

"I beg your pardon!" Vickie bellowed indignantly.

"Sorry. I, uh, I'm listening Vickie." Rachel held the cell away from her ear.

"Good! Robbie's teacher, Mrs. Harvey, called in sick today, and I was asked to substitute." Vickie still sounded quite put out and angry, which Rachel assumed was because Vickie couldn't see the confusion that had just taken place at Madam Na Na's.

"Oh, Vickie. I'm so sorry. I was just having a pedicure and my purse . . ."

"Rachel, this is an extremely serious situation!" interrupted Vickie. "It's very nice that you can afford the time in the middle of the day to take care of your, your *toenails*, but I insist that you interrupt your self-indulgence and come to Mrs. Harvey's classroom immediately." Vickie paused, took a deep breath, then screeched, "Immediately!"

"Oh, my gosh! Is Robbie okay?" Rachel felt her heart beat frantically.

"Your son is fine, but he is in *serious* trouble and you need to come to school directly to discuss his behavior!" ordered Vickie Mack.

"I'll be right there," Rachel said as she withdrew her feet from the water and squeezed them into the flimsy, pink flip-flops she'd worn to the spa.

"No, no, no! Not finish! You not finish," a Na Na protested, repeatedly motioning with both hands for Rachel to return her feet to the water.

Rachel pulled a soggy twenty-dollar bill from her wallet, pushed it into the young girl's hand and raced out the door to her car. She propelled herself into the driver's seat and jammed on her seat belt, oblivious to the fact that the entire front of her jeans was soaked with Madam Na Na's spa water and the legs of her jeans were still scrunched above her knees.

Rachel's mind was fixed on trying to figure out what Robbie had done to warrant such a phone call. He was a loving, enthusiastic child, overly enthusiastic sometimes, but he was a first grader. First grade boys are supposed to be enthusiastic. Like every growing child, Robbie had come home with a few inappropriate words and gestures he'd learned from other kids or TV, but Rachel and Conrad always made sure Robbie understood their meanings and the consequences of repeating them.

"Robbie would never give the finger!" Rachel gasped to herself, remembering when Vickie Mack had showed up at their front door a year ago, screaming that Robbie had just flipped 'the bird' at her as she drove by the Berger's house. Robbie, who was only five at the time, very sweetly explained that he was "just saying 'Hi' the cool dude way." Vickie Mack was not even mildly mollified upon hearing that Ruthie's nephew, Lawrence, seven years older than Robbie, had taught Robbie a greeting hand-signal that "all the cool dudes use." Vickie had stormed away from the Berger's front yard muttering something about bad parenting.

Selby looked up from his notepad. "So, Mrs. Mack called you while you were at Madam Na Na's Nail Nation, and you went straight to the school?"

"Yes."

"I can only guess if my wife had been forced to leave in the middle of getting her pedicure, she'd be pretty angry," said Selby.

"I, I was worried about Robbie. I wasn't angry."

"About how long did it take you to arrive at the school?" Roma asked.

"Less than ten minutes." Rachel sighed.

On the drive to the school it had occurred to her that Robbie might have tried to perform his newly discovered talent—the one where he held his right hand in his left armpit while flapping the left arm up and down like a chicken wing, causing a disgusting farting sound that sent Robbie and his friends into convulsive laughter each time the trick was performed.

"So, you got there pretty quickly," Selby said.

"Yes."

The moment she had parked her car Rachel did not walk; she loped through the halls of Calivista Elementary School unaware of her water stains and rolled up jeans. When she reached Room 27, she took a deep breath and peeked into the room. Robbie was sitting alone at his desk with his head bowed down. Vickie Mack sat stiffly at the teacher's desk. The other children must have been outside for recess.

"Tell us what happened when you got to the classroom," Selby said.

Rachel remembered every detail of what had occurred that day from the moment she entered the classroom.

*

"Hello," Rachel recalled saying to Vickie.

"Come in," said a very stoic Vickie Mack.

Rachel moved to where Robbie sat and placed her hand gently on his head. He wore a sad and confused look on his face.

Vickie pushed her chair away from her desk, angrily whipped a piece of paper from a pile of worksheets, and dramatically walked toward Rachel and Robbie.

Rachel noticed Cupertino Flores standing on a ladder in the far corner of the room, fixing one of the lights. She smiled at him as he nodded at her.

Vickie approached Rachel, getting so close that her perfume nearly caused Rachel to gag. "I gave an arithmetic quiz today and offered the children the chance to earn bonus points on the last question. I instructed the students to use their new rulers to measure just one item at their desks and then write down the name of the object along with its measurement."

"I see," said Rachel quietly.

"*This* is what your son wrote!" Vickie had slapped the worksheet down on Robbie's desk and pointed to the bonus question with Robbie's bonus answer.

*

"What was on the paper that made Mrs. Mack so angry with your son?" asked Roma.

"Oh Lord," Rachel said to herself. Embarrassed, Rachel proceeded. "Robbie had written, 'My penis **6** inches.'"

*

Rachel remembered staring at Robbie's first-grade printing and then at Robbie. She was stunned.

Vickie stared at Rachel, red-faced and indignant. "I told Robbie I would not discuss his bonus answer until you arrived. He was to sit here and think about his explanation for such a shameful answer!"

"But Mommy, it's not wrong!" cried Robbie. "I measured it really carefully and it really is six inches. I thought it was more but it's not. It's only six inches. I can prove it to you."

"You will do no such thing!" screeched Vickie. "How can you even think of doing such a thing?"

"But Mrs. Mack, you said we could measure anything near our desks." Robbie looked bewildered.

Rachel was simultaneously stunned and confused. *On the one hand*, she thought to herself, *Robbie had followed Vickie's directions. There was nothing in the instructions that said one couldn't measure a part of the body . . . even a private part . . . and it* was *something near his desk that he'd measured . . . and it is pretty normal for young boys to wonder about—*

"This is just unbelievable!" Vickie threw her hands into the air.

"Sweetie, what made you think of measuring . . . *that?*" Rachel tried to stay calm and not react in a way that would damage her child forever.

"Well," Robbie furrowed his brow. "I felt it in my pants and thought it would be a good thing to measure."

"This is just deplorable," blurted Vickie.

"But Mrs. Mack, you didn't say the object had to be in my desk or on my desk, so I just pulled it out," Robbie's confused, and oh-so-innocent voice pleaded for mercy.

"Rachel Berger!" Vickie Mack began with what would have been a firm, prolonged reprimand, except Robbie interrupted her.

"Look, it's right here. I can prove it to you." Robbie reached for his front right pants pocket.

"Stop!" Vickie screeched while she covered her eyes with one hand and thrust her other hand forward in the universal "halt" position.

Rachel stood frozen in time as Robbie pulled from his pocket a slender, blue writing pen. He held it up for Vickie and Rachel to see.

"That, that . . . that is not what you measured," snarled the substitute teacher.

"Yes, it is! See?" Robbie quickly laid the pen on top of his ruler and exclaimed, "Six inches!"

A mighty gust of physical and emotional relief spewed from Rachel's diaphragm.

"Oh my, you are so right, Robbie. Your *pen*," she emphasized for Mrs. Mack. "Your *pen is* six inches long." Rachel released a nervous giggle. Surely, Vickie could see the humor in the situation.

*

"That's actually pretty funny," said Roma, smiling. "Did Mrs. Mack understand the mistake?"

"No," said Rachel shaking her head. "Vickie was convinced Robbie had set her up to look foolish." Then without thinking, Rachel added, "Who knows what kinds of nasty rumors she would have spread about Robbie . . . if she hadn't died?"

There was silence in the room for a moment. Then Selby spoke. "Were you worried about that?" He looked directly into Rachel's eyes. "About Mrs. Mack spreading rumors about Robbie?"

"Of course, I was. Not even innocent little children were ever spared Vickie's wrath." Rachel realized she had sounded a little too angry.

"I hear you. I have children of my own, and I gotta' tell you, it's one thing if someone wants to spread rumors about me, but it's an entirely different thing if someone spreads rumors about my child." Selby looked directly into Rachel's eyes. "This must have been just about the last straw for you."

"What do you mean?" Rachel asked.

"Well, given how she hoodwinked you into caring for the dog, not to mention all the stuff she put into the local paper . . . things that were aimed at your reputation . . . and then, like you said, who knows what rumors Vickie Mack might have spread about Robbie?" Selby paused, then added, "That is . . . if she were still alive."

"Detective, I am not the kind of person who would murder someone just because of some ridiculous newspaper articles and nasty rumors!"

Both detectives stared at Rachel. Their silence was unnerving, and Rachel wondered if they were holding back something. But what? She suddenly remembered the night at the Mexican restaurant where she and Emily had gotten a little tipsy and playfully discussed the possibility of hiring a hit man . . . loud enough for anyone in the restaurant to hear. They'd even toasted to the demise of Vickie Mack more than once. Could someone within hearing distance have reported this to the detectives?

"Just a few more questions," Detective Roma said. "Would you say that you and Emily Fryze are close friends?"

"Emily is my closest friend."

"Close enough that she showed you the compromising pictures of her husband and Vickie Mack?" Selby asked.

Rachel was taken aback by Detective Selby's question. Of course, the detectives would eventually learn about the photos if the investigation continued. But it was information that neither Emily nor Pete had wanted out in the open. Besides, Pete and Emily's marital issues had nothing to do with Vickie's death.

"No, Emily burned them. She was beyond angry and humiliated."

Roma had a hard time picturing Emily angry.

"Understandably." Mick Selby knew that the mixture of those two emotions had led far too many people to commit murder. "Did Mrs. Fryze ever talk about any type of retaliation toward Vickie Mack?"

Every muscle in Rachel's body froze.

"Well, yes," said Rachel. "But so did I, and I'm pretty sure Emily and I aren't the only people in Calivista who had thoughts of revenge toward Vickie Mack. But—" Rachel swallowed hard. Now she was certain someone at the Mexican restaurant had overheard their *little joke* about hiring a hit man!

The two detectives remained silent which made Rachel feel certain they were just setting her up to confess. "Look, if you're talking about a night at the Tex-Mex restaurant when Emily and I were just being silly . . . we'd had one or two too many margaritas."

Roma nodded his head. "Now that you mention it, tell us a little more about your conversation at the restaurant."

"You have to understand that Emily and I were just joking around. I mean, we didn't really mean that we'd actually hire—" Rachel's voice trailed off.

She was now sure, by the detectives' expressions, that they didn't know anything about that night. *That's always how it happened on TV shows,* thought Rachel. *The police found ways to force a confession. Well, this wasn't going to happen to her.* Rachel braced herself. *No matter what, she would not give them what they wanted.* But then, she didn't have to worry because her cell phone vibrated and danced on the coffee table, ringing full throttle with the *Yes sir, that's my baby* refrain. Rachel grabbed the cell intending to silence it, but then she saw the name of the caller.

"Emily?" Rachel covered the mouthpiece with her hand, turned her back on the detectives and walked into the kitchen. "You and the Bubbles lady are what?!" Rachel glanced over her shoulder in the direction of the detectives. "How did this happen?"

Something hard slammed against the front door, startling the detectives and Rachel. It sounded like someone had thrown a sack of potatoes at the door.

"Oh Lordy," Rachel whispered into the phone.

A second *thud* banged into the door, prompting Detective Roma to get up from his chair, walk over to the door and look through the peep hole. Nothing there, so he twisted the handle and opened the door.

At that instant, Captain was already airborne. All fifty pounds of a soapy, soggy canine crashed full force into Aaron Roma, causing the unsuspecting detective to topple over backward like a human bowling pin. When the back of his head hit the marble floor it was lights out.

CHAPTER 31

AARON ROMA DID not remember a thing: not the fifty-pound creature who had slammed into him, not falling backwards and banging his head on the floor of the foyer, and certainly not passing out. Eventually, he became vaguely aware of two paramedics who were taking his vitals and asking him questions about what day it was and who was president. But in truth, what brought him fully back to life were the beautiful blue eyes of Emily Fryze staring into his heart with extreme concern. After a few moments, those warm, welcoming eyes caused him to become focused and alert.

Are you okay? her eyes seemed to be saying.

Better now, Roma's eyes seemed to respond.

The paramedics had arrived within minutes of the incident and soon determined that Roma had suffered a minor concussion but did not need to go to the emergency room. Keeping a cold ice pack on the back of his head, staying alert for several hours and then a good night's rest was their recommendation. With that, the paramedics packed up their bags and left.

Despite wanting to follow up on something Rachel Berger had said seconds before all the confusion, Mick Selby had decided, under the circumstances, to postpone any further questioning of her. He figured it was more important to drive his partner back to the precinct as far away from the follies and madness of Calivista as he could get.

Selby guided Roma down the front steps of the Berger house and into the detectives' car. But just as Selby was about to close the front passenger door, Emily appeared at Selby's side and offered Aaron Roma a fresh ice-pack to replace the one the paramedics had given him.

"Just in case you need another one," Emily said almost bashfully. She and Roma exchanged a look that expressed something more than gratitude.

"In a nutshell, here's how it all went down," said Selby while pulling away from the small gathering of concerned neighbors still hovering around their car and the paramedic van. With a bit of a smile on his face, Selby looked over at his partner. "While we were questioning Mrs. Berger, she gets a call from Emily Fryze and the dog groomer in the van, both saying that the dog had run away in the middle of his bath. The dog decides he doesn't like all the bubbles and would rather be at home. Mrs. Fryze, two doors away, *just so happens* to see the dog escape from the Bubbles and Buds van. She takes chase and arrives just in time to witness you becoming the front door that Captain loves to body slam."

They made the rest of their way out of Calivista and back into West Los Angeles in silence. Eyes closed, still throbbing with a headache, Roma realized he had not been dreaming. Those *were*, in fact, the blue eyes of Emily Fryze that had been locked onto his own eyes as he regained consciousness in the foyer of the Berger's home.

"Kind of convenient for Mrs. Berger to have our questioning interrupted by the dog, don't you think?" Selby said as he turned into the precinct's parking lot and pulled into a space.

Roma opened his eyes but did not respond.

Once inside the precinct office, Aaron wanted to ask why Selby had stressed the words *kind of convenient,* but he decided to wait until they were at their desks with a cup of coffee. Maybe his headache would be gone by then.

"Here's what we have so far." Selby calmly poured some cream into his coffee, reached for a packet of sugar and then continued with his train of thought. "We've got a whole town of knuckleheaded residents, every one of them with their own knuckleheaded motives for doing the deed."

Selby turned his chair to face the wall behind his desk. Small magnets fixed nine black and white photos against a five-by-seven white board. He pointed at the board. "But this group of knuckleheads wins the prize."

Roma looked at photos he and Selby had previously arranged into two columns. Rachel's was at the top of the first column, Emily's picture under

Rachel's, then came Conrad and Pete. At the top of the second column was a picture of Vickie Mack's dog breeder boyfriend, then Cupertino Flores, and Pedro the other janitor. Below these were photos of Lawrence and, at the very bottom, Aunt Ruthie.

"So, let's begin with Conrad Berger . . . *Doctor* Berger." Roma walked to the white board, picked up a red marker and wrote under Conrad's photo:

- Good dad
- Good doctor
- Good husband
- Motive: revenge for all Vickie put his wife through.

"Anything else we've got on him?" Roma asked.

"Yeah," Selby chuckled. "How about his fetish for female tampons?" Selby laughed as Roma added *tampon fetish* under *good husband*.

"I just don't see him being involved in the murder," Selby said as he opened another file. "There's nothing from forensics that suggests Dr. Conrad Berger was with Vickie Mack at the time of her murder. None of his fibers, hairs, fingerprints . . . or tampons on the victim or her clothes."

Roma chuckled. "I agree. Unless we're missing something, he doesn't fit the equation. One down, eight more knuckle-brains to go." Roma pointed at the picture of Peter Fryze. "This guy could be our man."

"He's an arrogant jerk, that's for sure. But that doesn't make him a murderer," Selby said.

"Are you kidding? Peter Fryze has motive written all over him. He had an affair with Vickie Mack, who then sent explicit pictures of their tryst to his wife, who then kicked him out of the house. Now he's living in a cramped apartment while his wife and kids are in a McMansion. Vickie Mack ruined his life. How angry would you be?"

It was clear to Selby, listening to Roma's rant, that his partner had gone from objective observer to emotional participant . . . as if he had some kind of personal investment in the outcome of the whole situation.

Roma turned to the white board and wrote under Peter's picture:

- Jerk
- Unfaithful husband

- Affair with Vickie Mack
- Vickie Mack sends photos to Peter's wife
- Separated from wife
- Motive: Pay back for the damage Vickie Mack did to his life

"But here's the problem: Peter Fryze was out of town the day of the murder," Selby said. "And we've checked his alibi with the Atlanta Airport Police. They confirmed his cockamamie story about being arrested on the plane. He was found innocent of any wrongdoing, was put on a later plane back to LA, and arrived after all the hoo-ha had taken place."

"Right, but—" Roma started.

"And we've contacted each of the women Mr. Fryze listed as *former* flings. Each one is alive and well, and . . . oddly enough, each one had *delightful* memories of Peter Fryze. None of those women knew or had ever had any contact with Peter Fryze's wife."

"Right, but—" Roma interjected again.

"But then," Selby interrupted, "there's Vickie Mack who happens to be the only one of Mr. Fryze's paramours that had any contact with Emily Fryze." Selby paused to let the point sink in for Roma.

Roma looked at the board again. He stared at Emily's photo, mesmerized by those blue eyes, by her natural beauty.

Selby stood up, took the red marker from Roma's hand and started filling in the obvious information under her picture. Roma took a seat, watching in pain as Selby wrote:
- Good mother
- Good wife
- Daily contact with victim
- Poor relationship with victim
- Motive: victim had an affair with her husband
- Alibi: working at beach club around the time of the murder

"How many wives have we investigated who had lost their minds and sought revenge on the cheating husband and/or their husband's *ladies of the night*?" Selby seemed more confident than ever.

"Let's go over the forensics on her again," Roma said, referring to the file in front of him. "No hairs, fibers, or fingerprints on the victim's person that match Emily Fryze. And her alibi checked out. She was at the beach club most of the day and night."

"Right." Selby pointed at the board again, directly at the picture of Rachel Berger. In the back of his mind, something continued to nag at him. Something Rachel had said just before her phone rang. "Let's focus on Mrs. Berger for a minute. *That* woman . . . I'm not real sure about her," he said, rubbing his chin. "Is she hiding something from us like she did from her husband? Seems like a devoted mother . . . but is devotion to her son enough motive to murder Vickie Mack?"

"For what? A few cruel attempts to humiliate her six-year-old son?" Roma asked.

"Not unheard of." Selby raised his eyebrows and began to write Rachel's profile:
- Devoted mother
- Son Robbie, a victim of Mrs. Mack's wrath
- Good wife?
- Caught in lie to husband
- Withheld truth about damaging his car

"Also, Mrs. Berger did not seem too pleased with how Vickie Mack conned her into keeping the crazy dog. And don't forget all the newspaper editorials accusing Rachel Berger of canine abuse," added Roma as he felt the bump on the back of his head.

"There's something else in all this: Not only did Vickie Mack humiliate and harass Rachel and Robbie Berger, but she also purposefully hurt and humiliated Rachel's best friend by her tryst with Peter Fryze. Selby added to Rachel's tally:
- Steamrolled into housing Captain, the dog
- Publicly harassed and humiliated by victim
- Best friend is harassed and humiliated by victim
- Son is harassed and humiliated by victim
- Motive: payback for all of the above

Roma tapped his fingers on the table. "Speaking of Vickie Mack's talent for harassment and humiliation, how about Vickie Mack dragging nutty Aunt Ruthie down the street with her car?"

"Good point," said Selby as he began to write under Ruthie's photo:

- Feigned friendship with Vickie Mack
- Humiliated by Vickie Mack/ dragged through town
- Possible romantic relationship with Vickie's dog breeder boyfriend
- Motive: Revenge for being humiliated in public by Vickie

"Do you think she'd attempt something like murder with the help of her nephew?" asked Roma.

Selby turned to the photo of Lawrence and wrote his profile:

- Nervous, insecure kid
- Loyal to Aunt Ruthie
- Weird friendship with Vickie Mack
- Motive: Revenge for Aunt Ruthie

Selby stopped and looked at his partner. "I want to go back to Mrs. Berger for a second."

"Okay," Roma said.

"This afternoon just before she answered her phone . . . she referred to a dinner at a Mexican restaurant. Remember?"

"Yeah. She said something about joking around but not really intending to hire something . . . or—" Roma stared at his partner. "Or someone."

"Someone to knock off Mrs. Mack maybe?" Selby finished Roma's sentence.

"So, who's an ordinary housewife going to hire?"

"The real question is, who would *two* ordinary housewives hire?"

Roma winced when Selby said this. He could maybe see Rachel Berger hiring a hit man but not Emily Fryze, whose photo was at that moment captivating him.

Selby tapped the photo of Cupertino Flores with the marker and began writing on the white board:

- Humble, nice man
- Hard worker

- Very loyal to Rachel Berger and Emily Fryze
- Humiliated and demeaned by Vickie Mack
- Motive: Loyalty to Rachel and Emily

"Cupertino said Emily and Rachel paid him extra money for all his after-hours help. You think he might have appreciated a little extra cash for bumping off Vickie Mack?"

"Holy cow," said Roma, immediately seeing this scenario as a possibility.

"And don't forget that Vickie Mack threatened to look into Mr. Flores and his family's citizenship status." Selby looked at the whiteboard, then added to Cupertino's profile:

- Extra cash for helping Mrs. Berger and Mrs. Fryze
- Threat of Vickie Mack looking into his and his family's citizenship

Roma quickly shuffled through some papers. "Forensics has the time of death at around four in the afternoon, which means the body had been dead for almost six hours before making its grand appearance at the auction."

"Okay, so we've got Lawrence placing Cupertino at the Berger house around four the afternoon of the auction. Lawrence says he saw the janitor go into the garage, come back out carrying a trunk, place it in his truck and then drive away. But Lawrence doesn't mention the other man, this Pedro guy, nor does Lawrence say anything about helping the janitors carry the trunk to the truck."

"Hah!" Roma chortled. "Remember how he kept saying, 'and that's all I saw'?"

"If it's true that Lawrence had actually gone into the Berger garage and had helped the two janitors carry the trunk to a delivery truck, I want to know why he failed to mention this to us."

"Let's not forget Aunt Ruthie who failed to tell us Vickie Mack had accused her of messing around with her boyfriend and then because of it, she dragged her down the street dangling from the car window."

"In front of the whole town to see," added Mick Selby. "That Aunt Ruthie must be a saint if she could call Vickie Mack a *dear* friend after something like that."

"I can't imagine Lawrence feeling any love for Vickie Mack either, especially after watching his aunt get dragged down the street."

"Don't you just wonder if there's anyone Vickie Mack didn't try to humiliate and shame?" Selby sighed.

Just then Officer Mew appeared in the doorway.

"Hey, Mew. What brings you off the street? You're not going to give us a ticket for parking our bodies here too long, are you?" Roma couldn't resist, and Mew was an easy target.

Officer Mew ignored the gibe and tossed a thin newspaper on the desk. "I thought you might be interested in this."

"Oh yeah?" Roma pulled the folded paper closer to him and noted the heading. "Oh, whoa, Mew, thanks for the delivery of the *Malibu Daily Post-Special Edition*," he said sarcastically.

"Open it up. Front page, bottom left corner," Officer Mew said before turning and walking out of the room.

Roma unfolded the paper and grimaced. "Well, well, well." Roma turned the paper around so that Selby could see what he saw: a photo of Lawrence and Aunt Ruthie at bottom left corner.

Selby grabbed the newspaper and began to read the article out loud. "Last night, Lawrence Hershey, fourteen, nephew of Ms. Hershey, told a reporter that he knew detectives were looking into the whereabouts of a school janitor who may have been the last person to see Mrs. Vickie Mack alive. The teenager and Ms. Hershey live on the same street as the two main suspects."

Selby continued reading out loud. "'All I can say is . . . Mrs. Berger and Mrs. Fryze had a very close friendship with that janitor. I mean, it was a little weird how he was always in and out of their garages,' said Lawrence Hershey. When asked why he thought the janitor was at the Berger and Fryze homes, he said, 'Well, I don't really know, but it kind of makes me wonder if their weird friendship had something to do with Vickie Mack's murder.'"

"Sheesch!" Selby breathed loudly, tossing the paper on the table.

"We told that zit-faced kid and his aunt *not* to discuss the murder with anyone?" Roma shook his head in disbelief.

"What do you say we make a surprise visit to Aunt Ruthie and Lawrence first thing tomorrow morning?" suggested Selby.

"Sounds like a plan," said Roma as he once again rubbed the bump at the back of his head.

"So, go home, take two aspirins and get some sleep," ordered Mick Selby.

CHAPTER 32

WEARING A BRIGHT purple tee shirt and tight black pants, his arms folded across his chest, Lawrence Hershey had the nervous look of a prisoner about to be sentenced. And compared to her earlier, defiant encounters with the two detectives, Aunt Ruthie was subdued as she sat quietly on her Pepto-Bismol pink sofa in the living room.

"Here's the problem, Ruthie and Lawrence," said Roma sitting next to Detective Selby on the matching pink sofa. "It's come to our attention that you both have withheld some very important information from us." Roma looked them in the eye using his most intimidating glare.

"Like what?" Ruthie sounded insulted.

"How about a car incident with Vickie Mack?"

"I already told you, I was afraid it made me look guilty!" Ruthie interrupted.

"Maybe," Roma said, not buying her excuse. "But it wasn't until Detective Selby and I further questioned you about a possible attraction between you and Vickie's dog breeder boyfriend that you or Lawrence mentioned something about an affair between Vickie Mack and Peter Fryze. Right?"

Both Roma and Selby looked at Ruthie.

"So?" Ruthie looked more disgusted than intimidated by the detective's question.

"And Lawrence," said Selby, turning his attention to the boy. "Until we questioned you the other day, you never mentioned having taken photos of Mr. Fryze and Mrs. Mack."

"So?" Lawrence whined.

"So, now I'm wondering, is there any other information you're holding back." Selby paused for a moment. "You know, anything *you* haven't told us that maybe you should have?" Selby measured every word, trying to get inside Lawrence's head.

The boy shook his head back and forth, as if shaking all information from his mind. "Nooo," said Lawrence, looking down to avoid eye contact with either of the detectives.

Selby looked at Roma, knowing he was getting somewhere, then stared at Lawrence, waiting for him to continue.

"Like someone else—" Selby started.

"Someone else?" Lawrence interrupted in a high-pitched voice.

"Yeah, someone else who came to the Berger house with Mr. Flores the day of Vickie Mack's murder?"

"Ummm, there was another janitor," Lawrence screeched as his neck turned blotchy red. "Yeah, and he acted weird, too. I'm sure I told you about him," Lawrence stammered.

"No," Selby countered while pretending to recheck his notes, "I'm pretty sure you didn't tell us about the second janitor."

"I guess I forgot, but now that I think about it, there definitely was another janitor there." Lawrence paused, then added, "But that's all I remember."

"Okay. Good." Selby nodded. "I'm glad we've got that clear. So, was it before or after the two janitors arrived that you saw Mrs. Mack park her car across the street and walk up to the Berger's front door?"

"Vickie got there before the janitors," Lawrence said.

"Got it. So, after Mrs. Mack knocked on the Berger's door, you said she walked to the side door of the garage and went inside the garage. Do I have that right?" Selby referred to his notes again.

"Yes," Lawrence said confidently.

"And you don't remember seeing Mrs. Mack leave the garage?" asked Selby.

"I never did."

"Did you see anyone leave the garage?" Roma asked.

"Just the janitors."

"Right. But before the janitors arrived, did anyone besides Mrs. Mack enter or leave the Berger's garage?" continued Roma.

Lawrence shook his head.

Selby looked at his notes, "Let's see, you also told us that the Berger's dog had been barking a lot?"

"Oh, that's right. He was barking a lot," Lawrence quickly remembered.

"And Mrs. Mack told you she was going into the garage to check on the dog . . . because of his barking?" Selby pushed.

"That's right! That's what she said." Lawrence was sounding more confident.

"So, Lawrence, do you remember if the dog stopped barking after Mrs. Mack went into the garage?" Roma asked.

"Ah, maybe. No! I mean, um, I think he wasn't barking anymore."

"Oh . . . so, what do you think would have caused the dog to stop barking?" asked Selby.

"I don't know. Maybe Vickie took him off the rope he was tied to."

"Did you see the dog tied to a rope?" asked Roma.

"No! I told you I didn't go into the garage."

"Okay," Selby said quietly, as if mulling over what Lawrence had just said. "Okay."

"And you're sure no one left the garage while you were watering your side yard?" Roma picked up the questioning. "I mean after Mrs. Mack went inside."

"Well, I don't know, but, um, maybe now that you mention it, I'm kind of remembering that I did see someone or something run out of the garage . . . but I can't be sure, because I only saw it with my peripheral vision." Lawrence's left eye began to twitch.

"Oh? I must have missed that from our last conversation," said Roma. "Is that in your notes, Detective Selby?"

Selby shuffled through the pages of his note pad and shook his head. "Not here. So, let me understand you correctly," said Selby looking directly at Lawrence. "You may or may not have seen *someone* or *something* dash out the side door of the Berger's garage?" Selby asked.

"Maybe. But that's all I know!" Lawrence's eyes darted to his aunt, as if looking for a place to hide.

"Okay. Even though you may or may not have seen something with just your peripheral vision, could you make a guess about the size of the person dashing out?" Selby asked.

"It wasn't a person. It was a dog!" Lawrence instantly replayed in his mind what he'd just said. "I mean, *maybe* it was a dog."

"Hum. Let's just say it was a dog you might have seen leave the garage. Any idea what dog that might have been?" asked Selby calmly.

"Maybe it was Captain, but how would I know?" Lawrence whined.

"You're referring to Captain, the Berger's dog?" Selby tilted his head to one side.

"Yes."

"So, from your peripheral vision you *may* have seen something like a dog run out of the garage." Selby spoke as if revealing facts for a jury.

Roma loved nothing more than watching Selby *play with the mind* of a hapless witness.

"Right!" said Lawrence, loud and confident.

"I'm curious. After that, do you recall hearing anymore barking from inside the garage?" Selby deadpanned.

"How could I? Captain had run away!"

"Now, you see, that makes sense to me. How about you, Detective Roma?" Selby looked at his partner.

"Well, yeah," Roma nodded his head. "*If* it was Captain that ran out of the garage, then it only makes sense that there would not be any more barking coming from inside the garage."

"So, here's what I understand so far," Selby summarized. "You, Lawrence, hear a dog, presumably Captain, barking in the garage. Mrs. Mack goes into the garage, because she wants to be sure he's not tied up. You can't be sure, but *maybe* Mrs. Mack unties the dog, and *maybe* the dog runs out of the garage. But then, you think maybe that's why you didn't hear anymore barking. Do I have that right so far?" Selby's voice had a comforting tone to it.

"Yes."

"And all during this time, you don't recall Mrs. Mack ever leaving the garage?" Selby asked.

"She might have, but I can't be sure, because my peripheral vision isn't so good." Lawrence's left eye continued to twitch.

"Understandable, but here's what I'm wondering," Selby said. "*If* Mrs. Mack went into the garage to check on Captain's safety and *if* Captain ran out the garage door, wouldn't you think Mrs. Mack would go running after him?"

Lawrence remained silent.

"You see what I'm getting at, Lawrence? I'm just trying to figure out why Mrs. Mack didn't leave the garage around the time the dog ran out."

"How should I know?" the boy squealed.

"Weren't you curious?" Selby asked.

"No! Besides, by then I think I'd gone inside Aunt Ruthie's house to get something to eat. Vickie must have left the garage after I went inside to get my snack." Lawrence looked pleadingly at Ruthie.

"Ohhhh, that makes sense," Roma said with feigned understanding.

The conversation stopped for a moment as the two detectives looked at each other, then at Lawrence and Ruthie.

CHAPTER 33

"SO, YOU CAME inside and grabbed a snack. How long would you say you stayed inside the house?" asked Detective Roma.

"Ah, I never went back outside," said Lawrence with conviction. His words hung in the air like a stench, just floating around all of them. "I came in here and sat on the sofa."

Roma rubbed his forehead with the palm of his hand, as if pushing his conclusion to his frontal lobe, then looked at Lawrence. "You know, here's another problem we have. Not too long ago, Detective Selby and I spoke with Cupertino Flores, you know, the man you described as . . . *weird*."

"Sooo?" Lawrence shrugged both shoulders as if it didn't matter to him.

"Sooo," Selby interjected as he glanced at his notepad, "Mr. Flores said that *the nice teenage boy next door,* and I'm guessing that would be you, helped carry the steamer trunk out of the garage and onto the flatbed truck."

Lawrence's upper body flinched. "Oh, that's right. *That's* right." Lawrence's eyes darted from Detective Selby to Ruthie, then back to the detective. "Now I remember. I didn't go get a snack, not yet, anyway. I was still outside when the janitors arrived."

Selby continued. "Okay. The two janitors arrive. No sign of Mrs. Mack. She may or may not have gone after the runaway dog. Then what happened?"

"I don't remember," said Lawrence, looking down at the carpet.

"It's hard to remember every little detail, isn't it?" said Roma.

"Of course, it is!" Ruthie said with fire in her voice.

"Okay, let me try to help you," said Selby. "You see, Cupertino Flores told us that you were hanging around, watering the grass between your aunt's house and the Berger's house."

"Well, yeah. I already told you that," Lawrence said.

"But Cupertino Flores also told us that moments later he saw you standing in the doorway of the Berger's garage and watching him and the second janitor attempt to pick up the trunk. Is that right?" Selby asked.

"I, I guess maybe I could see inside the garage from where I was standing," Lawrence stammered.

"You know, Mr. Flores was really complimentary about you. He said you were very helpful," said Roma.

"He did?" Lawrence's voice squeaked.

"Yeah, he did. He told us that the steamer trunk was very heavy, and you were such a nice guy that you offered to help them carry it to their flatbed." Roma was trying hard to win the boy over, to get him to relax.

"Oh, that's right! I forgot about that." Lawrence's jaw seemed to twitch to the beat of his jumpy legs. "Now I remember. I heard those two janitors grumbling about how heavy the trunk was and I knew they were probably in a hurry, you know, because Mrs. Berger was already at the auction waiting for them."

"I can tell you're one of those good guys, always ready to help out when needed," Roma said.

"Well, they looked like they needed help," Lawrence said.

"So, I gather you felt obligated to go into the garage in order to help them," Selby interrupted.

"Well, yeah! But that's the first time I'd gone in there . . . that day," stammered Lawrence.

"The janitor, you know, Cupertino Flores, said he was surprised the steamer trunk was so heavy. He thought he remembered Mrs. Berger telling him it would be light with just a few things inside it." Selby pretended to read from his notes again.

"Well, it *was* heavy," said Lawrence.

"You know what else Cupertino told us?" Selby continued.

"Noooo," Lawrence whined.

"He said the other janitor made a joke," Selby said this while looking at his partner.

"Oh, yeah," Roma said. "Apparently, Cupertino Flores told you and the other janitor that it felt like there was a dead body in the trunk."

"Cupertino said he and his partner laughed but you didn't," Selby said.

"Well, I didn't think it was very funny," Lawrence said quietly.

"You know what, I kind of agree with you, Lawrence," said Selby. "Sounds like a cold-hearted thing to say, especially since we *now* know that there *was* a dead body inside."

Lawrence's whole body began to shake. "Now that you mention it . . . I'm wondering if maybe those two janitors killed Vickie and stuffed her in the trunk before I got to the garage door."

"Whoa! Maybe," said Selby with feigned shock.

"In fact, now it makes sense that they might have done that, because they hated Vickie," added Lawrence with conviction.

"Now, how would you know that?" asked Selby.

"Well, before I went to help them, I heard them talking in the garage, and they were saying some pretty mean things about her," said the nervous teenager.

"Like what?" Selby asked.

"I heard one of them say he hated Vickie and hoped she was dead," Lawrence said slowly.

"Which janitor said that?" Roma asked.

"Not the Cupertino guy. It was the other one."

"This is really helpful, Lawrence," Roma said.

Lawrence breathed in and out, nodding his head, relieved the detective was writing this down.

Selby looked up from the notepad, "You're sure it was the other janitor, not Cupertino Flores who said he hoped Vickie Mack was dead?"

"I'm sure. Yes, I distinctly remember the other janitor saying that to Cupertino Flores." Lawrence nodded his head up and down.

"I'm impressed," Detective Roma said looking at Lawrence and Aunt Ruthie.

Ruthie and Lawrence seemed confused but nodded in agreement.

"Me, being Hispanic, I find it frustrating that so few Californians bother to become fluent in Spanish," Roma said calmly.

The aunt and her nephew remained silent.

"You see . . . the janitor who was with Cupertino speaks only Spanish. So, I commend you for being bilingual," said Roma looking directly at Lawrence.

Lawrence gulped and his Adam's apple rose and dropped.

"But just so we're sure of the words the janitor used, could you tell us in Spanish what he said?" Selby asked.

"I, I, let me think," Lawrence's voice quivered. "I don't remember the exact words, not in Spanish anyway. I'm better at understanding Spanish than speaking it."

A tense moment of dead silence hung in the air.

"Lawrence, you don't speak Spanish, do you?" Roma looked him in the eye, feeling a little sorry for him.

"Noooo." Lawrence's top lip was quivering.

Selby picked up the questioning. "Lawrence, I'm wondering if you just now made up the part about the Spanish-speaking janitor saying he wished Vickie Mack was dead."

With his eyes closed, Lawrence nodded.

"And, I have a hunch you knew Vickie Mack's body was inside the steamer trunk," Roma said in a soft voice.

"What!" Aunt Ruthie shouted. "How on earth could Lawrence have known that? Go ahead, Lawrence, tell them you didn't know Vickie was in there!"

"I did! I knew she was in there!" Lawrence jumped up from the pink couch and began crying.

"You did not!" Ruthie stood and faced her nephew.

"I did it! I killed Vickie Mack!" Lawrence opened his eyes and shouted at Detective Selby and Detective Roma. "I killed her!"

"Lawrence! Shut up, right this minute!" Aunt Ruthie screamed.

"Lawrence, why do you say that?" Roma asked.

"I didn't mean to." Lawrence was crying hysterically.

"We're listening," Roma said quietly to the boy.

"I didn't mean to," the boy whimpered. "After Vickie went into the garage, I heard her yelling at Captain."

"Do you remember what she was yelling?" asked Roma.

"At first, she kept shouting at him to hold still and about a minute later she started screaming for him to get off her," Lawrence said.

"Okay," said Selby.

"She sounded really angry, so I decided to look inside the garage."

"What did you see?" asked Selby.

"Just like it sounded. Captain was jumping all over the place, especially all over Vickie."

"Was Captain tied to a rope?" continued Selby.

"No, the rope was lying on the ground."

"Where in the garage were Captain and Vickie Mack?" asked Roma.

"In front of the big trunk. The top of the trunk was open, and Vickie was bent over, looking inside it, and Captain was jumping all around her. It looked like Vickie was shuffling around some stuff inside the trunk."

"Could you see what was inside the trunk?" asked Selby.

"No, because Vickie stood up and started kicking Captain really hard, over and over, and then she grabbed the rope and started to whip him."

"Whoa! I thought she went to the garage to be sure the dog was okay," said Roma. This was new information to both detectives.

"Yeah, well—"

"What happened next?" asked Selby.

"Captain ran to the other side of the garage to get away."

"Okay," Roma prodded.

"So, Vickie bent down inside the trunk again. But then out of nowhere, Captain ran and jumped on her back and her whole body fell into the trunk. That's when Captain ran past me and out the garage door."

"So, the dog jumped on Vickie's back causing her to fall into the trunk. Is that right?" Roma asked.

"Yes. I swear it's the truth." Lawrence sobbed.

"Okay. So, you see the dog run out the garage door. What next?" Selby stared at him, waiting.

"Well, I walked over to the trunk and kind of peaked inside."

"What did you see?" continued Selby.

"What do you think I saw? Vickie was in there all crumpled up."

"Was she alive?" Selby asked.

"I thought so, I mean, I thought she was a little unconscious but would wake up soon."

"Did she wake up?" Roma asked.

"No. I mean, I don't know."

"Did you check to see if she was breathing?" Selby asked.

"I didn't have time to check, because I heard a truck pulling into the driveway, and I panicked. I slammed shut the lid of the trunk and kicked the lock with my foot. Then I ran out the side door."

Roma looked at him. "Where did you go?"

"I ran to my side yard and pretended I'd been standing watering the grass all along." Lawrence plopped back down on the couch. His arms hung limply at his sides.

"I'm curious, Lawrence, what was going on in your mind when the janitors arrived?" Selby asked.

"I started thinking it would be pretty funny if Vickie was still inside the trunk when the auction started and she was screaming and yelling to get out. I mean, it would serve her right if all the auction people saw her climb out of it. I wanted everyone to laugh at Vickie the same way she made people laugh at Aunt Ruthie when she dragged her down the street. I mean, she deserved it after what she did to Aunt Ruthie."

Aunt Ruthie put her hand on Lawrence's knee.

"Mrs. Mack embarrassed your aunt pretty badly when she dragged her along Vista La Mar and accused her of messing around with her boyfriend," Roma said sympathetically.

"I really hated Vickie after that, and I thought it served her right to be stuck inside the trunk for a while," said Lawrence, looking first at his aunt, then at the detectives.

"Okay, you're standing in your yard next door and the janitors drive onto the Berger driveway. What happened next?" asked Selby.

"They got out of their truck and walked to the side of the garage. Cupertino Flores said hello, and I said hello, and then they went inside."

"Lawrence, why didn't you tell them what had happened?" asked Selby.

"I was afraid. And I guess I hoped they would get the blame for locking her inside. But I didn't think she was going to die!"

"So, when the two janitors tried to lift the trunk . . . is that when you offered to help them, knowing all along Mrs. Mack was in the trunk?" asked Roma.

"Yes." Lawrence bent his head. "But I really thought she was alive! Then the Cupertino guy said it felt like there was a dead body inside, and I got scared and told him he wasn't funny. I didn't want her to be dead. I just wanted her to be embarrassed in front of all the people at the auction."

"That's enough!" Aunt Ruthie shouted. "This poor boy doesn't know what he's saying. You two detectives have badgered him into a corner, and he can't be responsible for what he says!"

"Aunt Ruthie," Selby sighed. "You and Lawrence need to come with Detective Roma and me."

"Where?" shouted Ruthie.

"We just need to get this all sorted out at the police station," said Selby as he stood up and removed a pair of handcuffs from his belt. "You have the right to remain silent . . . and what you say can and will be used against you."

CHAPTER 34

JUST TWENTY-FOUR HOURS after Detectives Selby and Roma gave Lawrence and Aunt Ruthie a ride to Police Precinct #25, Detective Roma called Rachel and Emily and calmly requested that the two women meet them at Emily's house.

"I know what this is all about," said Rachel as she and Emily sat side by side on Emily's living room couch.

"What?"

"They're going to book us for Vickie's murder."

And because Rachel was certain the detectives were going to take their fingerprints and mug shots and then escort the two women to separate jail cells, she had come prepared. She had brought three very cold cans of Diet Coke from her refrigerator. Two were in her purse and the third sat opened and half full on the coffee table.

"Rachel, there's nothing to worry about as long as neither of the detectives starts reading us our Miranda Rights," said Emily, hoping this bit of police procedure she'd learned from TV detective shows would help relax them both.

Just as she offered those very informed words of wisdom, the doorbell rang. Emily immediately began to *hiccup* as she entered the foyer and opened the door.

"Mrs. Fryze." Mick Selby greeted Emily in a professional manner. "Thank you for meeting with us. May we come in?"

Emily responded with another robust hiccup. "Excuse me," she said, and then led the officers into the living room. Rachel stood up, caressing her can of Diet Coke as if it were a comfort blanket.

As they walked into the room, Detective Roma reached to shake Rachel's hand. "Good morning, Mrs. Berger."

Rachel nodded nervously, shaking Roma's hand while holding her Diet Coke even tighter. Then Roma reached out to shake Emily's hand. Emily looked into the detective's eyes, her knees wobbling slightly as their hands met for a second or two longer than normal . . . until she erupted with another sudden, loud hiccup. Detective Roma remained standing, certain he would have to get a cup of water for Emily.

"Excuse me," said Emily, her voice pitched a little higher than usual. "My hiccups have returned. It happens when I'm nervous. Please have a seat." She pointed to two high-backed chairs opposite the sofa, and the detectives complied.

"Well, here's the deal," Mick Selby said, looking first directly at Rachel and then at Emily. "We've come across some evidence that we think you should know about."

Emily gulped down a hiccup.

"Can I—" Detective Roma cocked his head toward the kitchen. "Can I get you a glass of water?"

Emily thrust her hands over her mouth and nodded her head *yes*. Roma walked to the kitchen, where he checked three different cupboards for a glass but found nothing. As he reached for another cupboard door Emily appeared beside him, one hand still covering her mouth. Silently, she reached into a cupboard next to Roma, brushing her hand, accidentally, against his. The two made eye contact for just a second.

"Here let me get the water for you," Roma said and took the glass from Emily.

He walked to the faucet, filled the glass and handed it to her. Emily smiled long and hard at Roma as she took the glass. Aaron returned the smile, locking his eyes with hers while she sipped the water. As soon as she placed the cup on the counter, Emily *hiccupped* again, and Roma cleared his throat motioning for them to return to the living room.

"Feeling better?" Selby asked Emily.

Emily withdrew her hand from her mouth and whispered, "Better, thank you."

"Good. So, Detective Roma and I need you to know that what we are about to tell you is extremely confidential at this point, and you are not to share this information with anyone." Selby paused and then added, "By court order."

Emily's hands shook while still clutching her mouth. Her eyes began to water, due to the hiccupping *and* her nervousness. Rachel's hands squeezed her can of Diet Coke so tightly it collapsed in the middle with a piercing crackling noise.

Selby and Roma were thinking the same thing: *these two women are way too easy and way too much fun to intimidate.*

"Once again, do you both understand that you are not to share the information we are about to give you with anyone?" Selby sounded threateningly stern.

Emily lifted her hands from her mouth to respond, but only a high-pitched, earsplitting *hiccup* emerged. "I'm sorry," she blurted quickly, which was followed by another ear-splitter.

"I do!" said Rachel as if saying her wedding vows, and then she lifted the can of Diet Coke to her mouth and gulped down the rest of her drink. "I do. Understand. Yes-I-do. So does Emily."

Emily nodded and then kept on nodding.

"Okay then," Selby attempted to proceed but was interrupted by Rachel.

"But don't you first have to read us our Miranda Rights?" Rachel glanced at Emily for endorsement.

Emily continued nodding, now in Rachel's direction. "She's right isn't she?" Emily managed to ask.

"Ahhh, well, if you'd like, Detective Roma here can pull out those rights and read them to you. But, ah, I don't really think he needs to."

"Oh, yes, he does, if you're going to charge us with Vickie's murder," Rachel said looking at Emily again for support.

"Well, okayyyy," Selby said, then looked at his partner. "Detective Aroma, could you please read the Miranda Rights to these two suspects?"

"It's Roma," Emily blurted out in Aaron's defense. Then she whispered, "Not Aroma."

Aaron Roma gave a nod of appreciation to Emily, then turned to his partner. "You really think I need to, Detective Selby?"

Rachel and Emily were confused by the obvious tongue-in-cheek manner with which the detectives were treating them.

Detective Selby placed both palms of his hands down on the coffee table. "I'm sorry if you thought we came here to arrest you for the murder of Mrs. Mack. We actually asked you both to meet with us so we could tell you that you are no longer considered to be suspects in this case."

Emily gasped with relief, followed by a doozy of a hiccup. Rachel stared at the detectives in shock and dropped the can of soda.

"But we know you will understand that what we are about to tell you cannot be repeated to anyone," Roma added.

Both women nodded their heads in silence. Emily placed her free hand over her heart.

"We now know that your neighbor, Lawrence Hershey, may have witnessed the dog, Captain, jumping onto Mrs. Mack's back, which caused Mrs. Mack to collapse inside the steamer trunk in such a way as to break her neck," said Roma very carefully.

"But I made sure the trunk was closed before I left for the auction," Rachel said softly.

"Well, apparently, someone opened it after you'd left," explained Roma.

"Vick—*hiccup*—ie!" blurted Emily.

"That stupid, stupid woman!" Rachel sounded angry.

"Why do you say that, Mrs. Berger?" asked Selby.

"Ohhhh, it drove her crazy that Emily and I wouldn't tell her what was hiding in the trunk," said Rachel. "She just had to sneak around and find out for herself." Rachel stopped to think before adding, "And Lawrence saw her fall inside the trunk?"

"It appears so," answered Roma.

"But why didn't he help her out?" squealed Rachel.

"Well, it turns out Lawrence believed she'd only fainted and thought it would be amusing if Mrs. Mack were discovered on stage climbing out from inside the trunk in front of all the auction attendees. He didn't realize

Mrs. Mack had broken her neck and died instantly." Selby leaned back in his chair and crossed his arms over his chest, a gesture of finality.

Emily let out a tiny, softer hiccup.

Roma smiled at her, and she smiled back.

"Now, if Lawrence were older, Detective Roma and I would be charging him with involuntary manslaughter. But because he's still a juvenile, we think he'll just get probation, mandatory counseling and public service work," said Detective Selby.

Rachel felt a little sorry for Lawrence, and for one fleeting moment she even thought it would have been comical if Vickie *had* only fainted in the trunk and was found alive, angry and embarrassed the moment Auction Item Number Four had been opened.

"Detective, are you saying Captain murdered Vickie?" Rachel was aghast.

"Inadvertently," Selby nodded his head, "and I guess we could charge your dog with accidental homicide and leaving the scene of the crime, since he ran out of your garage and disappeared."

Rachel worried for a moment that the detective just might do that, and then she envisioned Vickie Mack in hell, waving a fist at Rachel. *Wouldn't Vickie just love to have Captain in some kind of canine prison?*

"Well, seeing that Mrs. Mack was an intruder entering your garage without consent . . . and seeing that she went and released Captain from the rope you'd used to tie him down . . . and seeing that your crazy dog was probably just wanting some playtime with her, we're going to have to let him go without filing any charges," said Aaron Roma with a smile.

Rachel returned the smile. "Oh, my goodness, thank you," she said in a very weak voice. Was she really being spared another *Calivista Post* headline? One that surely would have read, "Vickie Mack Murdered by Rachel Berger's Crazed Dog." Rachel breathlessly repeated, "Thank you."

"I'm going to give you some free advice, Mrs. Berger. If you're thinking of keeping that dog, and I can't think of why you would, but if you *do* keep him, you'd be wise to hire a really good dog trainer before Captain breaks down your front door or pounces on anyone else," warned Detective Selby.

Rachel smiled. "That sounds like very good advice."

"Oh," Detective Roma interrupted. He pushed the small manila envelope across the table in front of Rachel. "I believe these are yours. They are no longer needed as evidence."

Rachel opened it. "My wedding rings," she sighed.

"So, okay, then. That's it. We're going to let you get on with your day," said Selby as he and Roma stood up and walked toward the front door.

Rachel and Emily stood up and followed behind. At the doorway, the two officers stopped to shake hands with Rachel and Emily, then made their way down the front steps.

Aaron Roma paused on the last step, then turned and looked at Emily. "It's been quite an experience. If we ever meet again, I hope it won't be regarding a murder."

Every muscle in Emily's body turned to mush. All she could manage was a soft, knowing smile and two words. "Me, too."

"Just don't go signing up for anymore chairmanships," said Selby over his shoulder with a meaningful grin.

CHAPTER 35

"OHHH," SIGHED RACHEL the moment the detectives drove away from Emily's house. "I wish we could celebrate with a bottle of champagne or something. I'm way too jittery to go home."

Emily squealed, releasing tons of pent-up tension, then grabbed Rachel's arm and dragged her into the kitchen. She opened the refrigerator door and pointed to the middle shelf.

It was Rachel's turn to squeal, for there, lying on its side, was a beautiful, unopened bottle of Monet champagne.

"I bought this for us to share the day after the auction. But then, well, there was nothing for us to celebrate that night, was there?"

"Oh, girlfriend! Open up that bottle!"

Within seconds, Emily had uncorked the bottle, and the two friends almost skipped to the kitchen table with water tumblers in their hands.

Emily poured some of the bubbly into each glass, and together, Rachel and Emily raised their glasses high into the air.

"So, who do we toast first?" Emily asked.

"Okay, here's to our dear Cupertino Flores!" Rachel said warmly.

The women reverently linked glasses and sipped.

"Ahhh," they said together.

"And let's not forget our *beloved* auctioneer, Ted Lloyd, who called us his ladies of the night," said Emily, again holding up her glass.

"Yes, and Tweedle Dee and Tweedle Dum!"

Rachel and Emily giggled as they took another sip of the champagne. Emily paused for a moment. "I think we need to toast Lawrence."

"What! And why?" Rachel squealed. "He was willing to let us go down as the murderers!"

"But remember, Rachel, Lawrence was only hoping Vickie would pop out of the voyager trunk for everyone at the auction to laugh at."

Rachel pondered this for a moment and decided that, actually, it would have been divine retribution if, in fact, Vickie Mack, the nemesis of all who knew her, had been forced to crawl out of Auction Item Number Four and onto the auction stage, screaming and wailing in full view for all to see.

"Well, okay, then." Rachel raised her glass. "Here's to Lawrence admitting what he saw happen in my garage, and here's to his demented sense of humor."

Rachel and Emily sat at the kitchen table clinking their glasses with toasts to the people who'd made their lives so miserable and to those who had made their lives easier over the past year and a half.

"And last but not least, here's to our lives getting back to normal!" said Rachel.

"More like a new normal for me," said Emily. "Tomorrow I'm calling my lawyer and asking him to finalize the divorce papers."

Rachel looked sympathetically into Emily's eyes and touched her knee. "Are you sure, Em?"

Emily sighed with a confident smile. "I'm sure. I don't like the old normal where I wondered who Pete is with whenever he leaves the house or goes on another business trip."

"Okay then," said Rachel raising her glass. "To a new and happier normal."

"And I had also been thinking that if we ever got through this ordeal, my new normal would also include me taking a few graduate level classes to get me back up to speed. I need to be a little more competitive when I start looking for a job."

"Really, Em?" Rachel asked with irony. "Well, I will place bets that *your* new normal will be a whole lot easier than *my* new normal."

"What?" Emily laughed.

Rachel took a deep breath. "Believe it or not, my new normal includes keeping Captain in the family."

"You're kidding, aren't you?"

"No," Rachel groaned. "Robbie and Conrad would never forgive me if I sent him packing. So, Captain and I are enrolling in *graduate* dog training classes . . . and by hook or by crook that dog is going to become the most obedient canine to ever live."

Emily laughed, "I'll believe it when I see it! But just in case Captain gets on the loose again, you'd better warn Detective Roma."

"Maybe you should warn him," said Rachel with a sly smile.

About the Author

Trish Evans is the author of *Katy's Ghost*. She was born and raised in Southern California in an eccentric family of journalists, writers and musicians. She graduated from Northwestern University in Evanston, Illinois. When not tapping on her keyboard, Trish can usually be found working in her garden, bike riding or walking along the sandy shores of Malibu with Ollie, a goldendoodle. She's married to her college sweetheart. They live in Southern California and spend as much time at the beach as possible.

Visit her at trishevansbooks.com.

Made in the USA
Thornton, CO
05/31/23 12:08:11

6aff92e3-df45-413e-85f6-755979f3182eR01